HE DIDN'T KNOW HOW MUCH SHE MEANT TO HIM UNTIL HE FOUND HER . . .

"Blue Duck?" Daniel stopped, sweeping his eyes over the clearing. "Blue Duck, you here?" he said softly. A motion caught his eye. He jerked around and saw the buffalo robe under a tree. He hesitated, then grinned and walked toward her.

"You sure are one lazy Cherokee gal, sleepin' in the middle of the . . ." He pulled the robe aside. Her wide, frightened eyes stared up at him. A cry stuck in his throat. He saw the gag in her mouth, the tight cords about her arms and legs and the welts and dried blood streaking her naked body. He threw himself away from her, bellowed a warning to Stewart. But it was already too late.

A Shawnee lunged at Daniel's left. Boone turned and fired blindly. His shot missed and he never heard the second Indian who attacked from behind him. The blow glanced off his head, numbed his shoulder and brought him to the ground.

He struggled to regain his feet, but a horrible weakness flowed through his body as the Shawnee's blows rained on his head and shoulders. His sight dimmed. He heard Stewart scream, but Daniel couldn't help his friend now. The darkness was coming over him fast, and he was falling into it. He was grateful he couldn't feel the blows any longer. . . .

THE AMERICAN EXPLORERS SERIES

Ask your bookseller for these other titles:

Jed Smith
FREEDOM RIVER

Lewis & Clark
NORTHWEST GLORY

Jim Bridger
MOUNTAIN MAN

John Fremont
CALIFORNIA BOUND

Kit Carson
TRAPPER KING

Zebulon Pike
PIONEER DESTINY

Marcus Whitman
FRONTIER MISSION

DANIEL BOONE

WESTWARD TRAIL

Neal Barrett, Jr.

A Dell/Standish Book

Published by

Miles Standish Press, Inc.
37 West Avenue
Wayne, Pennsylvania 19087

Dell ® TM 681510, Dell Publishing Co., Inc.

ISBN: 0-440-01654-1
Printed in the United States of America
First printing—January 1982
Second printing—September 1982

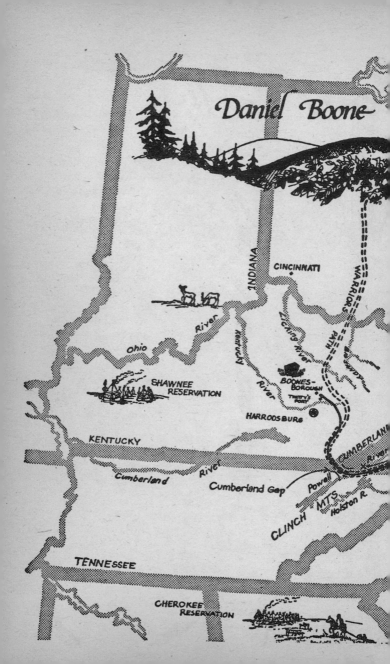

Prologue

The Dreamer: July 1755

The rainwater had already run off some by the time Daniel made his way down from the wagons an hour after the first light, but the encampment still looked like a swamp. His ruddy young face broke into a grin at the sight. The heavy summer storm that had pounded the camp until just before dawn was over. Braddock's troops looked more like ants plowed up from a furrow than tough British Regulars. Hundreds of tents had sagged and collapsed under the driving rain, and the bivouac streets were ankle-deep in Pennsylvania mud. A few fires crackled in the morning mist, but only in front of the officers' tents. Nobody had worried about keeping the wood dry the night before, and the officers had appropriated what little had escaped the rain. Some fifteen hundred redcoats would start this day's march with a cold breakfast in their bellies.

Daniel couldn't make sense of it, especially getting

wet when you didn't have to. A six-year-old man-child on the Yadkin River could sniff a downpour coming and pick high ground to sleep on. The boys from North Carolina and Virginia weren't dry as biscuits this morning, but they weren't hacking and blowing their noses all over camp either.

If someone had told Daniel Boone when he joined the trek northward that Braddock's famed grenadiers didn't have sense enough to keep out of the rain, he'd have called the man a liar. But the long march to Fort Duquesne had taught him differently. The redcoats were good soldiers, but they didn't have a spit's worth of sense in the woods. He had seen them make blunder after blunder on the long trek through the wilderness. They had even tried to march in straight columns, as if they were walking right across some flat green meadow in Europe instead of straight up and down the Endless Mountains.

Daniel skirted the worst of the mud and made his way to higher ground near the center of camp. Without thinking, he removed his brand-new black felt hat and held his long rifle high to avoid the heavy, dripping branches on his left. The big tent with soldiers clustered around it would be General Braddock's. Daniel was glad to find it so quickly. Now he could get rid of these damn papers and hike back to the wagons for some hot stew and dry moccasins. Carrying messages from one end of camp to the other wasn't Daniel's idea of proper work for a grown man. He had signed on in Fort Cumberland to do hauling—or, if he had to, fighting. This kind of business sure didn't seem like either to him. 'Course you couldn't tell that to Major Dobbs.

2

Even if he was a North Carolina boy, he was a Regular all the same.

The redcoat stepped out of line, brought his rifle down smartly and jerked it toward Daniel's belly. Daniel stopped, looked at the sharp bayonet and grinned.

"Hey, friend, I ain't Shawnee or French, neither. I'm on your side, near as I can tell."

The redcoat didn't smile. "This is officer country, farmer. Back away and go around."

Daniel ignored the insult. "Well, it's officers I got business with." He held up the packet of papers. "Where you reckon I can find Captain McKenzie or Dr. Walker?"

The soldier shook his head. "You got papers for the captain," he said tersely, "you can give them to me."

"That ain't exactly what the major told me to do," Daniel explained. He looked at the redcoat a long moment. "You made your point real good. Now I'm going to ask you to aim that thing the other way, boy."

The redcoat's mouth curled into a malicious grin. "You don't listen, farmer. I said go around." The sharp point of the weapon moved an inch forward, pricking Daniel's stomach. Daniel swung his own rifle up fast and slammed the barrel hard against the Britisher's head. The man's eyes went blank, then he dropped the weapon and folded like a sack. A shout went up and Daniel saw a short, stubby officer and three grenadiers bearing down on him fast, weapons at the ready.

"Hold off, Captain!"

The Regulars stopped at the sound. Daniel turned to see a tall, stern-faced young man standing in the entry to his tent. The man glanced at the redcoat sprawled in the mud, then looked sharply at Daniel.

"What the devil's going on here?"

Daniel respectfully tipped his hat, but before he could answer, the British officer stepped up smartly. "Sir, I'll handle this."

The tall man didn't look at him. "I'll handle it myself, Captain."

"Sir," the officer protested, "this fellow struck one of my men!"

"Need I repeat myself, Captain?"

The captain flushed and bit off his anger. With a dark look at Daniel, he turned and stalked off angrily through the mud. The soldiers picked up their companion and dragged him down the hill.

"Now," the tall man turned patient eyes on Daniel, "I'll ask again. What happened out here?"

"I got this ration list," said Daniel. "Major Dobbs told me to bring it to Captain McKenzie—sir." He added the last because the Regular had. The man wore no badge, but he clearly had some rank. "Reckon that feller didn't think I ought to be here, so he put his sticker 'bout a foot in my gut. I didn't much care for it."

"I see. And that's all?"

Daniel shrugged. "Yes, sir. Seemed like plenty at the time."

"What's your name, soldier?"

"Boone. Daniel Boone, from North Carolina, sir. Only I don't guess I'm exactly a soldier. More like a teamster. I do some smithin' work, too."

The man almost smiled. Daniel figured they were both about the same age, only the other's air of authority made him seem older. He wore a buckskin jacket like his own, only newer and a hell of a lot cleaner, Daniel thought. He had the sure speech of an educated man, and his deep blue eyes looked right through you when he talked. But when the man fell silent, the thin lips of his wide mouth pressed tightly together. Too tightly, Daniel decided. There was clearly something ailing the man.

"Sir, you all right?"

The officer gave him a short, piercing look. "Boone, you think you can make your way back to the wagons without felling any more grenadiers? We'll likely need them in the next few days."

Boone felt himself color and looked down at his feet. "Yes, sir. I'll sure do that."

The man reached out and took the papers. "I'll see these get to McKenzie. He's out of camp this morning."

"Thank you," said Daniel. "And I'm sure obliged to you for gettin' me out of that scrape."

As the man nodded, Daniel noted the tiny beads of sweat on his cheeks and brow.

"Take care, Boone. We'll likely need teamsters up north, as well. My compliments to Major Dobbs." With that, the officer turned and disappeared into his tent.

Daniel was halfway to the wagons before he remembered he hadn't learned the officer's name. He sure couldn't go back and ask. That would be plain foolish. But he would look an even bigger fool when he had to tell Dobbs he didn't know who he had given the papers to. Damnation!

Suddenly he stopped, alert and wary. He had heard a rustling in the woods.

"If I was a Injun, Daniel, I'd sure have me a fine scalp 'bout now," a voice laughed.

Daniel jerked around and brought up his rifle. The man stepped out of the trees. Boone grinned sheepishly and shook the man's hand. "Howdy, Mr. Gist. Guess I was dreamin' some."

"Guess you were, boy." He raised a disapproving brow. "Bad habit to get into. 'Specially 'round here."

There weren't many men who could stalk up behind Daniel that way, but Christopher Gist could, and Daniel felt no shame in it. Gist was a neighbor on the Yadkin, and his son Nat was Daniel's best friend. But more than that, Christopher Gist was close to being the best woodsman on the frontier. There wasn't a man anywhere better suited to head up Braddock's scouts.

"I got myself in kind of a mess back there," Boone explained. He looked curiously at Gist. "You know the general's officers, I reckon?"

"Most of 'em," Gist nodded. "Now tell me." The tall man turned curious eyes on Daniel. He saw a lean frontiersman near his own height, with dark sandy hair plaited at the back. His face was gaunt, hollow-cheeked, his wide mouth curled at one corner with a hint of mischief. "What happened out there?"

As Daniel told him the story, Gist managed to keep a straight face until he heard described the officer who had gotten young Boone out of the fracas. Then the scout's grizzled cheeks split into a wide grin, and he laughed out loud. "Goddamn, boy, you sure can pick 'em!"

Daniel looked blank. "You know him?"

6

"Hell yes, I know him. That's Colonel George Washington hisself that saved your hide, Dan'l."

Daniel was taken aback. He knew who Washington was, all right, but had never laid eyes on him. Everyone on the frontier knew how the colonel had fought the French all the way up the Ohio until he finally got cornered at Fort Necessity. Gist had scouted out that trek, too. Washington had to surrender in the end, but he marched his men back proud, with flags flying.

"The colonel didn't look so well," Daniel told Gist. "Appeared to me he was near to falling on his face."

Gist looked grim. "He's got hisself a fever, Daniel. Been carryin' him in a wagon since yesterday, which he don't take to at all." Gist shook his head and leaned on his rifle. "He's a stubborn son of a bitch, but a good man. Better'n these goddamn British, for sure. Not a one of 'em knows where the hell we're goin' or what's waitin' up there. The colonel knows, and so do I." He looked toward the north, then let his eyes rest again on Daniel. "Take a care, boy. Don't walk into no hornets' nests. You might get that pretty new hat dusty."

Daniel watched the tough old scout walk off toward camp. Everybody sure was worried about his health this morning. Both Gist and the colonel had already told him to take a care. Daniel figured it was fair advice. Like Gist said, he and Washington had been there and back again.

Boone silently hoped they would meet up with the French, and the sooner the better. A good fight couldn't be worse than hauling heavy wagons through the thick woods and rocky creeks of western Pennsylvania. Each day the pioneers scouting up front had to blaze a path for the train behind. It was slow going. More than a few of the hundred and fifty wagons they had started with had since fallen by the way, and the expedition was already near a month out of Fort Cumberland. At this rate, the French at Fort Duquesne would die of old age before Braddock could fight them.

One of the men who worked under Commissary Walker told Boone that Dr. Ben Franklin, Pennsylvania's postmaster, had warned Braddock against taking wagons in the first place. The trail to Fort Duquesne was tailor-made for an Indian ambush. Pack horses were a more practical solution, Franklin had insisted, but Braddock wouldn't listen. When he demanded a full wagon train to support the army, Franklin had relented and procured him the wagons. Now the general had to live with his decision. Or more rightly, Daniel thought darkly, he and the other wagoners had to, spending day after day mending broken wheels and axles with split wood and spit.

The best part of the trip, as far as he was concerned, was sitting around the evening campfire with the other teamsters. They were rough, hearty men, and he enjoyed their company. Most were hunters, traders or just plain roamers who had done a little of everything to provide for their bellies. They could tackle most any job that came along—shooting straight, blazing a trail or doctoring a horse if they had to, anything, Daniel figured, except sitting under one roof for too long. None of them were very good at that, especially Boone himself.

In all his twenty-one years, he couldn't remember when he hadn't spent the better part of his time out of doors and away from other people. Back in Berks County, where he had grown up, it seemed like the natural thing to do. There had always been buffalo, deer, bear and beaver to hunt, and plenty of land to roam free.

And always, Daniel remembered, there had been Indians about, Indians you could look at and talk to, and didn't have to shoot. Daniel understood them, and liked to be around them. Better than whites, sometimes, though it wasn't a good idea to talk that way these days, not with everybody's cousin having friends and kin who had been scalped or murdered.

It was hard to figure sometimes, especially now, with the Shawnees up there ahead somewhere, laying for white heads. He knew how the Indians felt. Hell, he thought that way himself more often than not. Knowing Indians, and now maybe having to kill a few, bothered him more than a little. He knew they had done plenty of killing, and worse. Somehow, though, that didn't ease his mind much.

Of all the men who could spin a tall tale around the fire, Daniel liked John Findley best. Findley was a short, wiry man with a bulbous nose, bright eyes, and a face lined with a map of his travels. He was a wagoner now, but he had spent the year before roaming about Kentucky, where he did some trading and hunting with the Indians. Boone listened in wonder when Findley spoke of it. Most of the men with the wagons had wandered a far piece, but there weren't more than a handful of whites anywhere who had seen that fabled land. It seemed odd to Daniel that three of those men were in this very expedition: Findley, Christopher Gist, and Dr. Walker, the commissary.

9

Kentucky was a rich and fertile land, said Findley, with soil so dark and moist in the long valleys that the Indians grew cornstalks twice as tall as a man and half as broad as his forearm. He told about white water rushing through deep clefts of granite, rolling hills and valleys shadowed green with ash, hickory, chestnut and every tree you could think of. He talked about fog on the river in the morning, deep forests full of ferns, streams thick with fish, and fields so full of cane that a fellow could get lost in one for years if he didn't mark his trail.

And hunting? Findley had a great deal to say about that. The land past the Endless Mountains was a veritable paradise for a man with a good eye and a long rifle. You didn't even have to track game there. All you had to do was to sit right still and let it come to you. Deer, bear, squirrel, fox and every kind of fur you cared to trap. There were more buffalo in Kentucky than anyone could hope to count, herds so big they made the earth tremble. Why, a man could stand and watch them pass all one day and the next, and never see the end.

"It's like nothin' you ever seen," Findley told his audience. "Once I set out some trade goods for a bunch of Injuns, and tossed the wrappin's aside, not thinkin' anythin' of it. Well, don't you know, when I come back to that place later, the whole valley was sproutin' grass I never seen before. I couldn't figure what'd happened. Then I recalled the goods I'd opened up was from England, and it come to me like lightnin'. Them wrappin's was dried up bluegrass, which grows real good over there. It just come back to life in Ken-

10

tucky, and took hold right off. Whole damn place is covered with it now."

Boone wasn't sure he believed that, but he didn't laugh like some of the others. He sure believed everything else Findley had to say, and kept him talking long after the others had gone to sleep. How, Daniel wanted to know, had he made his way to Kentucky in the first place? Had he crossed the Endless Mountains? Everyone said they rose up sheer as a wall and that no man had ever managed to scale them. Findley had a ready answer for that. He hadn't come through the mountains at all. He had traveled down south from Ohio, with a Shawnee party. "When they were a mite friendlier than they are now," he added wryly. "Or 'bout as friendly as the Shawnees get."

"So that's the way in, then?"

"That's one way," said Findley. He grinned at Boone and spat in the dying fire. "There's another, if a man could find it—a trail that starts up north somewhere on the Blue Ridge an' winds west out of the mountains. It's a secret way the Indians call the Warrior's Path. Ever heard of it?"

Boone shook his head.

"It curls down south, then cuts through the Endless Mountains, or it's supposed to, anyway. I reckon it's true, 'cause the Cherokees been usin' it since God was a chile to pounce on the Shawnees an' anyone else they can find north of the Ohio. Probably plenty of other Injuns found it 'fore that."

Daniel sat up straight, his blue eyes bright with interest. "Mr. Findley, you think there is such a trail? Truly?"

"I think there might be."

11

"Then by God," Daniel blurted, "let's find it!"

Findley gave him a patient smile, but Daniel didn't notice. John Findley wasn't the first man to talk about Kentucky, but there was a magic in his words that touched Daniel and held him spellbound. The wonders of that land behind the mountains filled his head, crowding everything else aside.

The fire had dwindled to charcoal and a wisp of grey smoke by the time the pair stopped talking. It was Findley who finally brought the conversation to an end, for Daniel would have rattled on all night and then some. Sleep wouldn't come to him even after Findley's snores had settled into a long, easy rhythm. Kentucky was there, just past the mountains, waiting to be taken—if a man was big enough to do it.

It sounded like heaven the way John Findley talked about it. Only heaven was likely a little easier to get to, and a safer place, for sure. Daniel didn't figure there would be any Shawnees in the hereafter. A couple of tame Delawares maybe, but certainly no Shawnees.

He wondered what Rebecca would think about his dream. She liked him, he knew, but maybe Miss Rebecca Bryan wouldn't want a man who would haul her off to a wilderness full of Indians. He thought of her all night and wondered. He had gone without sleep before, and didn't miss it when he arose at dawn. As ever, there was a full day's work on the wagons to be done, enough to keep a man's hands busy and his mind off the wonders of Kentucky. By late afternoon, there were other things to think about. Rumor reached the wagoners that the trip was nearly over. Advance troops would reach the river late that night, or early the next morning. That meant Fort Duquesne was just ahead. Would the French come out and do battle? Maybe they didn't know Braddock was coming. Hell, they had to, one teamster laughed. The army's trek north was about as secretive as a herd of buffalo stampeding through Boston.

Rumors grew as the day wore on. By nightfall, Daniel heard that the French had given up and there would be no battle at all, that the Shawnees had turned on their allies and slaughtered them all in the fort, that the French army was twice as big as the British had expected, and that Braddock himself was surrendering his sword at that very moment.

After supper, Daniel walked up ahead to the encampment to try to find Gist, who would know the truth of the situation. But the scout was nowhere to be found, and all Boone got for his trouble were more rumors.

At least one story, however, turned out to be true. The river was there to slow them down. Early the next morning, Braddock's troops started across the Monongahela. Boone could barely see the tips of their banners, they were so far ahead, but he could hear the crisp beat of drums and the shrill whistle of fifes in the morning air. The stirring sound of the Grenadier's March wafted through the thick woods and rolled down the valley. Boone thought it must be a stirring sight and wished he could be up front for a better look.

Linc Morgan, the dour old Virginian who rode beside him on the wagon, was less impressed. "Reckon you ought to be damn glad you're where you are," he scowled.

"Why?" Daniel asked curiously. "My God, Linc,

there's near two thousand of 'em, countin' the militia. Whatever we run into . . ."

Linc spat over his shoulder. "Damn redcoats ain't got the sense God gave a gopher, that's why. Where you think the militia is, Dan'l?" He nodded ahead and flicked his reins. "Right up ahead of us is where. Ol' Stiff-Nosed Braddock don't want 'em to take no glory from himself. What does that tell you?"

Daniel frowned. Linc was right. It didn't make much sense. You didn't have to be a gold-braid general to know it was a good idea to spot Indians before they spotted you. And the seven hundred boys from North Carolina and Virginia were the only troopers on the trek who had ever fought redskins. The rest had more than likely never even seen one. "Well," Boone replied finally, "there's more'n a thousand rifles up there. I don't reckon the French or the Shawnees'll want to walk into that."

Linc Morgan looked at him cynically, but didn't answer.

The column was long, and as usual, moving slowly. The sun was almost straight up in the sky before Daniel's wagon splashed into the waters of the Monongahela. Its banks had been churned to mud by the boots and wheels that had passed that way all morning. Urging the horses up the other side, he glanced ahead, past the other wagons. There was a narrow, sloping defile ranging up the hill, crowded close on either side by dense woodland. It was just like every other hill they had climbed for the past four weeks, thought Daniel.

Suddenly, the wagon ahead came to a halt. Morgan cursed, and shouted at the driver. Daniel shook his head and laughed at Morgan's frustration. Not thirty yards past the river and already another delay. Some wagon had a busted wheel, or maybe tangled traces. Standing, he squinted at the wagon in front, and the one after that. It was like riding on a caterpillar through the grass. The front end stopped, dragged its back end up behind, and waited for the middle to make up its mind.

Daniel stopped, peered intently at the hill, and grabbed Linc's shoulder. "Great Jesus, look at that!"

Linc stood. Dense puffs of smoke mushroomed out of the woods up ahead on either side of the ridge. At first, Daniel thought the trees were on fire. Then he heard the unmistakable chatter of rifles echoing down the hill. It was a terrible, devastating sound, more guns going off at once than he had ever imagined, followed by high-pitched calls of alarm and shouted orders.

Just ahead, Daniel made out the mounted figure of Colonel Washington, and beside him, Christopher Gist. He had thought the colonel was still confined to a sickbed, but there the man was, swinging his saber to left and right, spreading his militiamen out of the column and into the cover of the woods.

It was difficult to tell what was happening on the ridge. The smoke was as thick as a cloud come to ground, but the redcoats marched forward in orderly lines and columns, disappearing into the pall. What the hell were they doing? And where was all the shooting coming from?

Suddenly, as Boone watched, redcoats came pouring out of the smoke, tearing back through their own ranks. The lines held for a moment, then broke. In half a minute, a ragged mass of crimson flowed like a river

15

of blood down the hill. Gunfire mixed with the shouts of the dying echoed across the ravine. Panic swept like a tremor through the wagons. Teamsters yelled and whipped their horses about for the river, while militia officers sprinted down the line, shouting angrily for the wagoners to stand by their teams and hold.

"Goddamn," Linc Morgan muttered, "hold what, for Christ's sake?"

A loud cry went up ahead, as the word passed from man to man: "Indians!" Through the smoke they charged after the fleeing redcoats. The hill was covered in an instant with red-painted Shawnees, snapping at the Regulars' heels, shrieking like devils and waving their tomahawks high.

Washington's militia, dispersed in the woods, slowed the enemy and gave a good accounting of themselves, but it was too late to turn the tide. The battle was clearly lost as soon as it began.

Redcoats by the hundreds poured past the wagons, fighting their way to the river. Daniel was near deaf from the din of screaming soldiers and the steady crack of rifles. His strong hands held his own weapon high, searching for a target, but there were none to see, only choking smoke and dust. He heard his own name above the noise and jerked swiftly about. John Findley reined up beside him on a dappled mare. Findley shouted again, but Daniel couldn't hear. He didn't need to. Findley's gestures were plain as day. The Shawnees had already reached the lead wagons. Daniel waved at Findley and leaped to one of his team horses. Morgan took the other. Slashing the traces that bound their mounts, the pair charged through the redcoats for the river.

General Braddock was dead. Four days after the somber remnants of the army fled across the Monongahela, they stopped to bury him near Fort Necessity, under the road they had built only a few weeks before. It was Christopher Gist's idea to put him there. The old scout knew the Shawnees. A scalp as famous as Braddock's would be worth looking for, and the Indians would surely sniff it out if they could.

Rumors of what had happened flew thick as flies all along the long trek back, but Boone was home on the Yadkin River before he heard the full story. Two-thirds of Braddock's army had been felled in the massacre—a thousand men, dead or wounded. Everyone said Braddock could have beaten the Shawnees easily if he had only had the sense to listen to Washington. But instead of sending his men to cover, the general had galloped back and forth through the hail of gunfire, keeping his troopers in straight, even lines, making them easy targets for the Indians.

Much later, Christopher Gist told Daniel the rest of the story. The French, horrified by Braddock's superior force, were ready to wave the white flag when an officer named Beujeu had a better idea. He talked eight hundred Shawnees into setting up an ambush, tempting them with the promise of British scalps, plenty of bright red coats and all the rifles they could capture.

The Regulars who had died straight off were the lucky ones, said Gist. Those who surrendered to the Shawnees had gotten the worst of it. The Indians had not yet heard about the European tradition of courtesy for prisoners. The hapless Britishers had been stripped, painted black, tortured and burned at the stake.

"Don't guess Pennsylvania's a hell of a lot like Europe," said Gist.

"This ain't the kind of country a man can just come into and admire from afar," observed Daniel, watching the flames lick wood in Gist's fireplace. "You got to live in it, and listen to it."

"You're right as you can be," agreed Gist.

In the radiant warmth of the hearth, Daniel's thoughts wandered away from Braddock and Fort Duquesne. "You mind tellin' about it again, Mr. Gist? How it looks when you first catch sight of Kentucky?"

Gist shook his head. "Damnation, boy. How many times you got to hear it?"

"A thousand, if I can. That's the part I don't never get tired of," said Daniel.

PART ONE

1768–1770

Chapter 1

Daniel stood quietly in the shade of the big oak. Bright sun filtered through the heavy branches and dappled his strong, sun-leathered face. He adjusted the brim of his black felt hat, tattered now from fourteen years of use. Just beyond the trees, the small meadow caught the first light of morning, yellowing the tips of high grass and thin spears of second-growth ash. A squirrel chattered overhead. Half a mile away, a crow rose out of the trees, cawed a loud complaint, then dove back into the woods.

"You see that buck yonder?" Daniel said softly. The boy nodded without looking up. Daniel waited a moment, then slid the rifle out of his arms. "Reckon you better take him now, James."

The boy glanced up, startled. His eyes went bright with pleasure. "Me? You want *me* to bag it, Pa?" he whispered.

Daniel looked solemn. " 'Less you can spit that far, boy."

James reached up and took the rifle, holding it as if it were a sacred artifact. Without turning his head, his eyes flicked toward the far side of the clearing. The buck was just visible through the saplings, frozen at the edge of the forest. The sun colored his back the same shade as the brush around him.

"He's a nice one."

"Ten points, maybe."

"Might be twelve," James said hopefully and looked up with a dozen questions in his eyes.

Daniel knew what the boy was thinking, and he was pleased. The boy didn't want help on his first deer. He would take all the credit for a hit, or the blame for a miss.

Quietly taking his father's horn and pouch, James moved off. It was the right time of day, early enough for the dew to wet the grass and soften the sound of his footsteps. The buck was at least seventy yards off, and James wasn't sharp enough to try a shot like that. He would have to cover half that distance to make a clean kill, and there was scant cover to help him.

Daniel watched his son with a critical eye. Whenever the buck put his head down to feed, James moved, keeping low to the ground, knowing every place his moccasins would touch without looking, never taking his eye off the animal. Just before the deer brought his head up, James caught the slight bunching of muscle at the shoulder and froze. The deer raised his muzzle, sniffed the air, and looked right at him. The buck knew something was wrong. He stared at James for a full three minutes. Daniel saw a dark swarm of gnats drift past the deer's head. The deer twitched one ear. Then the gnats moved off, smelled the boy's sweat, and settled around his head, but James never moved. Daniel grinned with pride. Goddamn! The boy was better than the buck. The animal had moved, but James hadn't. The gnats were likely stinging his eyes, now, and crawling up his nose.

Finally, the deer looked away, searched the rest of the meadow, then lowered his head again. James waited. Sometimes, a wise old buck would look away from something he found suspicious, then jerk up to catch it moving.

In a few moments, James moved forward again, taking a few short yards at a time. When he stopped and carefully brought the rifle to his shoulder, Daniel figured he was a good forty yards from the buck. The boy was right. Any closer and the animal would bolt for sure.

The deer raised its head and James squeezed the trigger. Powder flashed in the firing pan just before the gun jerked against his shoulder, and a puff of smoke rose from the muzzle. Daniel saw the buck rise up straight, shake its head, and bolt for the brush behind. He looked at James and smiled. The boy was likely wetting his trousers, itching to go look for that deer. Instead, James dropped to his knees and started reloading the long rifle. Holding the weapon between his knees, he ran the ramrod quickly down the barrel, poured powder in his palm and filtered it into the muzzle. The ball on its patch of linsey went in after, and James ran the rod in to tamp it. He put the hammer on half-cock, charged the pan again and shut the frizzen.

When the boy stood up, Daniel walked out into the clearing. He was pleased. His son had remembered the most important rule: Unless there's an Indian breathing down your back with a scalpin' knife, don't do anything till you load again. An empty rifle makes a passable club and nothing more. James hadn't forgotten.

The deer, a good ten pointer, had been hit under the right ear and had died no more than four yards into the trees. Daniel hefted the animal up on a branch and let James dress it.

"It's a good buck," said James, stepping back to look at his work.

"It's a fine buck," Daniel agreed. "Fine as they come."

James knew he had been lucky to get such a fine animal for his first. They had roamed nearly fifty miles from home during the past three weeks, and the buck was easily the best they'd seen. Game was to be had, and they had trapped their share of skins, but you sure had to work for it. Things weren't like they used to be, as his father was fond of saying. When the Boones had come to the Yadkin nearly twenty years before, a man could shoot thirty deer a day without leaving the valley. It wasn't like that now. And Pa said it wouldn't ever be again. When people moved in, deer, bear and everything else got hard to find.

They were halfway home before James brought it up.

He had gone over the problem a dozen ways to Sunday, then decided to just come right out and say it.

"Pa, you were twelve when you got your first rifle, ain't that right?"

24

"That's right," said Boone.

"I'm eleven now."

"I recall you are, son."

"That means it'll be 'bout another year, won't it?"

" 'Bout that." Daniel couldn't keep his mouth straight. He stopped on the trail and grinned down at his son. "James, how long you been thinkin' this over in your head?"

James wet his lips. "Guess since I shot the deer."

"An' before that, too, I imagine."

"Yes, sir. I reckon so."

"James, I don't reckon twelve's any kind of magic number. Somethin' could happen before then. I mean, if we was in Salisbury takin' down skins and just happened to see the right kinda rifle . . ."

"Yes, sir," James replied as he tried to keep from whooping like an Indian. "I sure hope that's the way it happens."

Sometimes it scared Daniel just to look at the boy. His hair and eyes were dark, like Rebecca's, but inside he could see nothing but himself. He had once taken the boy hunting in the dead of winter, carrying the small, trembling frame against his chest under his own heavy jacket. James had been barely eight, but his big black eyes had searched out the forest like a creature born to the wilderness. Daniel could see it plain, and he thrilled at the sight. That was the first time he'd noticed. It was like seeing a part of yourself flow into someone else.

Of course, he and Rebecca were linked together too. Some peculiar power was always there between them, no matter how many miles apart they were. But this was different. Loving a woman was a strange and wonderful thing, but Daniel wasn't sure the mysterious cord that bound him to his son wasn't stranger and more wondrous still.

Chapter 2

They knew he was coming. The dogs didn't bark that way at strangers. Even before he and James stepped out of the trees into the hollow, the door to the cabin erupted with small, screaming figures. In a moment, Israel, Jemima and Susannah were all over him, laughing, jumping and climbing up their father's legs. The last to reach him was little Levinia, stumbling twice before she toddled up to him. Daniel set the others aside and hefted his two-year-old daughter high, laughing as she squealed in delight, churning her short legs in the air.

"I got a deer," he heard James solemnly tell his brother. "All by myself." Daniel lingered long enough to see Israel's eyes go wide, then he strode up the hill to meet Rebecca. Carrying baby Becky in her arms, she came to him. He grabbed her around the waist and kissed her soundly.

"Damnation, girl, you're fillin' out some." Grinning, he held her back to look at her and pat her belly.

Rebecca flushed. "Daniel, the children!"

Boone laughed. "They growed up in the woods, Becky. They seen plenty of wild critters, so I reckon they know what I'm doin'."

"Well now, we don't have to show 'em right here, Dan Boone." Concern creased her brow. "Anyway, I'm not fillin' out, I'm thinnin' down, if anything."

"You look just fine," he assured her and reached down to let the baby grab his finger. "Better'n ever." It was the truth, too. At twenty-nine, Becky seemed no different than the tall, black-haired beauty who had captured his eyes when she was just fifteen. She still had the power to set something stirring in him. Full-figured yet coltish, she was lean in the right places and soft where it counted. Her flashing black eyes could put more in a glance than a full day of talking. He could leave her for a full season, but when they held each other again, the need between them was as strong as ever, old and familiar, yet strangely new again.

"You have a good hunt?" Rebecca looked over his shoulder to see Israel and James leading the mounts and pack horse to the rear of the house.

"Fair to middling," Boone shrugged. "Thirty, maybe forty hides. James got a buck all his own."

"He didn't!"

"Good one, too. Tracked and downed it like an Indian. You'd have thought it was ol' Christopher Gist himself out there."

"More like ol' Daniel Boone, I imagine," she teased him proudly.

Daniel grinned. "He's a fair shot. Takes after his

mother, I reckon. 'Course, he didn't kill no horse, but he'll come along fast." His blue eyes twinkled.

"Daniel Boone!" Becky stepped back and put her hands on her hips. "You are not goin' to start that business again!"

Daniel threw back his head and laughed. She was a good shot all right, but he never grew tired of telling how once while perched in a tree branch, she had downed her own horse. He usually failed to mention that she had also killed seven deer in the bargain.

Later, when supper was over and the children had been sent off to sleep, Daniel and Becky talked awhile before the fire, then went quietly to their own bed. As always, neither said a word as Daniel slipped under the heavy bearskin cover and waited while Becky changed in a small corner of the room. She kept her back to him, and he could hear the soft rustle of clothing as she slipped out of her dress and drew the long cotton nightgown over her head. When she was beside him, he reached over and kissed her. Becky's arms came up to hold him.

He murmured to her a moment, then she moved up close against him, her body trembling at his touch. Daniel reached down gently and let his hand roam under the gown, over her legs and to the softness of her belly. Becky moaned and came to him, pulling the nightgown quickly over her shoulders and flinging it out of the way.

Daniel never ceased to marvel at the warmth and fury of this woman of his. Quiet and soft-spoken in the day, she was likely as not to blush clear to her brow if he touched her in a familiar place. But at night, the fires smouldering in her body came alive, and it was all he could do to match her needs. It had always been that way, right from the beginning.

He knew other men looked at Rebecca. She was a beauty, and worth a second glance. But they could never see the woman inside. Becky didn't show that side of herself to anyone but her husband. Not ever.

Daniel had been with other women—just a few. He neither cherished nor regretted those times. The truth was, all the others had ever done was sharpen his desire for Rebecca. She had touched him first, and put her mark on him forever.

"Sure is nice to see you again, Becky," he murmured to her softly.

"See me, Daniel?" Her black eyes looked amused in the dim firelight. "Well, now, I been wondering what it was called. Sure didn't seem like *seein'* to me. Seemed more like *feelin'*."

"Good feelin', Becky?"

"Not too bad, Dan Boone."

"I'm pleased to hear it."

Her raven hair touched his cheek, and she reached down and ran her fingers past the flat of his belly. "Lordy, Daniel. You ain't quite through lookin', are you?"

Daniel laughed and joyously pulled her to him.

Early in the morning, Becky woke and looked at him. It was still a good half-hour till dawn, but even in the dim light she could see his eyes were open, and guessed he had been awake for some time.

"You all right?" she asked.

"Just thinkin'."

She rose and rested one hand on her chin. " 'Bout what?"

He was silent a long moment. "It wasn't a good hunt, Becky."

"I know that, Daniel."

"Thirty skins. Damnation! Might as well live in Boston or Fredericksburg. People comin' out of the woods like flies, an' more every day."

It wasn't quite that bad, Becky knew. A person could still walk up the Yadkin River for days without meeting a soul. But Dan Boone had his own idea of crowded.

He reached out and touched her. "It's not the same, Rebecca. It's changin'. The country ain't ever goin' to be the way it was."

Rebecca didn't answer. She knew her man well, and the sound of his voice told her all she needed to hear. Something churned in the pit of her stomach—an old familiar fear, one she had never let him see and never would.

Even if Daniel had brought in a thousand prime skins it would still be the same. He hadn't yet been home a whole day, and it was already gnawing at him, pulling him from her. She loved him with all her heart, and she knew full well there wasn't another woman who could hold him. Sometimes, she almost wished there was. She could fight a real, live rival. But she was helpless against an enemy she couldn't see, that great and fertile whore across the mountains, Kentucky.

She had seen her rival's shadow in his eyes the day he came back from the war in Pennsylvania and asked her to marry him. At first, she guessed it was another woman. Later, when she learned the truth, she fled alone into the woods and cried until she could cry no more. It was one of the few times in her life she let her tears flow freely. Daniel was hers, but even when he held her, when he lost himself inside her and gave her life, she could feel the bitch named Kentucky somewhere near. And if it came to deciding between his two loves, Becky knew whom Daniel would choose.

He put off taking the skins into Salisbury, telling himself he would get to the task soon. Or maybe, as he told James, they would rest up awhile and go out again. But three weeks passed, and they went nowhere.

James knew his father's moods, and he understood, or tried to. But the image of a new long rifle with his name on it seemed to fade farther and farther into the distance. He could see someone marching into the store and buying the only one in stock, right before he and Pa got there. "Sorry, James," old Mr. Wells would smile, "that's the last of 'em. Won't be makin' any more, I hear." James knew it was only a bad dream. There wasn't any way in the world they would quit making long rifles. But he couldn't help waking up sometimes with that thought on his mind.

Going into Salisbury was about the last thing on Daniel's mind. Not because of the skins, either, though that was part of it. Walking in with three dozen hides for a month's work irked him no end. But there was more to it than that. It was getting harder and harder to face folks in town. He could scarcely turn a corner anymore without running into someone he owed money to. The trip up the Big Sandy had yielded enough skins to ward off some of his creditors, but there were always more debts than he could pay. Like Dick Henderson said, Boone had the honor of having more suits against him than any other man in North Carolina.

Stepping off the porch, he stalked off down the hill and into the woods. Leaves were spread red and gold on the ground, and the evening air was crisp and clear with the promise of winter. All the signs told him it would be a hard one this year, but Daniel still hoped it wouldn't be. A long winter meant holing up inside, except on the few good days when a man could get out for a few hours without freezing his tail off.

There would be some good hunts, Daniel knew, but there would also be long weeks of boredom and waiting. That was more time than a man needed to think about things he wanted to do, things left undone from years before. There was too much unfinished business behind him now, Daniel decided. The last days of October were falling away fast. In November he would be what, thirty-four?

Damn, and damn again, he thought. The years were passing him by, and what had he done with them? Hunted, scratched out a few crops, and this time last year, tried for Kentucky and failed, all the while piling up debts in Salisbury.

A sound through the trees suddenly interrupted his thoughts. He dropped the stick he was whittling, walked across the dry leaves and peered down the road. A man was riding a mare and leading three pack horses, bony animals laboring under a load of boxes, sacks and clanking pots and pans. The peddler heading this parade was only a shade better off than his animals. A short, gaunt old fellow in worn buckskins, he rolled half-asleep in the saddle. Only grizzled white whiskers poked from under the coonskin cap that covered his head.

Daniel took a step forward and shouted out a hello. The peddler stopped, pulled off his hat and scratched his crown. "You know where I might find a feller name of Daniel Boone?" he asked, squinting against the sun. "Folks said I'd likely find him out this way."

"Looks like they was right," said Daniel.

The man raised a brow and stared, then a wide grin spread across his features. "Well I'll be goddamned. You growed up some, Dan'l. What's it been now—twelve, thirteen years since we showed our tails to them Shawnees?"

Daniel was puzzled for only a moment. Then the years fell away and he was back in Braddock's camp, listening to tall tales around a campfire. "Findley," he shouted, "Christ A'mighty, John Findley, or I'm an Indian dog!"

Boone ran to his old companion, whooping and scaring the horses. In a moment, they were pounding each other on the back like no time at all had passed since the war. Daniel couldn't remember when he had been happier to see a man.

Chapter 3

Daniel's stern Quaker upbringing didn't leave much room for belief in portents and omens. According to Scripture, true signs from heaven were few and far between. It was usually the Devil himself who set out sweet-smelling traps for a man. Still, it seemed to Daniel that John Findley's sudden reappearance in his life had to be a godsend. Otherwise why had Findley showed up now, right on the heels of Daniel's trip to the Big Sandy, which had taken him clear to the door of Kentucky?

Findley's eyes had lit up plenty when he heard about that. He wanted to hear the whole story, over and over, and as they sat before the hearth, he interrupted Boone again and again with questions about the trip. What did the country look like? What kind of game had Daniel seen?

Finally, Findley leaned back and narrowed his eyes thoughtfully.

"You're right," he told Boone. "If you'd kept on going, I figure the Sandy would've took you to the Ohio. You'd have run into more'n tame Cherokees, too. That's mighty close to Shawnee country." He shook his head and looked into the fire. "I still say that ain't the way, Dan'l. Too far north, and the long way 'round to boot. Isn't much better than my way, down the Ohio. The Warrior's Path is the answer, if only a man could find it."

"And you still think you can? You believe there's a way through the Cumberland?"

"There is," Findley said firmly. "Isn't any question, boy. The Indians ain't been *flyin'* over those mountains all these years."

Findley hadn't been in the Boone household two nights before Daniel sent for his younger brother, Squire, and his brother-in-law, John Stewart. Squire had been up the Big Sandy, and Stewart, only months before, had traveled with Ben Cutbirth southwest across the mountains clear to the Mississippi, then rafted down to New Orleans to sell furs. Stewart brought along a map, and Daniel pulled out another. Neither chart seemed worth much, but the four men knew enough together to make a few sound guesses.

Findley knew where the Warrior's Path ought to be. If there was a way through it all, he said, it had to be over the Blue Ridge and past the Clinch Mountains. If he was right, they should hit the north-south branch of the Warrior's Path somewhere near the Powell River.

From the beginning, none of the four said anything about actually making the trip, but Daniel knew, since Findley had come riding down the road from Wilkesboro, rattling pots and pans behind him, that the trip was fated to happen. This time, Daniel was going to make it happen.

Rebecca knew. Right from the start. She didn't need more than one look at Daniel coming up the road with the bearded man in tow. Dan's eyes were shining and there was a spring in his step. Lord God—the way he walked, he looked more like Israel or James than a grown man.

Becky didn't like John Findley, but if Findley noticed, he was smart enough to keep his mouth shut. And why shouldn't he? He had food in his belly and a bed to sleep on. And not just for the night, either. Daniel asked him to stay the winter.

Rebecca understood that. It was the custom on the frontier. If there was extra food in your cupboard, you shared it with those in need. She didn't fault Daniel's generosity. Eight mouths were no harder to feed than seven, and she didn't resent Findley for taking up bed and board. She resented him for bringing Kentucky inside her house. The whore was winning again, pulling Daniel away, and this time, she wouldn't easily let him go.

The winter was milder than Daniel had figured, but the cold, dark days seemed to drag on forever. Spring was the time to try for Kentucky—in April or May at the very latest. He vowed to wait no longer than that.

Meantime, there was so damned much to do! Good horses to buy, and traps, extra rifles, a hundred-

and-one things that had to wait for a break in the weather. Till then, all he could do was wait. And of course, the debts kept piling up higher while he sat there.

Sometimes he wondered how he could even think about Kentucky. Here he was, worried about buying pack horses, when the truth was that he would be lucky to feed Becky and the children through summer. And Stewart, Findley and Squire were just as broke as he was—or damn near. They were a fine crew, the four of them.

Sometimes he thought about picking up his rifle and just walking out the door straight for Kentucky, Rebecca and everything else be damned. He wouldn't, of course, and the thought fairly shamed him, but what was a man to do? Wait till the time was right? Hell, it never would be! There would always be another bill to pay, another crop to bring in, more hunting after skins to buy lead and powder so you could get more skins, and start the whole business all over—there wasn't an end to it. No end at all.

Early in March, he rode into Salisbury with Squire, hauling the skins he had taken with James through the fall and winter months. There were more than a hundred now, not what he would like to bring, but better than nothing. It was all the country would give, thought Daniel. The land was closing in, filling up with people, and not the kind who belonged there. The newcomers were men in a hurry, men who tramped through the woods, destroying nests and chasing away game. Daniel had moved his family farther up the Yadkin three times in search of wilder country, but still the strangers came, plaguing the Yadkin with their lawless ways.

"It's time," Daniel finally told Squire. "Time, and then some."

Squire looked up curiously. "Time for what, Dan'l?"

"Nothin'. Just talkin' to myself." Through the trees he could see the outskirts of Salisbury. It was early yet, but the streets were full of people. Besides the market trade, there were extra folks in town for court—just where he would be in the morning, Daniel reminded himself. What in hell was he going to tell his creditors this time? They had heard just about every tale he could spin already.

"Go on over to the store and find Findley and Stewart," he told Squire. "I'm goin' to have me a talk with Dick Henderson, if I can find him."

"About court or Kentucky?"

Daniel grinned. "A little of both, I reckon."

Squire brought his mount up close and shook his head. "You're fair wastin' your time, Dan'l. You been plaguin' Henderson for four years about Kentucky, and he hasn't done nothin' but sit on his tail, far as I can see."

"Dick Henderson's land hungry. Don't you forget that, little brother. He's slow, but he's hungry."

Squire made an irreverent noise with his tongue.

"He knows I'm goin' to get there with or without him," Daniel insisted.

"I heard that before somewhere."

"Well, you'll likely hear it again," Daniel replied.

Urging his mare forward, he jerked the pack horses down the hollow and into the streets of Salisbury.

When the skins were sold and the few supplies he dared to purchase were loaded on the horses, he stabled the animals and started after Henderson. The clerk in Henderson's office said his boss was out, probably down at the sawmill with a client. If Daniel cared to wait . . . but Daniel didn't. He had already waited all winter.

The sawmill was half a mile down the hollow, on the far edge of town. On his way, Daniel passed by Miller's Tavern. The laughter and fiddle music inside was inviting, but the place was full of disreputables, so he kept on going.

Suddenly, from behind, he heard a girl scream. At first he thought nothing of it, but then she screamed again, this time crying out his name.

Sprinting back up the hill, he cut through the trees to the front of the tavern. The sight that met his eyes turned him rigid with anger.

Three roughnecks were playing cat and mouse with a young girl. Two of the men on foot would let her run for the trees, then the third man, on horseback, would herd her back.

The game could end only one way, and the girl knew it. Her hair was disheveled and an ugly bruise colored her cheek. Her blue blouse was torn off one shoulder, exposing a breast.

Daniel recognized her. Her name was Mindy, and she was a second cousin of Becky's. She was a pretty girl, not a day over fifteen.

When Daniel stepped forward, the girl saw him and screamed his name again. The two men on foot instantly froze in their tracks, and the horseman glared, then clutched his reins and jerked the mount toward Daniel.

"Don't," Boone said calmly, leveling his rifle at the man's chest. "I'll kill you sure and quick, mister."

The horseman reined back and sat easy, as if nothing had happened. Daniel looked the three over. He knew Billy Girt, a drunk and a ne'er-do-well, the worst of three brothers. The second, stocky and mean-eyed, looked half-Indian.

Boone moved his gaze from Girt and the half-breed to the rider. Lean and wiry as a wolf, he was a breed like the other, but obviously had more white blood than Indian. His deep-set blue eyes were as cold and blue as river ice, and he looked a hand taller than Boone.

Daniel glanced at the man's buckskins. They were common enough, but no frontier wife had stitched them together. They were made by Indians, for certain, like his moccasins and horse gear.

"Mindy, get over here with me," Boone said quietly. The girl struggled to her feet and stumbled to him. "Billy Girt, you got to answer for this."

Girt forced a tight grin. "No harm meant, Boone. We was just . . ."

"I know what you were doin', Billy." His tone was hard and uncompromising. Out of the corner of his eye, Daniel saw the rider suddenly sit up straight.

"Hold it!" As Boone swung the rifle to cover him, the stocky breed charged from behind. Daniel turned and fired. The ball parted the breed's hair, but he kept coming. His head met Daniel's belly and bowled him to the ground. Daniel sucked in air and tried to roll away,

41

but the breed had a grip like a bear. Daniel clawed his face, found an eye and jabbed a thumb in hard. The man yelled and tossed Boone aside. Daniel came to his feet, pulling the tomahawk from his belt as the short man staggered and shook blood from his eye. A long blade flashed in the breed's fist.

Daniel glanced to one side. Billy Girt was gone, and the rider was bringing his horse around hard to get behind. A pistol waved at the end of his arm, following Daniel for a clear shot. Daniel stepped quickly away, putting the short man between himself and the rider. The breed feinted, tossed the knife to his left hand and lunged at his opponent's stomach. Daniel skipped aside and came in fast. The tomahawk whistled. The breed ducked, but not fast enough. The weapon ripped at his sleeve and tore flesh.

"Goddamn it—kill him!" he shouted hoarsely as he backed away.

The rider looked amused. "Kill him yourself, Rafe."

The breed raged and charged again. Boone moved away easily. The man was strong but slow. Daniel knew he could take him anytime. He also knew that the rider had no intention of staying out of the fight. He'd kill quickly when he felt like it.

Swinging the tomahawk in wide circles, Boone went for the breed. When the man crouched to meet him, Daniel shifted to the right, lashed out with his foot and kicked him solidly in the crotch. As the breed doubled up, Daniel buried the tomahawk in the back of his neck. The man staggered, then dropped like a sack. Daniel wrenched the weapon loose, turned swiftly and tossed it at the rider.

The rider instinctively brought up his hand to ward off the twisting weapon. It glanced off his shoulder and spun in the air. The pistol exploded and the horse bolted. Daniel leaped for him. The tall man cursed, kicked out and drove him back, then swung the mount around fast and crashed through the brush.

Daniel wiped his brow and looked around. The breed was dead. The fellow had asked for it plain, and Boone had no regrets. Miller's Tavern had gone suddenly quiet, as if the men packed inside had disappeared.

Daniel brushed himself off, found the tomahawk and stuck it in his belt. Billy Girt would have to get a talking-to, and that meant taking on his brothers. Damnation! The whole business irritated him no end. He had plenty to do without fooling around with Girts. He picked up his rifle, walked to a tree and sat down to reload. It was then that he noticed Mindy had taken to the woods as well. The party sure had died quickly. There was no one left but him and the breed.

Chapter 4

It was well past noon when Daniel finally tracked down Dick Henderson. Henderson welcomed his old friend into his office, but Daniel knew better than to accept. This wasn't talk he wanted interrupted. As a Rowan County judge, Henderson was busy enough on ordinary days. On the day before court, everyone in town wanted his ear, so Daniel guided him quickly out of the building and down the street to a table at Steele's Tavern.

When they were settled over a pitcher of ale, Henderson leaned back and gave Daniel an amused smile. He was a tall, portly man who always gave Boone the impression of relaxed authority.

"The way you're acting, Dan, I'd say you're a man with something on his mind."

Daniel grinned. "I guess it shows, don't it? Well, you're as right as you can be."

45

"We've known each other a long time, my friend."

Daniel nodded absently, glanced back over his shoulder, then leaned toward Henderson. "It's time for us to do it, Dick. It's time to get to Kentucky." He laid his fist solidly on the table. "You recall me talkin' about John Findley, the feller that was with me on the Monongahela?"

Henderson nodded. Boone told him how Findley had shown up at the start of winter, and what he had said about the Warrior's Path. Daniel ended by telling how he and Findley, along with his brother Squire and John Stewart, were bound and determined to find the Path. They were ready to go, and to go now.

"I never saw a time when you weren't ready, Daniel," Henderson remarked warily.

"This is different."

"You believe in this Warrior's Path, do you? It's an old story."

Boone started to protest, but Henderson held up his hand. "I'm not saying it is or isn't there. If it's not, though, it wouldn't be the first Indian legend that didn't hold water. You have to admit, old friend, a secret path through the mountains . . ."

Boone swallowed his impatience. Sometimes it was difficult to remember he and his friend were as different as night and day. Dick was a town man, not a wanderer. His round, full features spoke of too much good whiskey, and even his fine, well-tailored clothes failed to hide an ever-expanding middle. Only Dick Henderson's eyes spoke of his love for the far side of the mountain. It was a look Daniel knew and understood, the one thing that brought them together. "It's there, Dick, and it's more than a goddamn Indian story." He borrowed Findley's words. "How do you think the Cherokees been gettin' to the Shawnees all this time? They sure ain't been flyin'!"

Henderson frowned thoughtfully. Daniel didn't give him time to argue. "It's time, Dick, you know that as well as I do. Look what's happenin' on the Yadkin, and here in Salisbury—all over North Carolina and Virginia, too. Folks are goin' to cross those mountains to find land. Whoever gets there first will get the best pickin's. If it isn't us, it'll be someone else."

Henderson grinned and shook his head. "You know how to get to me, don't you, Daniel? Right to the throat, eh?"

"I reckon I do. And you can't argue it, Dick."

Henderson took a stiff pull on his drink, then looked carefully at Boone. "It would have to be done right, Daniel."

"How's that?"

"I mean proper. There would have to be legal foundations for settling up land . . ."

Daniel made a face. "You're talkin' like a lawyer, Dick."

"Why, damn you, I *am* a lawyer!"

"Well stop actin' like one a minute and talk like Dick Henderson, who's as eager to get his toes wet in Kentucky as I am!"

Henderson smiled. "You're not such a bad lawyer yourself, Daniel."

"I'm nothin' of the kind, but I know the man I'm drinkin' with. Hell, Dick, I been scoutin' out land for you for how long? Ain't any big secret—everyone in North Carolina knows it."

Henderson cleared his throat. "There is no law against scouting or surveying," he said evenly. He caught Boone's expression and broke into a laugh. "All right. You've made your point."

"Fine. My old grandpa used to say thinkin' about sinnin' was the same as doin' it. Besides, I won't exactly be goin' in there and layin' out towns behind my horse, Dick. This is a huntin' expedition, and nothin' more. If there's as much as Findley claims, we'll more'n pay for the trip."

"Of course," Henderson said with a straight face. He raised a brow at Daniel. "But in case you should happen to stumble across some land in Kentucky you would like for your own, it would be prudent to arm yourself with some authority to claim what you've seen. Though at present, I must admit I don't know where that authority would come from, Daniel."

Daniel grinned. "Hell, you'll think of somethin'. Lawyers always do, Dick."

Henderson pretended to cringe, but Daniel could tell by the gleam in his eye he was interested.

"What do you need from me?" Henderson asked. "I know you want more than just my moral support."

Daniel tried to swallow his relief. "Two things, Dick. Money for the trip, first off. Enough supplies to hold us till we can get our own meat." Daniel hesitated. "And I got to get these damned suits off my back. I can't leave Becky with that hangin' over us."

Henderson nodded. "You want me to get a continuance."

"If you can. I don't see how I can go without one."

"No. Nor do I." He sat up straight and looked

48

squarely at Daniel. "You'll go, my friend. By God, you will go. Rest assured of that!"

Henderson watched his friend leave and ordered another ale. He knew Boone was likely the happiest man in North Carolina right now. Daniel didn't give a whit about the business of acquiring land. He might think he did, but Dick Henderson knew better. All Daniel really wanted was the chance to find his promised land. He'd do that, and willingly, even if he never took one acre of Kentucky for himself.

Henderson treasured his bond with Boone more than any other. In one respect, they were worlds apart. Boone's life was in the forest and on the plain. His friends were scouts and backwoodsmen like Findley. Boone cared nothing for the undercurrents of colonial society that were Henderson's element. Only once had Henderson tried to mix their worlds. His friends had been fascinated by Boone, but, although Daniel would never say it, the small talk of lawyers and businessmen had bored him. When Daniel spoke of buffalo and endless forests, Henderson's friends saw only acres of profit, new settlements and new industry.

Still, Henderson recalled with a grin, Daniel had no trouble at all communicating with the women at that gathering. The aristocratic ladies there had swarmed around him like moths around a flame. The aura of danger and excitement that seemed to surround the rough backwoodsman set many eyes fluttering, and brought a flush to the cheeks of even the most sedate colonial lasses. Even his own wife, the daughter of an Irish lord, had not been immune to Boone's charms. Daniel's presence at the party had clearly been a feather in her cap. Who else could boast a guest who had actually killed a buffalo and had lived with savage redskins?

Barely through his second cup of ale, Henderson spotted his partner, John Williams, making his way through the crowd. Henderson waved him over.

"Been looking all over for you, Dick. For Boone, really. The office said—"

"You just missed him. Sit down. What's the trouble?"

Williams looked concerned. "Nothing, maybe. But Daniel ought to know about it. That little fracas he got into this morning. One of the men in it was . . ."

"Wait." Henderson held up a hand. "What little fracas are you talking about?"

"Didn't he tell you?" Williams frowned, then quickly recounted the tale.

"Well, by God!" Henderson shook his head in amazement. "We sat here for half an hour and he never said a word. Killed a man, you say?"

"His name was Rafe Flint. A wagoner who works for us saw the whole thing, and he swears the one who got away is Rafe's half-brother, Henry."

Henderson sat up straight. "Henry Flint, the renegade?" He shook his head adamantly. "That bastard wouldn't have the nerve to show himself among decent men!"

"Maybe not, but if it's true . . ."

"Damnation!" Henderson slammed his fist on the table, staining the wood with ale. If it were true, Daniel had made for himself a bad enemy.

There was more than enough to do, and as far as Boone was concerned, scarcely any time to do it. The first smell of spring was already in the air. Provisions had been packed, and Squire had bought a team of pack horses. There were bearskin blankets, pots, kettles, salt, flour, lead, powder, extra rifles, skinning knives and spare moccasins. Plenty of rope and leather were also packed, as well as traps and rifle tools.

Daniel wouldn't have left the tools behind for anything. He had learned to work metal from his blacksmith father, and the knowledge had saved his life more than once. A sharp eye with a rifle was important, but a weapon was nothing more than worthless wood and metal if it wouldn't shoot properly. A man who had his own bellows and files and knew how to use them could damn near build a whole new rifle in the woods if he had to.

Daniel had thought long and hard about who else to bring along on the trip. With him and the others spending all their time exploring and trapping for skins, someone else would have to keep camp, and prepare and pack the hides. Boone finally settled on Joseph Holden, James Mooney and Will Cooley. They had always been good neighbors and reliable men. They would have to be paid, of course, but the time they would save the others would make them well worth the expense.

In mid-April, Daniel had one of the few arguments with Squire he could remember. Someone had to stay back to bring new supplies in the fall. Squire agreed, but didn't think he ought to be the one.

"Hell, I been part of this thing from the start, Daniel. You know how I feel about goin'."

"Isn't anyone else I can trust," Daniel told him. "That's the truth, Squire."

51

"Ha!" Squire forced a laugh at Daniel's expression. "I'm your brother, remember? You don't have to rub no grease on me!"

Still, in the end he agreed. Someone had to get the crops in and look after Daniel's family, as well as John Stewart's. And there was the other matter, too. Daniel had quickly dismissed Henderson's news about Henry Flint, but he was more than a little worried about the renegade. Squire could read it plainly on his brother's face.

Nat Gist, or any number of friends or relatives for that matter, could have looked after the families till fall, but Daniel had more faith in his own brother. Daniel told him so. That decided it for Squire. He gave Daniel no more trouble about staying behind.

A few weeks earlier, he had ridden out with Daniel to give Billy Girt a stern warning. They had nearly scared the life out of Billy, but when Daniel asked him about Flint, Girt denied knowing the man. Obviously, by the look in his eyes, he was more frightened of Flint than he was of Daniel. And with good reason, Squire decided.

Flint was a name frontier mothers uttered to scare their children. "You go too far into the woods, ol' Henry Flint'll get you, child!" Squire knew more than one family who had lost someone to Flint and his Shawnee friends. Folks in Salisbury refused to believe that the man the Indians called Black Knife would come down this far south, but Squire knew better. And so did Daniel.

On one of the last days of April, Daniel strode into the pantry and told James to get the horses ready.

Though his father didn't say where they were going, James had a fair notion. He kept his silence, even when the two reached Salisbury and hitched their horses outside the store. Just thinking about it could ruin everything—the whole town might disappear and he would wake up and find he was dreaming.

When Mr. Wells took the brand-new long rifle off the rack and handed it to him, James held it tightly and stared at it for a long moment.

"It's a good one, James," Mr. Wells said solemnly. "I guarantee it. Top quality."

"Does it suit you, boy?" asked his father.

"Yes sir," James murmured in awe. "It suits me just fine, Pa." He could scarcely take his eyes off the long rifle. It was shinier than his father's, and longer than James was tall, but he could handle it. That he knew. And he wouldn't be here in the store, holding it in his hands, if his father didn't think so too.

"It cost me seven pounds sterling," Daniel told him. "That's a lot of money. I'm tellin' you that 'cause I want you to know how hard you worked last winter to help earn it." He looked squarely at James. You know what I'm sayin', son?"

"Yes, sir. I reckon I do."

"No, don't just reckon, James. You got it 'cause you worked for it. A man who's worth his salt don't get a rifle given to him free."

"No, sir. And I thank you, Pa."

Daniel nodded. "You're a fine young man, James. You make a father proud."

The two didn't speak again till they were well out of town, when Daniel stopped and let the boy wipe down and clean the rifle. Then he gave him the new powder horn and pouch he had hidden in his saddle-bag.

While James loaded up, Daniel stepped off twenty-five yards down the creekbed and fixed a little patch of leather to a tree. James fired six times. After each shot, Daniel inspected the rifle thoroughly, then took the boy out to the target.

"First three shots veered about a gnat's hair to the left and above, but that was your fault, James, not the rifle's. You took better care with the last three." He slapped the long barrel and handed it back to his son. "It's a good one. Like Mr. Wells said, top quality."

James carefully cleaned and reloaded the rifle, then polished it again. Daniel finally had to stop him. "Lord, boy, you keep that up and you'll wear her right through to the bore! Let's get crackin' 'fore it's dark."

James flushed. "Yes, sir. Guess you're right." As he stood up, his father laid a hand on his shoulder.

"You haven't said anything about the trip, James, not since you knew I was going."

James looked steadily at his father. "No, sir."

"Wish you were comin', I expect."

"Yes, sir, I purely do."

"You know you can't. Not this time."

"Yes, sir."

Boone looked away and poked at the earth with a stick. "I want you to know I wish you could. I'd be proud to have you with me."

James' eyes nearly filled, and he bit his lip. "I—someone's got to look after Ma and the others."

"You're right." Daniel looked at him. "And don't ever think that I'd be leavin' you with such a burden if I didn't think you were ready. Your uncle Squire'll be around for a while, but that ain't the same. It's in your hands, James. And don't you worry none. I'll be back. Then you, me and the whole family'll head out for Kentucky together, and you'll ride right up there in front beside me. I promise you that right now. I'd be pleased to shake on it."

James gripped his father's hand and squeezed hard. He couldn't remember a prouder day in his life. The rifle had pleased him, but his father's respect was something you couldn't buy for seven pounds sterling, or seven thousand. A man didn't shake on a bargain with a mere boy. That was a pact between men.

Daniel knew something was wrong.

He could feel it, even before they got to the cabin, like a sudden chilly wind blowing over the back of his neck. There was nothing to see or hear—it was just a feeling he trusted and feared. He looked at James, dismounted quietly and handed the boy his reins. Then he cocked his rifle and walked quietly into the clearing.

Wood smoke curled out of the chimney, not enough for a cookfire, though. The dogs dashed out and barked wildly, but there were no children to greet him, no little ones laughing, running, shouting his name.

Daniel froze. Israel, his face pale as death, appeared in the doorway. He had the big wood-axe clutched in his small hands. Jemima, eyes wide as saucers, peered out fearfully from behind him. When Israel saw his father, he dropped the axe and came running, tears breaking loose and streaming down his face. Daniel raced forward and grabbed him up.

"Israel, what is it?"

"Ma," he cried, choking out the words, "they took Ma!"

"Who did, Israel? Who!"

"The—the men—Billy Girt and his brothers. Pa, I think they hurt her bad!"

Chapter 5

Daniel grabbed James' rifle and sent him riding hard for Squire's place. Then he put Israel and Jemima atop a farm horse and set them at a trot for John Stewart's in the opposite direction. He prayed silently one of the two would be home, and that maybe John Findley or Nat would be nearby.

Daniel wouldn't let himself think about Rebecca. He forced her out of his mind and concentrated on Billy Girt. The knot in his stomach hardened. He knew full well Girt wouldn't dare do a thing like this on his own, not in a hundred years. Someone had put him up to it. Flint?

Jesus God, Daniel prayed, *let me get to her before he does!*

Girt's tracks were clear, and as Israel had said, not a half-hour old. At least there was still time. Three sets of hoofprints were pressed into the mud—Billy's and his brothers'. One set of tracks looked deeper than the others. Becky was riding double, or more likely, tied on like a sack. Flint wasn't with them. Not yet. That's the way he would do it, Daniel was sure. Get Billy to handle the dirty work, then meet him somewhere up north with a band of Shawnees.

There was no question in Daniel's mind what all this was about. Boone had killed Flint's kin, and now Rebecca would clear the debt. But Boone himself coming to get her, that would be even better. The French and Shawnees would both honor Black Knife for a scalp like that.

Daniel pushed his mount hard. He wasn't worried about the Girts yet, or the Shawnees either. The Indians wouldn't try an ambush this close to the Yadkin, and all Billy and his brothers wanted now was to put plenty of miles behind them. That gave Daniel the advantage he needed. He knew the country well, every tree and hollow. The Girts weren't woodsmen. He could guess where they were going, and which trail they would take.

Still, something nagged at the edge of his mind. No matter how this business came out, the Girts had cut themselves off from North Carolina or anyplace else where decent folk settled. They had committed themselves to Flint and left everything behind. What the hell had Flint offered them? More than he planned to deliver, most likely. Billy and his brothers would be of no use to the renegade after this. Maybe their scalps might, though. Flint always delivered to his Shawnee friends.

The tracks led into a thick stand of trees, then stopped. Daniel left his horse and stood for a long moment, sniffing the air and peering in every direction. Finally, he went to his knees and carefully studied the ground. The three horses had taken different paths. One went northwest, the other two, including the mount carrying Rebecca, went straight on to the north.

He knew what they were trying. They would split up here, then come together again somewhere farther up the trail, figuring he was alone and could follow only one path. Daniel let himself smile for the first time since he had left the cabin. The trick was as clear as glass. Maybe the Girts figured he couldn't read sign any better than they could.

Daniel cut a notch to show Squire, or whoever followed, where he had gone. Then he moved on, ignoring both trails and pushing his horse fast. He could guess where they would join again, and he intended to beat them to the spot. For a while, before he turned back east, the shortcut would put him in danger of running into Flint. Still, the Blue Ridge country would hide a whole army in one of its pockets. With any luck, he would miss the Shawnees completely.

The sun was high over the western mountains when he came down off the ridge and plunged once more into the thicket. A shallow creek sparkled on his right. He knew that it ran due east for some miles, and that unless the Girts turned back, they would have to cross to open ground. If they kept to the trees, they would have to go miles out of their way. When they crossed the creek, they would leave clear tracks. Daniel had cut the distance between them fast, and when he spotted their trail he would be only minutes behind.

In a few minutes, he found the tracks. They plunged up the soft bank on the north side of the creek. But he instantly knew something was wrong. His heart jumped up in his throat and he cursed himself soundly. The Girts had already met—and switched again! The two riders who had taken the eastern route had joined the single rider somewhere south. The lone rider had taken Rebecca and gone off on another path. Neither of the animals he was tracking now was carrying an extra load.

He couldn't credit the Girts with a trick like that. Indian sense was behind this kind of business. Had they already met Flint, somewhere behind him, or the Shawnees? Hell, he couldn't have missed their tracks. He was a better tracker than that.

He had two choices: He could double-back on the rider's path south and find where they had met and switched, which would take him to Rebecca but add hours to the search; or he could follow the two men north. The Girts, he decided, wouldn't feel easy in the wilderness. They would want to meet up again fast, even if Flint had warned them not to. Either path was a gamble with Becky's life. He knew, though, he had to follow the tracks he had found and pray they would lead him to her. He didn't dare let the Girts meet Flint before he found them. Even if Squire brought the whole Yadkin Valley, they would never make it in time. Daniel would have to take them on himself. And if he ran into both Girts and Flint, he would never get Becky out alive.

He followed the tracks straight for a few miles, then started crisscrossing in ever-widening circles until he was convinced they were keeping to the natural lay of the land. Finally, he ignored the tracks entirely and headed north. After an hour of plunging through deep clefts strewn with rock and tangled growth, he came to a ridge. He left his mount and climbed twenty yards up. He recognized the valley right off. He and Nat Gist had taken some good deer there several years back. It was a wide, natural bowl between the ridge and the woods beyond. One end butted up just below, the other curved out of sight in a long half-circle northwest. If he was right, the riders would come out of the woods here and into the valley. They would either keep on going, or wait there for Becky and the other rider—and for Flint. Daniel hoped they would wait. The valley was fully in shadow now, and darkening fast.

Daniel watched as twilight slowly descended. He tried not to think about Becky, but her face kept creeping into his thoughts. Maybe he was wrong. Maybe he had outwitted himself good this time, and the Girts had gotten past him. If Becky was in Flint's hands, she was dead already—or soon would be after the renegade got through with her. Jesus God, if he and James hadn't stopped to sight the damned rifle, if only he had been there a little sooner!

Daniel went rigid. Suddenly, just to the south, a flock of crows rose noisily out of the trees. Then, moments later, an owl flew up and flapped swiftly off to the west. Boone grinned and let out a deep breath. Damn! The Girts couldn't have announced themselves better with a drummer boy marching out ahead.

In a few moments two riders came cautiously out of the forest. Daniel waited. Then a third rider rode up behind the others, with Becky—still alive and well! Daniel's heart started beating again. She was bound, and sagged wearily behind Billy Girt, but by God, she was all right.

Even before they began to settle in, he was off the ridge and making his way down into the valley. There was no time to wait or to get his horse. Flint might come out of the valley at any moment.

The Girts would stay put, but they weren't foolish enough to make camp. They knew someone was after them.

Boone hated to lose his horse, but if his plan worked, he would have the Girts' mounts, and maybe time enough to get his own. If not, hell, he wouldn't need horses anyway.

Daniel stalked slowly, silently. Before he could get up close, one of the brothers walked right out to him, stopping behind a tree not twenty yards away. In a moment, Daniel heard a stream of water splattering on leaves.

The man never heard him. Daniel slapped a hand over his mouth, slipped the scalping knife under his ribs, and lowered him gently to the ground. The Girts didn't even look up. Billy was squatting down rummaging through his pack. Becky was under a tree. The other brother, hearing someone behind him, turned around and grinned. The grin faded and the man went pale. Boone's tomahawk whistled through the growing dark and caught him square in the chest. Billy jerked up, took one look and crashed through the brush with a startled yell. Daniel slung the rifle off his shoulders and calmly laid the bead on Billy's back.

Then he stopped and eased his finger off the trigger. With Billy on foot in the woods, Daniel was safe enough, and a shot would tell Flint exactly what he would want to know.

Bending quickly to Rebecca, he brought her to

her feet and slashed the leather about her wrists. "Becky, you all right?"

Becky wound her arms tightly about his neck and sobbed into his shoulders. "Oh, God, Daniel!"

He took her by the hand and plunged into the trees. Damnation! Two of the horses had spooked and run off. The Girts hadn't even bothered to hobble them. He would have to go back for his own horse now. Riding double, they would be an easy catch for Flint. Pulling Becky up behind him into the saddle, he quickly explained their situation and passed her the extra rifle. Then, urging the mount on, he took them swiftly back south through the trees. There was a gap there, not a quarter-mile back. If he could find it in the dark, it would take them safely to the other side of the ridge.

He missed the gap twice, then found it. The horse didn't like stumbling over sharp rock with two strangers on his back, but Daniel urged it on, cursing under his breath. Branches whipped out and tore at their faces, but Becky hung on tight. Finally, the growth thinned and Daniel stopped. His eyes were used to the dark now, but with all the racket they had made, if anyone was up there, seeing wouldn't be much help.

Something moved, froze, moved again. Daniel let out a deep breath. The pale shadow took the shape of his own horse, waiting where he had left it. Becky touched him and said something, but Daniel never heard. Her words were lost as a blood-curdling yell suddenly split the night. Boone jerked up in time to see a dark figure leap off the ridge to his left.

The shadowy figure hit him hard and tackled him to the ground. Daniel saw the long knife flash in the

Shawnee's hand and felt the Indian's hot breath against his cheek. Boone kicked out savagely, driving the warrior back. The knife sparked as it scraped against stone. A rifle exploded, scalding Daniel's cheek. Then fire lit the hollow and he saw a second Shawnee drop to his right, a few yards from Becky, who picked up a rock, snuck up behind the Indian, and smashed the back of his head. The Indian with the knife came at him again. Daniel searched frantically for his own rifle. It was nowhere in sight. As the Shawnee jerked his blade around in a wide arc, Daniel sucked in his gut, leaped back and went sprawling over a root.

The Indian flew after him, but this time Daniel swept out his arm and caught him on the shoulder. The knife whispered again, and Boone yelped as pain burned down his side. He scrambled back and tore at his waist for a weapon. His knife was gone—it had slipped out in the dark—and the tomahawk was back there buried in one of the Girts. Daniel's hand touched something hard. He clutched at it, recognized the barrel of James' rifle. It was the wrong end, but better than nothing. Jerking it up fast, he caught the Shawnee's arm just below the elbow. The Indian grunted, dropped the knife and took a step back. Boone went down on his knees, grabbed the barrel in both hands and swung out blindly. The stock hit the Indian's head and splintered. Boone felt the blow clear up to his shoulders. That Shawnee was out for good. Grabbing the reins of both horses, he led them quickly back down the hollow.

When they were past the gap again, he held Becky briefly, then swung her up on his horse. In a moment, they were cutting quickly through the trees, skirting the edge of the dark valley and heading south.

Black Knife could follow if he liked; Daniel knew they would make it now. He was just as dangerous in the dark as Henry Flint or any damn Shawnee. And by God, so was his Becky, for sure!

They rode hard all night without stopping and by noon of the following day, they were once again safely at home. And for the first time in his life, Daniel Boone was happy to be out of the wilderness. But not for long.

Chapter 6

"You take care of yourself," he told Rebecca. They were lying in bed the day before he was to leave. "Squire'll be here awhile. James too. And Dick Henderson, if you need him."

"I don't expect I'll be calling for help." Her voice was hard, cool. "I never have, Daniel."

"Becky, what's wrong?"

"Nothin', Daniel. Not anythin' at all."

"There is. There's somethin'. Becky, if it's Flint you're worried about, that's over with. By God. I sure wouldn't leave if I thought there'd be problems with that feller. You ought to know that."

"Wouldn't you, Daniel?"

"What? Now what the hell does that mean?"

When she turned over slowly and faced him, the brittle coldness in her eyes shocked Daniel. The woman lying beside him didn't look at all like his Rebecca.

"You wouldn't leave if you thought there was danger, Daniel. But what if I thought there was? Or if I figured there was another reason you shouldn't go. What then?"

"Hell, I—I can't even tell what you're tryin' to say," he mumbled gruffly.

She held his eyes a long moment, then turned and looked away.

"Don't worry," she said evenly. "I won't ask you to stay, Daniel. Maybe I have a right to, and maybe I don't, but I'd never put that burden on you."

"Well, damn it all," he said crossly, "you know if you—I mean if you was to—"

"No." She laid a finger on his lips. "Don't, Daniel."

After a moment, she slipped out of bed and left him. For a long time, he could hear her rocking on the porch. Finally, when he had nearly fallen asleep again, she returned, snuggling close and affectionately nuzzling him. He turned to her, and they made love. Afterwards, he held her close, and everything was like it ought to be.

Only it wasn't. Not really. Something wasn't there that should have been. He didn't like that. He wanted all of Rebecca, without even the smallest part of her gone. He suddenly knew she might keep that something from him, hold it to herself always. It scared him to think about that.

Damn it all, it didn't seem right. A man ought to have all of his woman. He gave everything to her, didn't he? He sure wasn't holding anything back he could think of.

The next morning looked to Daniel like anything but the start of a hunting trip. It reminded him more of a spring fair, or a wedding celebration. Folks had come from up and down the Yadkin and all over Rowan County to see them off. There were plenty of Boones—cousins, uncles, aunts and whatever, and enough Bryans to start an army. Dick Henderson and his partner came, as did many other people from Salisbury.

Hell, even people he owed money to had come to wish him well!

He felt uncomfortable about the whole business. There were too many people bunched around the small cabin, all wanting to shake his hand and talk. Still, it touched him deeply that they had bothered to come. All the yelling and shouting put excitement in the air, and a feller couldn't help getting caught up in it.

"You take care of your kin, now," he told James again and again. "You got a man's job to do."

"I will, Pa."

"Squire, I'll see you in the fall. We'll blaze a trail for you plain and clear."

Squire gripped his brother's hand and forced a smile, but Daniel knew how disappointed he was.

"Hold on to your scalp, Daniel," yelled one of the Bryans.

"In case you don't," Nat Gist called over, "we'll send a couple of extry wigs out with Squire!" The crowd laughed, and Daniel laughed with them. John Stewart gave his pretty wife, Hannah, a long good-bye kiss and the folks around them cheered. Stewart, a big

69

bear of a man with dark eyes and a great mane of black hair, turned red as a beet and let go of his wife. The pint-sized Hannah sternly pulled him back in her arms and kissed him soundly again.

Daniel had already hugged his children a dozen times and lifted the young ones up onto his horse for a ride around the yard. Finally, he held Becky tight and whispered his good-bye to her, then mounted his horse and started down the slope for the river. Findley, anxious to get started, had already walked the pack horses as far as the hollow. Boone caught up, looked back once more at the cabin, waved, then followed the others into the woods.

It's happening, he thought. I'm finally on my way to Kentucky. By God, it's happening right now!

Boone and Stewart knew every turn and hill of the first stretch. The long, westward valleys that cut through the Blue Ridge peaks were as familiar to them as the streets of Salisbury. Following the curl of the Yadkin River south, they crossed the rough, high country down to the headwaters of the Watauga and started the trek northwest. Daniel loved this part of the country. There were so few people here, and game was still easy to find. He, Stewart and Findley took turns going out after meat, ranging away from the path the others would take, then catching up in the evening. Deer were plentiful, but chasing them down was difficult. The land was wild and rocky, thick with trees, and crisscrossed with rushing water. And the game thereabout knew the best, most treacherous places to hide from a horse and rider.

From the start, Daniel was glad he had decided to

bring along Cooley, Holden and Mooney. They were good men, easy to get along with and content with their duties in camp. Nor had any of them a desire to ride out alone. The Cherokees were supposed to be friendly at the moment, but you never could tell.

Findley was fond of advising them that the friendliest of Indians were the ones you didn't see.

"And what about the others?" asked Cooley.

"Oh, you don't see them, neither."

"What's the difference, then?"

"Well, you're dead when you don't see the unfriendlies," said the old peddler. Daniel and Stewart laughed at the ancient joke, but the three campkeepers weren't amused.

At night, Daniel and his companions took turns spinning yarns, each trying to top the other. Stewart regaled them with the wonders of the Mississippi and the sinful joys of New Orleans. For the first time, Findley loosened up and talked about his long years of misfortune after his trek with Braddock. He told how he had wandered about from one odd job to another, always aiming to make another try at Kentucky. Once, he had almost got a big enough pile together, but that disappeared when a trading-boat venture went bad.

Daniel and Stewart nodded in understanding. It was the sort of bad luck that happened to a man now and then. There was no shame in it.

John Stewart knew all of Daniel's tales, but Findley had heard only a few, so Daniel related what had happened to him during the past fourteen years. He had returned home from the war with the Shawnees only to fight another with the Cherokees after they had ravaged the Yadkin Valley. Then he had gone back

north with General Forbes and had seen the end of
Fort Duquesne, come south to see the Cherokees make
peace, wandered off through Tennessee a spell, and
made a trip down to Florida.

"Don't sound to me like you been sittin' 'round
much," grinned Findley.

"Guess not," conceded Daniel, looking at him
across the fire. "But what good was all that rovin'? It
sure didn't come to no account."

Daniel was impatient to get on to new, unfamiliar
lands. But even though he knew the path ahead, it
wasn't country you could hurry through. One towering
peak led to another, and in between were deep, dark,
wooded valleys. And always the Endless Mountains
ranged far to the west, looming up like an impassable
barrier against travelers to Kentucky. Sometimes it
seemed to Boone as if they got farther away instead of
closer every day.

Finally, the twisting water of the Holston appeared, and past that, through another range, the
Clinch River, flowing swiftly southwest through the
dark, rocky land. At last, the wild desolate beauty of
Powell's Valley lay before them. Here was Martin Station, a final lonely settlement in the very shadow of the
great range ahead. Beyond Martin's, there were no
clear paths to follow. From here, the only trail would
be the one they made.

The blood in Daniel's veins surged at the sight.
The air above the mountains was crisp and clear and
as he watched, an eagle soared high over the peaks,
then vanished westward into Kentucky. It was there,
just beyond Daniel's reach. Once again, he felt the

deep, unreasoning fear that it would somehow be gone when he got there, that the dream would disappear.

It was already late afternoon, and in the hollow of the mountains, shadows crept quickly over the land. Still, Daniel insisted they leave the outpost behind and make camp in the wilderness. Even if only a mile or so farther, at least it would be at the edge of the unknown.

The country south of Martin's seemed to close in around them and push them back. They camped on a ridge near the base of the mountain, a place so thick with trees that Findley said it was all a man could do to stretch out straight.

Daniel lay awake, watching the stars through ragged branches. Somehow, his mind wouldn't turn to Kentucky. Instead it strayed back East, across the long valleys to the Yadkin. Becky had been on the edge of his thoughts since they had parted. It hadn't been easy to leave her. She had gotten her dander up good and really given him a time. It was something she had never done before, and it puzzled him, made him angry. In fact, it frightened him.

The terrain grew rougher, as rough as Boone had seen anywhere. In places, the steep, wooded ridges were almost impenetrable. It took a whole day to get the mounts and pack horses through one especially difficult stretch of tangled trees and spiny rock. When the job was finished, they found they had cut a path right to the rim of a deep, impassable gorge. Peering over the edge, they saw a white, angry river thundering below, a river tucked so tight between the high granite walls of its canyon that the sun touched its waters only a few minutes out of the day.

Frustrated and tired, they made their way back through the growth to find another route.

Still, if it was wild and difficult, the country was awesome, spectacular to look upon. It seemed to Boone that neither God nor man would ever tame it.

When it happened, it happened quickly, surprising them all. They had forded a rushing river that morning, nearly losing their pack horses and supplies to the current, and had come up against another tangle of woods that looked as solid as a fortress wall. Stewart, scouting ahead on foot and cursing up a storm, suddenly let out a whoop. The whole party rushed up to him, rifles at the ready, but when they reached him, they found him laughing uncontrollably. They followed close as he plunged through the trees. They had gone less than twenty yards when they found themselves standing in a narrow, open way that wound like a snake through the forest. A high ridge, sharp as a razor, had split the woods there and fallen over on itself, leaving a pathway free of growth and tangles. It was no Boston Road, for certain—in places it was scarcely visible to any but the practiced eye—but they understood at once what they had found. Here was the Warrior's Path, the clear, honest-to-God trail to Kentucky.

Curbing his excitement, Daniel bent down to show them sign. "We came to the right place," he said dryly. "There's more goddamn Indian tracks here than you'd see after a war dance."

"Cherokee?" asked Stewart.

"Uh-huh. And not real old, either. Goin' that way, mostly," he said, pointing northeast. "Back to Martin's Station, or past it. No wonder them redskins come an' go as they please. I ain't surprised they was able to keep this place a secret."

"Ain't any secret no more," grinned Findley.

"It will be again," Stewart remarked soberly, "if they catch us out here."

They followed the path south, keeping silent and staying in shadow whenever they could. Sometimes the way seemed to disappear completely, or to end at a high, rocky wall. Always, though, they found it again, twisting off in what inevitably proved the easiest way. Finally, the path widened, spreading out into a long valley that turned abruptly northwest. The valley was overshadowed by a sheer wall of stone, rising to an awesome height before it vanished into the dark, grey clouds overhead.

The party stopped, gazing up the valley at this wondrous sight. As they watched, the clouds scudded away, blew into bands of mist and left ragged tails behind. As the veil slowly lifted, Daniel saw it, a deep cleft in the wall, as if some great tooth had been pulled from a monstrous jaw.

"Great God A'mighty," breathed Findley. "There's your door to Kentucky, Dan'l, and I reckon it's standin' right open."

Chapter 7

Daniel stopped a moment to let his horse take water. The creek deepened where it trickled through a dense draping of willow, hiding darting schools of sunfish and perch. Beyond the bank was a rolling pasture of grassland, and past that, foothills that led to a higher range. The light colors of spring had darkened now, and the land about him was rich with the deep, green shades of summer. There were still good months of hunting ahead, plenty of time to add more skins to the pile.

Damn, what a haul they would take back to the Yadkin! He still marveled at the rich supply of game in the area. The cache in the camp, piled high into bales, grew bigger every day, and his camp-keepers had all they could do to keep up with the hunters. Besides collecting pelts, they were also storing a supply of smoked meats for the winter. Deer, buffalo, bear, squirrel, rabbit and a dozen other kinds of game abounded in Kentucky, so the men were in no fear of starving.

Bringing the horse out of the willows, Daniel started off north, keeping a sharp eye on the open stretch of land all around him. In the two months since they had crossed the mountain gap and set up camp, they had seen no fresh sign of Indians, though there were old fires and stale traces in the woods. Daniel figured they were still around somewhere, but not in great numbers. He figured the Indians were here for the same business as his own party—hunting and roaming about.

Leaving his horse in a thicket, Boone started up the big hill he had sighted from the willows. It was an easy slope to climb, rising some seven or eight hundred feet above the rolling grasses. At the top, he stood on a flat table of stone and peered out over the land. The sight nearly took his breath away. Below, the great river blazed like copper in the sun, and past it, Kentucky seemed to stretch out forever.

When he had first stood in that high gap between the mountains and looked down on the land he had so long sought, Daniel thought he had seen the loveliest sight Kentucky had to offer. Yet, each new vista he came upon put the one before it to shame. Drinking in the great, sprawling scene before him, he longed to strike out for the farthest point he could see. What was there, where the land disappeared past the soft blue horizon?

Daniel shook his head in wonder. If this wasn't Paradise under his feet, where was it? Dick Henderson, and a thousand other men, would look no farther. But Daniel knew it was there just past that far blue haze. It would always be just past him, and he would always yearn for it.

It struck him then that this was what Becky had told him with her eyes. She knew what he was as well as he did—a wanderer. She had hidden her fears a long time before finally letting him see them. Daniel couldn't blame her. A woman needed a man to be all hers, and maybe she was entitled to that. But he couldn't be something he wasn't. If he changed to someone else, Rebecca sure wouldn't have the same Dan Boone she had loved and married.

On the way back to camp, Stewart came up to meet him. "Findley says he saw what looks like fresh sign just west of here, where you found that old skinnin' ground."

Daniel nodded. He knew right where it was. The Indians had taken buffalo there a season back. "Not too surprisin'. We knew they was here. How many does John figure?"

"Half a dozen, no more'n that. A huntin' party, most likely."

"Shawnee or Cherokee?"

Stewart shook his head. "No way to tell. Wasn't that much to see." He stopped, and looked at Daniel. "You thinkin' we ought to move?"

"Kinda late for that, ain't it?"

Stewart didn't answer. The edge in Daniel's voice was clear enough.

"I'll talk to Findley when he gets back," Boone said quietly.

The whole business irked Daniel no end. They had been expecting sign all along, and it was a damn wonder they hadn't seen it before now. They were too close to the Warrior's Path—had been from the start. Daniel had been against it, but the spring rains had set in hard and sudden, so they had stopped and put up a shelter. They should have kept going, he thought, west, east, anywhere but right here. There was nothing to do about it now, except keep their eyes peeled. It meant they would have to hunt farther from the main camp, and the outlying camps as well. He, Stewart and Findley would be doing more traveling than shooting, which would cut down considerably on what they could take and carry.

Daniel wondered how he could warn the campkeepers to be more careful when they went for water, and watch how they lit their fires, without alarming them. Maybe there was no good way to do both.

"Squire'll be comin' in a couple of months," he told Findley and Stewart as they sat by the campfire that evening. "We'll figure what to do then. I don't see makin' no move right now."

Findley agreed. "We leave this place an' the Injuns find it, ain't no way they won't know we're here, and they'll sure come lookin'."

Boone stirred up the fire and chewed on a tender strip of venison. "If they don't spot us before the cold sets in, they won't be movin' 'round enough to find us. Squire'll bring plenty of traps, and we can start after fur. Trappin' makes a hell of a lot less noise than shootin'."

Daniel didn't sleep well that night. He wasn't nearly as confident as he tried to sound to the others. Findley and Stewart, he decided, were likely to be thinking the same thing. Their luck had been running too strong for too long. Now they knew for certain there was a party of Indians close by. Kentucky was a big chunk of country, but not that big. It was just a matter of time before one of them walked around a tree and saw someone wearing a scalp lock instead of a hat.

Throughout July and into early August, Daniel and his companions roamed far from camp to trap and to hunt. They stayed far away from the Warrior's Path, and often, when the country looked too open, they hunted in pairs.

By late September, the main camp was inundated with skins. They were packed and baled on high scaffolds, far enough off the ground to keep wolves or curious bears from tearing them down.

One day, while hunting with Stewart in the country east of camp, Daniel found a rich section of land where three rivers snaked down from the highlands and emptied their waters into a fourth. When Daniel put all the maps he had together, it looked likely that this great river ran clear across Kentucky.

"If it does," said Stewart, "it comes south from the Ohio. That's a far piece, Dan'l."

Boone scratched his head and looked at the maps. Hell, there were so many empty spots a man could do near as well by guessing. "It could. Like you say, that's quite a ways." Stretching his legs, he wandered out of camp. Far off to the east was a faint grey blur on the horizon where the Endless Mountains began, and past them, North Carolina. He wondered how Becky was, and the children. Squire would be along soon with news of them.

Daniel searched the horizon a long time. It gave

him a great sense of accomplishment to finally look at those mountains from the Kentucky side. It was now close to October and they had left the Yadkin on the first of May. As near as he could reckon, they had set up camp the seventh of June. Five months from home. They had put a lot behind them in that time.

If they could keep their scalps through the winter and get back to Salisbury with the cache of skins, he would pay back every debt he owed and then some. And he would walk into Dick Henderson's office to tell him he had found the biggest damn country out there a man could ask for! The year 1769 would sure be one to remember—the year he had stopped being poor. Why, he could. . . . Something bothered him, something familiar in the look of those mountains.

Suddenly Daniel gave a loud, high whoop to the sky. John Stewart came tearing out of the brush, rifle at the ready.

"Goddamn, Dan'l—I thought the whole Shawnee nation was on us!"

Daniel grinned and pounded him on the back. "Hell, John, it just come to me what a fool I been. I knew for dead certain I'd looked at those mountains before, an' now I know when. The Big Sandy's got to be 'bout a hundred or so miles up north, and I stood right there like I am now." He threw back his head and laughed. "If I ain't wrong, I already been in Kentucky two years ago. Only I didn't even know it!"

When the days grew crisp with the snap of autumn in the air, Daniel took off alone, following a stream far to the west of the Warrior's Path. He was alone because it was a time of year he couldn't bear to share with other folk. The whole world was spangled with red and gold and yellow. The chattering of squirrels and cawing of crows carried farther in the clean air. Every smell was sharp and clean. Sometimes he came on a broad meadow full of prime deer and, putting his rifle aside, sat down to watch them. If he died right then, he decided, he would have seen near everything worth seeing.

On the fourth morning of his journey, Daniel woke up to an acrid smell that was alien to the crisp air. Quickly wiping out every trace of his camp, he led his horse deep into a hollow and tied him there under a cropping of stone. Then he silently made his way back up the hill and started circling the place where he had slept.

The smell was clear enough. It was wood smoke, and close by. He thanked his luck he'd built no fire on his own the night before. If he had, he would scarcely have noticed the other.

It had to be Indians. Findley and Stewart were at least twenty or thirty miles distant. Was it the same party Findley had found? The sign wasn't this far east, but Indians were traveling folk.

Two hundred yards to the south he found their trail. They were being careful enough, but it was hard to cover your tracks in the fall, 'less you could find some way to stay clear of the leaves.

There were four of them, Daniel guessed, maybe five. He stopped in a thick stand of maples and leaned against a tree, letting his eyes study the terrain ahead. The land dipped south and west, which likely meant water nearby. The camp would be there. Under a bluff, perhaps, or in a limestone cave near a stream.

Leaving the woods, he circled to the north and crossed the creek so that he could come in behind the wind. Bellying up slow, he came to the edge of the creek and parted the brush under a big oak. The Indians were just across the stream, camped against the step bank. They were Shawnees, and there were four of them. There was a low fire on the bank, near a stand of young trees. Tied to one of the trees was a naked Indian girl.

Chapter 8

He knew he should just mind his own business, back out of there, scoot back to his horse real quiet and make tracks east.

Indians were always stealing someone else's woman—that was the way they lived, and it wasn't any concern of his. Still, he found it hard to take his eyes off the girl.

Damn, she was a pretty little thing! Tall, long-legged and slim as a willow. Black hair hung loose over her shoulders, framing taut little breasts, and her dark skin was as bright as new copper and as slick as an otter. Daniel guessed she was about seventeen. It was difficult to tell at this distance. But he could see by her beads that she wasn't Shawnee. Cherokee, more likely, or Catawba.

Something else about the scene held him there, something more to do with the men than with the girl.

She'd likely been their captive for some time now, as she wasn't kicking and screaming. Yet, it was clear they hadn't touched her. When the Shawnees took a woman, they didn't leave her looking like this one. By now, all of them should have had her a dozen times over, leaving her bruised and bloody, at worst with her nose sliced off, or her thighs cut to ribbons with a knife. There she was, though, naked and tied to a tree, as ripe a beauty as any man could ask for. What, he wondered, was holding the Shawnees back?

Even as he watched, the Indians below started stowing their gear away and carefully covering the fire pit. Boone knew he was going to try to help the girl. It didn't make a damn bit of sense, but he was going to do it anyway.

He had two rifles, but so did the Shawnees. He could quickly down two of them, but the other two would be after him in a second. Still, they couldn't be sure he was alone, which meant they wouldn't come straight at him over the creek. What they would do was go to ground, one heading for the horses while the others circled around to catch him dodging through the woods, trying to reload on the run.

That's what ought to happen, he told himself wryly. It damn sure better, too, because he had to get all of them. If one got away, he would dog Daniel's heels clear back to the main camp.

Carefully, Daniel lined up both rifles on the edge of the bank. It was an easy shot, no more than thirty or forty yards. Squeeze off the first one, drop the rifle, grab up the second. . . .

The muzzle roared. Echoes cracked down the hollow. Daniel saw the Shawnee stagger. Before he hit the ground he had the second rifle against his shoulder, a startled Indian's face over the bead. He squeezed the trigger again. Fire flashed in the pan, then—nothing! Daniel groaned. Misfire! A goddamn misfire, and the Indians knew it too!

The Shawnees yelped with glee. All three came at him across the creek. One paused, fired into the brush. Daniel screamed. "Bright Fox is hit," he shouted in Cherokee, "get to their horses!"

The Shawnees stopped and looked at each other, then one ran past the girl for the mounts. The other dodged into cover and scampered up the bank to flank him.

It took all the nerve he could muster to lay right where he was and reload. They'd figure he was well into the woods, trying to put distance at his heels. They'd come in fast, knowing he needed a good fifteen seconds to ready his weapon. Of course if he were wrong, they wouldn't flank him at all—they'd catch him right where he was and split his skull.

He heard the first one scrambling in the brush to the left. Now where the hell was the other one? Daniel rammed home the ball and patch, charged the pan, and slammed the frizzen as softly as he could.

The Shawnee heard him, sprang up with a blood-curdling yell and came at him. Daniel brought up the rifle and fired without aiming. The Shawnee's face exploded, spattering dry leaves with blood. Without looking, Daniel turned and leaped over the bank into the creek, fell hard into shallow water, rolled and came to his feet. The girl screamed when she saw him. Too late Daniel realized she was staring wide-eyed over his shoulder. He turned, saw the second Shawnee on the bank above him downstream. Fire flashed in Daniel's face, and pain knifed into his side as the bullet slammed him hard to the ground.

Lights danced before his eyes. He shook his head to clear it. The Shawnee splashed through the water, sun flashing off the knife in his fist. Daniel forced himself to his knees, grasped for the tomahawk and found it. The Indian kicked him in the face and sent him sprawling. Daniel felt his weapon fly, and heard it hit the bank. Then the brave was all over him. Daniel grabbed the Indian's hand and forced the blade from his chest. Boone felt the brave trying to knee his groin and rolled away, sending them both tumbling into the creek.

The Shawnee got a mouthful of water and gagged. Daniel pulled himself free and clawed for the bank. The Indian was right behind him and he still held the knife. Boone was sure he was finished. Even if he could find the damn tomahawk, his strength was draining from him fast. He ran, stumbled and fell. The pain was numbing as his hand slapped down into the smoldering remnants of the campfire. The Indian grabbed his leg, spun him over and dropped down fast with the knife. Daniel dug his fingers into the bank and threw hot coals and sand in the warrior's face. The Shawnee staggered back, dropped his knife and slapped his hand to his eyes. Daniel ignored the knife. He picked up the largest rock he could lift and brought it down hard on the Indian's head.

Daniel sank to the ground, then brought himself up again quickly. Jesus God, there was another one still running loose! What was he going to do with that one?

The girl spoke to him in Cherokee. "He is gone. I heard him take the horses."

"You sure?" Boone felt his stomach knot up.

"Yes, I am sure."

"Hell, I better go see anyway."

"You can see if you like," she said calmly. "But he is gone."

Daniel tried hard to keep his eyes on hers, but they kept dropping down to her body. The girl was even more breathtaking up close! He staggered around behind her, cut the leather thongs, then made his way back through the brush. The girl was right. The horses were gone. The Shawnee might try an ambush, but Boone didn't think so. He'd be more likely to hang back and trail him. Somehow, Daniel would have to find the Indian and kill him, no matter what. Until he had done that, he couldn't go back.

The girl had been busy in his absence. She had gone across the creek and gathered everything worth taking from the dead Shawnees. An assortment of knives and tomahawks was piled on the sand, and she was cleaning and reloading the rifles—Boone's and the Indians'.

Daniel stared at her. She was still stark naked, sitting on the bank with a rifle pressed tightly between her legs, diligently scraping dirt off the hardwood stock.

"There was wet powder in the pan of the gun that didn't go off," she explained without looking up.

"I kinda figured," replied Daniel. "Look, ah—you got any clothes or anything 'round here?"

The girl glanced up curiously. Eyes as big as a doe's studied Daniel. The high planes of her cheeks curved down gracefully to a small, delicate chin and a questioning mouth. "It is important to get the weapons loaded first, is it not?" She looked thoughtfully at the spot of blood on the side of Daniel's buckskin jacket. "When I finish with the guns, I will tend to that."

"Oh, no you won't," he spoke crossly. "What we'll do is get the hell out of here." He walked over to her and started gathering up the weapons, but the pain made him gasp, and he went to his knees.

The girl sighed. "You see? It is as I said. First we must fix the wound."

Boone picked himself up. "Goddamn it, quit tellin' me what to do!"

The girl walked past him and found her buckskin dress. When she started squirming into it, he flushed and stared down the creek. Damnation, he thought, the way she went about it was more like taking clothes off than puttin' them back on.

Daniel didn't stop moving until they were deep into the forest. He pulled every trick he knew—doubling back, riding downstream and coming out on stone, starting false trails that led nowhere. If that Shawnee was any good at tracking he would find them, but it would take him a while to do it.

Finally, Daniel grew so tired that when the girl told him to lie down and be still, he didn't even argue. She tended the wound deftly and gently. The ball had gone in the flesh of his waist and come out again clean. He had lost a little blood, but some rest and food would fix that. Mostly, the wound was stiff, and his feet jarred it something awful when he walked.

"Bind it up," he told the girl. "Tight."

The girl looked puzzled. "Why? It does not need to be bound up tight."

"It does," Daniel said patiently, "if I'm goin' to sit a horse."

"Why would you want to do that?" But she saw the look in his eyes, clamped her lips shut and started to work. The binding made it hard to breathe, but held off the pain.

"What will we do now?" she asked him.

"Now we sit tight an' wait till dark."

"Then what?"

"Then we light a fire."

The girl swept hair from her eyes and looked at him. "To cook? Is that wise?"

"You sure are full of questions, aren't you?" The girl started to pout and Boone laughed. "No, you're right. It ain't wise. The fire's not for cookin'. It's to give that Shawnee out there somethin' to look at."

"Ah . . ." The girl's face brightened. "Wide Mouth is very wise."

Boone raised a brow as she spoke the name the Cherokees had given him. "Now where'd you hear that?"

"I saw you two seasons ago, when you visited the camp of my people on the Nolichucky."

"Well, sure . . ." He'd made the trip many times that year. "Though I don't recall you right off. If I'd seen you, I'm sure I wouldn't have forgot."

She blushed and lowered her head. "Wide Mouth only speaks from pity. In truth, he thinks I am so ugly he puts clothes on me quickly."

Daniel laughed too loud. "Hey, come on now. You're right pretty, and—the thing is, uh . . ." She raised her head and smiled. She was close to him; her black eyes burned into him, and he could sense the strong, womanly smell of her. Daniel could feel himself growing aroused, and backed away from her quickly, pretending to fix the binding on his waist. The girl said nothing, but busied herself gathering sticks for the fire.

"You never told me your name," Daniel finally said.

"It is Blue Duck." She straightened up and looked at him. "Wide Mouth, may I ask a question? What do we do after we light the fire? Is that a question I should not ask?"

"No, you can ask it," Boone told her. "We're goin' off a ways where I can rest up some. When it's dark, I'm comin' back up here to wait for that Shawnee."

"I see," Blue Duck nodded. "Thank you for telling me, Wide Mouth." She turned away and began quietly gathering sticks again.

That night he slept restlessly. At first his dreams were pleasant. There was a quiet bubbling stream in the shadows of some thick-bodied oaks. A woman was there, laughing and clinging to him. Black hair flew over her shoulders and veiled her little-girl breasts. He held her to him, marveling at the silk of her skin next to his. When he suddenly entered her she gasped, then wrapped strong legs tightly about his back. Sometimes she was Rebecca, and sometimes the Indian girl, Blue Duck. It didn't seem to matter.

Then his dream turned bad. The Shawnee with the red-painted face pounced on his chest and split him from belly to throat. In numb horror, Daniel watched his insides spill out onto the ground. As fast as he could pull his belly together, the Shawnee cut him open again.

Daniel sat up, a scream starting in his throat. The girl's hand clasped gently over his mouth. He looked at her, then stared up at the sky. "My God, I got to get up there!" He turned angrily on the girl. "Why the hell didn't you wake me when I told you to!"

Blue Duck hung her head. "Wide Mouth, I tried to, very hard. But the fever was upon you and I could not. You struck at me and cried out. Still I tried to wake you, even though I feared the Shawnee would hear. I was afraid I could not wake you before he came down upon us." She looked at him with fear in her eyes. A single tear coursed down her cheek.

"It's all right," Daniel told her. "Hell, it's my fault, not yours. Damnation!" He slammed his fist into the ground. There was no use chasing after the Indian now. He'd either taken the bait, then left, or smelled a trap and stayed away. Whichever it was, it was too late to catch him now. The Shawnee would simply wait and pick up their trail.

Lightning flashed in the east, and thunder rumbled down through the hills. Daniel hoped it would rain hard. If it kept up all the way back, they might lose the Shawnee. But Daniel didn't really believe that. The Shawnee had the debt of a blood-fight now. He'd stay on the trail no matter how long it took.

Billowing thunderheads rolled in quickly, turning the sky to black. Blue Duck huddled behind Boone, her head pressed close against his back. The rain pelted her hard, stinging all over like tiny stones, but she didn't complain. Instead she wrapped her hands around him. He could not object to that. If she told him she was frightened of the thunder, or afraid she would fall off the horse, he would believe her.

She thought about the thing she had done. She was not sorry she had lied to him. Wide Mouth was hurt, more than he cared to admit, but he was brave, too, and if she had told him when the Shawnee was up there by the fire, Wide Mouth would have tried to kill the warrior. And he would have failed. He was a better man than the Shawnee, but he was hurt, and the Shawnee would have won. She could not let him die.

She wondered, as she clung tightly to him, how long it would be before he made love to her. Not long, she hoped. She would have to be very careful. Wide Mouth would have to be certain it was his idea, and not hers. . . .

She stayed close to him until the rain stopped, then walked quietly and proudly by his side as he gritted his teeth against the pain and made his way back to camp.

Chapter 9

Daniel figured that if he hadn't lost a day somewhere, today was his birthday, but he sure couldn't think of a damn thing to celebrate. He felt more like sixty than thirty-five. The cold November wind crept under the bearskin and chilled him to the marrow. He had slept on his bad side and the moment he awoke, the dull ache spread from his chest down to his legs and made him sick to his stomach. He thought about just lying in his bedroll till it got warmer. If he did get up there wouldn't be a thing to do, except watch Mooney skin game, or maybe ride out and see how Stewart was coming.

Cursing himself soundly, he kicked the covers aside, stretched, and stood up. It was a full hour past dawn, but the earth and sky were the same shade of grey. The trees were nearly bare, etched black against the horizon. Blue Duck was heating venison and

95

corncake over the fire. The smell of food made his mouth water, but he walked past her without stopping. Gritting his teeth against the pain, he took long strides over the ground to stretch his muscles. He walked down to the hollow and circled the thicket around camp.

Daniel didn't like being slowed down. Though he could understand and tolerate weakness in others, he couldn't allow it in himself. That wasn't his way, and by damn he wouldn't have it!

His fight with the Shawnees had drained him more than he cared to admit. The wound was healing, but traveling with it had stiffened him up badly. Trotting through two days of rain had only made it worse. He had been determined to shake the Indian and hadn't stopped more than an hour all the way back to camp. Finally, when he rode in with Blue Duck clinging behind him, he had fallen right out of the saddle.

While the fever had him down, Stewart and Findley did all they could to help him get well. Blue Duck wouldn't let them do much, but they would sit and talk and joke with him. Once he was on his feet, however, Daniel noticed a chill in the air that had nothing to do with the season. It was clear that neither of the two men approved of the girl. Findley, though he knew Indians well, didn't much like them. Stewart was another matter. Daniel's brother-in-law often spun a yarn or two about big-busted women in New Orleans, but that was all so much tongue waggin'. Daniel's sister had her husband trained, and Stewart mirrored his wife's disapproval. Daniel wasn't bedding Blue Duck, and Stewart damn well knew it. Still, she was there—a desirable, sensual young woman.

Daniel figured there was more to Stewart's problem than prudish disapproval. Maybe Stewart was too stiff-necked to admit it, but Boone had seen the way he looked at the young Indian girl. That was probably why he had stayed out so long—two days now—on this latest hunting trek.

The camp-keepers wouldn't come near the girl. They remembered too keenly the Cherokee Wars, and what had happened on the Yadkin. It amused Daniel that Mooney and the others were so dead certain that Blue Duck would sneak up and scalp them in their sleep.

Stewart didn't come in that day, or the one after. When four more days went by, Daniel grew concerned. None of them kept any regular hours, but staying away so long wasn't like John. Boone was relieved when he finally saw his friend's mare trot up the hollow with a loaded pack horse behind. He helped unload the hides, then sat by the fire while Stewart thawed out.

"It's a good load," said Daniel, " 'specially for this time of year."

Stewart nodded and blew on his hands. "Yeah, but you see how they're getting, Dan'l. They're not prime, not all of 'em. Looks like an early winter, an' likely a hard one."

" 'Bout time to start beaver. In a month or so, anyway. We got some traps, and Squire'll bring more."

Stewart looked up at him. "We haven't talked about that, Dan'l. Maybe we ought to. Squire said fall, and the season's 'bout over."

"Squire'll be here," Daniel replied sharply, "don't you worry none about that." He saw Stewart stiffen and shake his head. "All right," admitted Daniel, "he's late. Hell, I'm worried too."

"I know you are. But it don't mean somethin's wrong, does it? Maybe the crop was late, or he had some fixin' to do."

Daniel didn't answer. Squire knew they couldn't start winter trapping until he got there with supplies. They were short on lead and powder. They could do without new traps, but they were risking their lives if they ran out of ammunition.

Stewart guessed his thoughts. "One of us could backtrack, if you want. Go on east a ways and take a look . . ." He looked candidly at Boone. "Wouldn't do a damn bit of good, would it?"

"No. Not much."

"He'll turn up," Stewart said. "Hell, you know Squire." Stewart smiled at the thought of his other brother-in-law marching into camp next week, late as usual.

Daniel turned and stared at the man with sudden, unreasoning anger.

"God A'mighty, Dan'l. What'd I do?"

Daniel looked away. "John, let's just forget it."

"No, goddamn it, let's not. Sit down, Dan'l."

Boone hesitated, then squatted on the log and looked squarely at Stewart. "All right. You want to hear it, I guess you will. You smiled at me, John. That's all. An' I damn near hit you for it. You want to know why?"

"I reckon I better."

" 'Cause you haven't turned a kindly face my way in 'bout three weeks, that's why. You been treatin' me

98

like I come in collectin' taxes, John. You want to end this, fine—but don't act like nothin' ever happened."

Stewart let out a breath and looked at his feet. "Hell, Dan'l, I guess you got a right to get your dander up."

"I sure feel like I do, John. You're one o' the best friends I got, but you're steppin' on me some."

Stewart nodded. "You're due an apology, an' you got it."

"I'm not beddin' the girl. You oughta know that. An' if I was, there's nothin' another man has to say about it. I'm full-growed, and you ain't old enough to be my daddy."

Stewart laughed. "Ain't anyone old as you, Boone. 'Less it's Findley."

"You're right as you can be. Today's my goddamn birthday."

Stewart brightened and let out a whoop. "Son of a bitch. Let's see if we got a drop of that corn-squeeze somewhere!"

"Wait a minute." Daniel held him back. "Suppose it was you that found the girl tied up naked by the Shawnees? Would you have left her there?"

"Huh-unh." John shook his head firmly. "That's guessin' games. One man ain't another, Dan'l. You want the truth, I don't know if I'd've had the guts for it. I've thought about it some, but I've got no answer."

"All right." Daniel nodded. "That's honest enough. An' while we're on the subject of apologies, you got mine for puttin' the Shawnees on our ass."

"Hell," Stewart spat on the fire, "you already apologized for that 'bout two hundred times. I'm plain sick o' hearin' it." He offered his hand and Daniel took it. "One thing, though," Stewart added soberly. "If one of those bastards comes in an' scalps me in my sleep, I ain't ever goin' to speak to you again, Dan'l, and that's the truth!"

Blue Duck could not understand their words, but she knew by Wide Mouth's anger with his friend that they were talking about her. She covered her ears against the sound of their voices and squeezed her arms tight against her breasts. Wide Mouth's friend frightened her. Maybe he would make Boone send her away. She knew the friend didn't like her, even though he craved her with his eyes.

Boone's eyes were not like his friend's, nor those of the other men in camp. Boone tried to hide his hunger for her. He had done this even when he had first seen her naked by the stream. That he now fought so hard to keep her out of his blanket brought joy and sadness to her heart. Joy that he wanted her so badly, sorrow that he was waiting so long to take her.

Sometimes, the ache in her body became more than she could bear. She longed to touch him. She often remembered when they had fled the Shawnee, and she had wrapped her arms tightly about him. Then there had been nothing he could do to stop her.

It would happen soon, she told herself. It was not right for a man to keep a woman about and not take pleasure from her. She had never known a man, but her mother and sisters had told her these things. Waiting too long could make a man like Wide Mouth hurt as much as she was now hurting.

She set her lips firmly together. If he did not decide soon, she would have to help him. Sometimes, she knew, it was up to a woman to do that. Two days later,

Wide Mouth's friend left to hunt for game. Blue Duck was overjoyed. Perhaps now was the proper time. White men were so peculiar, it was difficult to tell. Perhaps Wide Mouth would feel more comfortable now that his friend was gone again.

But on the day after the first friend left, the other one, the gray-beard, returned from his hunt. And on the day after that, Boone left with him. Blue Duck ran into the woods and buried her sobs against the frozen ground. At first she thought about tearing holes in her face with little sticks, but Boone clearly thought she was much too ugly to bed already. There was no sense making things worse.

Chapter 10

At first, Rebecca dutifully carved a notch in her cutting board for every day Daniel was gone. It was a practice she always started after he left her, and one she always quickly abandoned. The days dragged slowly by whether you marked them or not, and she had better things to do. With six children under foot and another on the way, plus a whole farm to look after, there was plenty to keep her busy.

It hadn't been that way in the beginning. Daniel hadn't been gone a day when neighbors and friends started flocking in to help. Rebecca wasn't to worry, they had all said, her husband was doing something important for every family on the Yadkin. They couldn't all take off for Kentucky, but they could each and every one lend a hand back here.

And lend a hand they had, till they nearly drove Becky crazy with six men and a dozen women trying to do every job and people fighting over chores like milking, planting and cutting wood. They had nearly worn out the plowing horse and had tromped all over her garden trying to fence it in. There were more pies, cakes and sweetmeats on her table than Becky had seen in a month of Christmases. Of course the children found them all, stuffed themselves and got sick.

Rebecca had waited. After the first week, more than half her helpers had dropped off. A few staunch supporters had hung on through the second week, but by the third she had been left gratefully on her own again.

Poor dear Squire kept coming, doing the best he could to help her. Besides Daniel's farm, he had his own to look after, and John Stewart's. All that work kept him going in circles like a mouse in a barrel, till Becky was sure he was going to drop. Besides, it was plain as day that Squire was itching to have done with farming and follow after Daniel.

James tried hard to be a man, and Israel, two years younger, did his best to help James. Neither did as well as they wanted, but she was proud of them both.

But Rebecca was worried about James. Sometimes she would catch his eye and see in it the very image of his father—and always the worst qualities, never the best. When the boy lapsed into a dark, brooding silence, he was so like her husband that it frightened her.

Finally, as the months wore on, she realized James was doing his own brooding, not Daniel's. Something had a hold of him, and wouldn't let go. When she sat the boy down and asked him, he clammed up tight. Rebecca grew angry, and demanded an answer. He silently defied her, something he had never done before. Finally, she gave up and let him go. Whatever was bothering him would come out on its own—an untreated sore will always fester, she thought.

Summer passed more slowly than any she could remember. She kept as busy as she could, but nothing took her mind off Daniel. Was he alive or had he been taken and slaughtered by Indians? That was both the harshness and the kindness of long waiting. Your man could be long dead while you thought him still alive. By the end of October she was swollen with child. She turned over more and more of her chores to James, Israel and Susannah. On November second they celebrated both Daniel's and Susannah's birthdays. How was Daniel spending the day, she wondered? More than likely, he didn't even remember the date. Counting time or the money in his pocket wasn't Daniel's favorite pastime.

'Course, there was one time when he counted well enough, she recalled. When he came back from the Cherokee War he had found little Jemima in the crib and had known for certain she couldn't be his. He had just stood there looking at the child for a long, long time.

"Who's the father, Rebecca?" he asked her finally.

"Ed Boone," she told him. "Your brother, Daniel."

"I see," he nodded, still not looking at her.

"I thought you were dead, Daniel. The other Yadkin men came home, but you didn't. I'm not goin' to put it on Ed, and neither are you. It's my doin' as much as his."

Daniel bit his lip thoughtfully, then looked straight in her eyes. "Might put some of that blame on me, Becky. You're a growed woman with needs, and I left you here alone."

Then he picked up the child and held her. "She's a fine-lookin' girl, Rebecca. An' she's a Boone. I'll settle for that."

Daniel had never since reproached her, and he plainly loved Jemima as much as the others. He didn't ask if there'd been other men before Ed or after. There had been. One. And only once with him. Not that she wasn't tempted. Her urges didn't stop when Daniel went wandering. If anything, they grew stronger as the months dragged by.

She wondered if Daniel had ever found a woman when he was gone. Likely he did, she had decided long ago. But not too many. Somehow, she was certain of that.

Rebecca had noticed something unusual down by the woods for a good month or so, but she had said nothing to James or the others. It was never much, just a shadow that shouldn't be there, but it set her heart to racing. The business with Henry Flint had frightened her more than she would ever let on to Daniel or to anyone else. And this wasn't the first time she had spotted someone lurking about the farm. It had happened once before, early in the summer, a month after Daniel had gone.

Squire was supposed to come by, but he didn't. Becky decided he was down with the fever again. It had to be a real bad spell, or he would have left with the fresh supplies for Daniel long before now.

Well, Mrs. Boone, she told herself firmly, if something's down there, you had better waddle your pretty self on out and see what it is. She thought about sending James, but a mother didn't send her young out to look after her.

When darkness settled over the cabin, she slipped quietly out the back door and made her way past the barn into the hollow. Cradling the long rifle in her arms, she leaned against a tree and waited in the blackness.

At first there was nothing unusual—only the sounds and shadows of birds and small animals. Then suddenly, she saw it. Her heart leapt up and nearly choked her. A shadow seemed to peel off one tree and slide silently into the darkness of another.

Rebecca fought back her fear and the numbing cold. Holding her hands steady, she slowly raised the rifle. Then, barely breathing, she let the bead down to just where the tree met the dark.

"Missus Becky," the voice said softly, "I sure do hope you don't shoot me with that thing. I know you're good enough to do it, and I ain't comin' 'way from this tree till you say so."

Rebecca's mouth dropped open. "Nat? Nat Gist, is that you out there?"

"Yes'm, it is."

"Well, for heaven's sake, come on out here!"

"You sure?"

Becky laughed. " 'Course I'm sure!"

Nathaniel Gist stepped out of the shadows and

walked toward her. Rebecca set down her rifle and drew the shawl snug about her shoulders.

"You shouldn't be out here in this cold, Becky."

"You are, Nat. You mind tellin' me why?"

"I, ah—come out here sometimes and take a look around. Me and a couple of others."

Rebecca tried to make out his features. "What for, Nat? Is there somethin' I ought to know? Lord God, you're not out here every night, are you?"

"No, Becky, we ain't. Just times when we figure we ought to be." He hesitated, set down his rifle and blew on his hands to warm them. "And there's nothin' special for you to worry 'bout, neither. If there was, I'd say so."

"Nat," Becky said firmly, "if there's nothin' special, you wouldn't be standin' out here in the cold. I'm a growed woman. Is it Flint? Or Billy Girt?"

Nat looked at her. "To be honest, I got no idea. Sometimes we hear 'bout things that maybe don't mean nothin'. Like this summer, one of the boys thought Girt showed his face up north, only as it turned out, it wasn't him."

"And now?"

Nat looked down and studied his feet. "There was some Shawnee sign west of here, over by Sycamore Shoals. Probably nothin'. If there's any around, they're likely to be botherin' the Cherokees, not us."

Rebecca laid a hand on his arm. "Thank you, Nat," she said softly. "It's a great kindness, and I appreciate it. Won't you come in for somethin' hot to drink?"

"I'd better not," he told her, "but I'm obliged. I'll

just wander 'round here some, then head back home. You ought to get in out of the cold, Becky."

Rebecca made her way back to the cabin and huddled before the fire. The warmth came slowly back to her limbs. Finally, when she had sipped a cup of broth and quieted down her shakes, she went to her bed, lay down and buried her face in her hands. When the tears came, it was impossible to hold them back. They burst from her in a great wave that racked her body and left her helpless and limp all over.

Why, she hadn't even known! Lord God A'mighty, they all loved Daniel as much as she did! In a different way, but it was love all the same, near as strong and fierce as her own.

Chapter 11

Stewart returned to camp. Both Holden and Cooley had complained to him about spending the winter in outlying posts. The hunting season was over, they had argued, and there'd be no more skinning or curing till spring. They could easily handle the furs from one camp, and saw no reason why they couldn't hole up at Station Camp with the others.

"I got a reason," Daniel snapped. "That's what they're bein' paid to do."

"They're farmers, not hunters," Stewart reminded him.

"I guess I know what they are, John."

Stewart caught Boone's dark look and ignored it. "I know you do, Dan'l. I'm just sayin' to you what they said to me. Leave 'em out there if you want. It's all the same to me. Just remember we got to live with them again come next spring."

"There ain't no reason we couldn't haul what

111

skins we got back here," said Findley. "Put 'em with the big cache and let them two come back in."

Daniel looked at him. "That what you want?"

"Don't matter to me one way or the other."

"Fine," said Daniel. "Since just about anythin's all right with you boys, why the hell don't we quit talkin' 'bout it?" He stood up abruptly and stalked away.

Stewart waited, then shook his head and spit on the fire. "Goddamn, Findley, if Squire don't get here soon, Dan'l's goin' to scalp the both of us. The man ain't fit to talk to!"

Findley gave him a curious look. "What's Squire got to do with it?"

"Well hell, everything. We're runnin' out o' powder and lead; we got no traps to work with—"

"—and Daniel thinks Squire's dead," Findley finished. "I know that, boy."

"Then why you askin'?"

"'Cause Squire's got nothin' to do with Daniel acting like a bear with a burr up his tail end. That kind of mad comes from the head. But ole Boone's temper's hangin' right between his legs." He grinned at Stewart through his grey-white beard. "If he'd bed that goddamn squaw, 'stead of all the time thinkin' about it, we'd have us a grinnin' fool on our hands."

Daniel strode right over to his blanket and started tossing trail provisions together in his pack. Stopping by the food cache, he tore off a long strip of jerked venison and poured two handfuls of parched corn into a leather pouch. Hefting the pack and two long rifles, he started down the hollow for his horse. He had everything loaded and strapped when Blue Duck came up behind him.

"Wide Mouth is leaving again?" she asked.

"Yep. He sure is." Daniel averted his gaze from her.

"Can Blue Duck ask where he is going?"

"Huntin'."

"But there is nothing to hunt. The land is cold and empty. Even a poor woman knows the deer's meat is lean and its skin unfit in winter."

"That's right."

"Then why does Boone . . ."

"Goddamn it!" Daniel turned on her savagely. Blue Duck quickly backed away.

"You got to know everything, woman? Get away from me. Go on, get out of here! Leave me the hell alone!"

Blue Duck turned and fled up the path. Boone glared after her. In a moment, she was nearly lost in the hollow, a shadow against the trees. He saw her reach the top of the hill, turn and look back at him. She made a small, almost childish figure in the fading light, but she was no child. No child at all, Boone thought. Even the heavy furs she wore failed to hide the full figure of a woman. Daniel clamped his teeth and turned away. In a moment, he was out of the hollow and into the open, driving the mare hard over the frozen ground.

Late in the afternoon, he saw the rider galloping behind him. Boone pulled out of the wind and waited. Stewart looked like a bear riding a horse, with only his deep brown eyes squinting from under the furs. He stopped near Daniel and blew on his hands.

"Mind some company?"

"Nope. Don't mind at all."

"Figured you might be goin' after buffalo."

"I was thinkin' on it."

Stewart nodded. "The trace that snakes down across the river oughta show a few shaggies 'bout now. There was sign there a week ago."

"They'll be there," Daniel said confidently. "If they ain't, we'll look somewhere else."

The ragged line of trees skirted the valley for another five miles, then fell away to open, rolling meadow. The thick, lush grasses Boone had seen there in summer were now turned to a stiff matting of brown, frozen against the earth. Kentucky lay dark and silent under a colorless sky.

"What day you figure it is?" asked Stewart. "I know it's December, but that's about as close as I can get."

"You're on it," Daniel told him. "It's December 22, 1769."

"Hell, I *know* the year, Dan'l."

Boone laughed. "Just tryin' to be a help."

"Three days, an' it'll be Christmas." Stewart made a show of sniffing air. "Hell, I can smell Hannah's pies. I sure to God can."

"It's a far piece to the Yadkin."

"Hannah makes big pies."

"She does that, John."

Stewart sighed and blew a breath of frosty air. "This is the only life for a man, Dan'l. But there's times when you oughta be home, you know?"

Boone grinned. "Quit talkin' about those pies. I'll get you a nice buffalo tongue and a steamin' slab of liver."

Stewart made a face. "Ain't nothin' real Christmas-like 'bout that."

"Will be. Why, I'll stick a piece of holly on that old tongue and it'll sit right up and sing you a hymn."

"Huh. I reckon that'd be worth seein', all right."

They reached the river in another hour. The buffalo, moving sluggishly down the long valley, looked like a rolling sea of shaggy black humps blotting out the land. The herd was enormous, its flanks swelling hard against the woods on either side. The tail end was somewhere far past the curl of the hills.

"Goddamn," breathed Stewart, "must be a good mile from one side to the other!"

"Enough to make our supper, I figure." Daniel, squatting on the crest of the ridge, watched in fascination as the thousands of great beasts shuffled by below. It was a big herd, all right, one of the biggest he'd ever seen. It looked like a long, furry caterpillar bellying down the valley.

"They're funnelin' south and west," observed Daniel. "Movin' nice and easy. We get us into that little side valley on the right an' we can pick some off as they pass without makin' everybody nervous."

" 'Cept me, Daniel." Stewart raised a brow. "That little valley you're talkin' 'bout's got straight-up walls."

Daniel looked pained. "John, them buffalo ain't interested in runnin' through there. They got a fine road straight out ahead."

"Right now they do," Stewart muttered.

Boone grinned and started down the hill. Well, you wanted to get him smiling again, Stewart told himself ruefully. You oughta be pleased with yourself.

As Stewart had expected, the valley was a dried-up riverbed with high limestone banks. If Daniel noticed there was no way out of the place, it didn't seem to bother him. He knelt down seventy-five yards behind a line of dead trees, which masked him from the animals thundering by. Stewart squatted beside him.

"You shoot and I'll load," John said.

Daniel nodded, took aim, picked the animal he wanted and dropped him solid. In a few moments, he had four. Stewart knew what Daniel was doing—the son of a bitch was showing off, dropping buffalo in a nice even line across the river bed to build a barrier between themselves and the herd!

"That's a real nice fence," Stewart said dryly. "Don't see how you're goin' to get 'em to hop up and die on the second row, though."

Daniel fired again. The rifle jerked against his shoulder and a big bull folded on its short front legs and dropped dead, kicking up dust.

"I'd have put him 'bout three inches to the right," observed Stewart.

"What you don't understand is the next one goes right over the—"

"Oh, Jesus, Dan'l!" Stewart squeezed his partner's shoulder and jerked up fast. Daniel's eyes went wide. He snatched up the other rifle and sprinted off down the draw. In the blink of an eye, one arm of the herd had shifted abruptly out of the valley and started straight for them. Stewart didn't dare look back, but he could feel the beasts shaking the earth at his heels. Boone shouted something, grabbed his arm and pulled him to the ground. Stewart rolled and came up shaking. Daniel was on his knees, steadily taking aim.

116

"Goddamn," yelled Stewart, "we don't need another buffalo!"

Daniel waited. A wall of shaggy backs and beady red eyes thundered toward him. His muzzle flashed. The hit animal staggered and tumbled twice, stopping no more than two yards from Daniel's gun. Stewart suddenly understood and leaped after Boone. Huddled against the big furry mound, he could feel a million pounds of meat roaring by on either side. Hooves pounded the riverbed only inches away from his head.

It seemed like forever before the last of the beasts thundered past, leaving the pair choking in the dust. Daniel looked at Stewart and burst out laughing. Glaring back at him, Stewart wiped the dirt off his face.

"Well hell, it worked, didn't it?" Daniel asked.

Stewart, scared and disgusted, refused to answer. Daniel knew that splitting a herd that way had about a thousand-to-one chance of working, and they'd both seen more than one poor hunter who'd tried it squashed flatter than spilled soup.

It was nearly evening before they finished skinning the animals and hauling the heavy hides behind the trees. The night was getting cold, and Daniel decided to make camp. In the morning, one or the other would ride back to the outcamp to get Cooley and a pack horse.

Boone woke early. Lying quietly under his blanket for a long moment, he peered up through naked branches at a low, heavy sky. There was no wind, and the air was so quiet he could hear a bear scratching wood far down the valley. Sitting up slowly, he let the sounds work through his sleepiness. He heard one

117

sound that worried him. Pulling his hat down tight, Boone roused Stewart.

"Get up and make your way to the horses. We'll worry later 'bout the skins," he whispered.

"What is it?"

"Don't know. Don't want to wait 'round and see, neither."

Stewart nodded and scampered off. When the horses were ready Daniel came quickly down the hollow. He motioned down the steep path and started off, leading his mount quietly, keeping a calming hand on the animals' muzzle. At the end of the twisting path the trees thinned out. There was a narrow meadow to cross, then cover again. Boone studied the place carefully before moving forward. Stewart followed him silently into the open.

There wasn't a sound to be heard except the hoofbeats of their own horses. The lead-grey sky looked swollen with snow. Boone watched small puffs of vapor drift from his horse's nostrils. He heard the loud creak of his saddle and the gurgle of water running somewhere ahead.

Suddenly, from the woods to their left, a jackrabbit burst out of cover and ran a crazy pattern over the meadow. Stewart went stiff and jerked up his rifle.

"Hold it." Daniel laid a hand on Stewart's arm. "Too goddamn late for that, friend." He motioned with his eyes and Stewart looked east across the meadow. A party of Shawnees stood there on their ponies, not thirty yards away. There was a good dozen of them. Five or six of them had long rifles aimed steadily on Stewart and Boone.

Chapter 12

It might be the last move he would ever make, but it had to be done. Handing his rifle to Stewart, Daniel walked straight across the field toward the Shawnees, keeping his steps bold and sure. Indians never believed what they saw in a man's face, but his would tell them he wasn't afraid. At least he hoped it would. He had never been much of a liar either talking or walking.

Boone knew which Indian to approach. The man sat tall and straight, well in front of the others. He was square-faced with piercing eyes and a broad slit of a mouth. Under his bearskin robe he wore a bright crimson British officer's jacket. The Shawnee might have bought or stolen the coat, but Daniel figured he had more likely killed for it.

"Well, brothers," Daniel said in fluent Cherokee, "it's a fine day for huntin', ain't it? We have been havin' some luck, and hope you're doin' the same. Got

119

some good buffalo meat yesterday. I'd be pleased if you'd take some. It'd be a real pleasure to—"

"Wait." The Indian held up his hand and narrowed his eyes at Boone. "Speak to me in English. The tongue of the Cherokee is a dog language."

Off to a good start, thought Daniel. "I'm right sorry I don't talk Shawnee," he apologized.

The Indian nodded gravely. "It would be well if you did. You walk the Shawnee's land, fish in his rivers and piss on his trees. You hunt his game and make fires in his forests. It seems strange to me that you do not speak his tongue, Boone."

Daniel tried not to flinch. "I'm shamed that you know my name, and I don't know yours."

"I am called Captain Will by the white man."

"Well. It's a pleasure, Captain Will. My friend here's . . ."

The Indian pointed his rifle between Daniel's eyes. "You are a good talker, Boone. Now I see why the Cherokees call you Wide Mouth. But you will stop the talking. We will ride together to the camps where you keep your pelts. I am anxious to know how well you have done in the land of the Shawnees."

Daniel's heart near stopped. He kept his eyes on the Indian's but said nothing. Captain Will's stony look told him all he needed to know. The Indian plainly meant business, and there wasn't a damn thing he and Stewart could do about it.

The cold December wind sang through the trees and cut through his heavy clothing. Still, Daniel hardly noticed the chill. He was seething with anger inside, and trying hard to keep the Indians from seeing it. Stewart rode beside him. Their horses were tied together, making it impossible for them to make a run for it. And if they tried, the two braves riding beside them and one behind would slow them down.

At first Daniel figured Captain Will knew everything about him—where the skins were, how many men he had, everything. Now, on sober second thought, Boone wasn't so sure. The meeting in the meadow happened by pure chance—one hunting party coming across another. More than likely, the Indians too had been after buffalo. They had probably found the carcasses or heard the shots, and tracked Boone and Stewart from there. The Captain's mention of the camps was straight-faced bluffing and nothing more. He and Stewart were clearly hunters, and it didn't take much to figure that hunters would have a couple of caches of skins.

Something else worried him. Did Captain Will know about the Shawnees Daniel had killed? And about Blue Duck? Maybe the warrior who got away and had put him on the lookout. If Will knew about that business, he and Stewart were goners. They would live only until the Shawnees took all the skins they could steal. Or worse still, the Indians might take them up the Ohio as trophies to give to the folks back home for sport. Either way, the future looked dim.

Still, Boone thought doggedly, they weren't dead yet. If the Shawnees didn't know what he'd done, he and John might come out clean and healthy. If there wasn't a real war underway, most Indians would let a white man go after they had robbed him.

Boone knew what he had to do—lead the Indians first to Cooley's outcamp, but make enough fuss to warn Cooley off and to give him time to haul out for

121

Station Camp. If he and Stewart could stall and wander about long enough, Findley and the others could get the main cache moved. That way they wouldn't lose more than a few skins in the outpost camps. Damn it, it had to work that way. He wasn't about to lose six months of hard work to a bunch of thieving Shawnees!

Still, one thought kept gnawing at his mind. How did they know who he was? The only answer he could think of was one he didn't like. Black Knife, the renegade Henry Flint.

Captain Will sat on his horse and stoically watched his warriors ransack the camp. Cooley was gone, but it was clear he'd just scampered off. The embers in the fire pit were still hot, and there was a pan of spilled beans soaking into the earth.

"Boone." Will pointed at the pile of skins his braves had made in the clearing. "That is not enough. You will take us to the others, and quickly!" He poked Daniel hard with his rifle. "This time, you will not pretend to lose your way, Wide Mouth. The Shawnees are not children. Do you understand?"

"Yeah, I reckon I do," Daniel replied evenly.

"We will see if you do." He jerked around and spoke to a warrior in rapid Shawnee. The warrior rode up beside Stewart and kicked him savagely to the ground. Stewart clawed at the air and hit hard. Before he could move, three more Indians pounced on him. Stewart struggled and yelled. The Shawnees shouted with glee, tearing at his clothes with their knives until they had his trousers in shreds. Stewart realized what they were doing and screamed out in fear. The Indians ran their blades over his belly and thighs, leaving

122

wicked streaks of red. Finally, one brave grabbed Stewart's genitals and shook a knife in his victim's face. The message was clear enough. Stewart went as white as a fish's belly and threw up his supper.

"All right, goddamnit!" Daniel shouted angrily. "We get the idea! Leave him alone!"

Captain Will nodded to his warriors, then looked solemnly at Boone. "Now Wide Mouth will be a better tracker, I think. We will see more man-trails and chase fewer rabbits." Turning his pony about, the Indian trotted through the camp and joined his warriors, leaving Boone to see after Stewart. Daniel knew better than to try the same trick twice. Convinced that Captain Will would castrate him if led astray, Stewart was shaken to jelly. But Daniel figured there was no need to worry. He had bought all the time he needed. Cooley had now had time to ride to the other outposts and to warn Station Camp. There was no need to push for more time.

Daniel took off straight for the second camp. It was a long ride north past the big river, but Captain Will was satisfied Boone had led them by the quickest route.

"Your tracking improves, Wide Mouth. I am pleased." Captain Will's dark eyes looked over the campsite. "There are signs that another man was here. One fled the first camp before we arrived. That makes four in your party. How many more do you think there might be?"

"One other," said Daniel, "if he ain't hightailed it into the woods."

"And where is he now? Hiding with the first two?"

"Might be. Or could be he's still waiting at the third camp, the one you ain't seen."

Captain Will grinned broadly. "Wide Mouth speaks the truth at last. If you had not, I would be angry with you now. It is clear there is another camp. You have been in the Shawnees' land a long time. I know this is so. Five men can skin many more hides than we have seen. Now, lead me to this other place." The Indian's mood seemed almost jocular.

Daniel sighed and shook his head. "Captain Will, I been kinda hesitatin' to tell you this, knowin' you won't be happy 'bout it, but by God, it's the truth."

The Shawnee's face clouded. His eyes shifted from Boone to Stewart and back again. "Tell me what, Boone? Do you pretend with me again!"

"Now, damn it all, there ain't no pretendin' to it," Daniel protested. "It's just that you ain't goin' to find any more skins where we're goin'. There was plenty there, I won't try an' fool you 'bout that. But they're gone. Packed back east." He nodded to his left. "Over the mountains to North Carolina."

Captain Will stiffened. His eyes grew dark with rage, and he leveled his rifle steadily at Daniel's head. "You are foolish to lie to me, Boone."

"Hey, now." Daniel held up his hand. "How do you know I'm lyin' when you ain't even been there? Hell, I'm goin' to take you to the camp right now, and you can see for yourself."

Captain Will brought his mount up close. "There are no more skins? Just these!" His mouth curled and he spit at the small cache on the ground. "Pray to your white god, Boone. Ask him to send an eagle to fly many skins back over the mountains. I think you should do this now!" Will glared at him and jerked his mount away.

"Just a damn minute!" Daniel reached out and pulled him back.

The Shawnee stopped, surprise spreading across his features. The warriors about him lifted their weapons and turned angry faces at Boone. "I heard a lot about the Shawnees," said Daniel, bringing all the indignation to his voice he could muster. "But I never heard they were two-faced."

Captain Will stared. "What is this you say, Boone?"

"What *you're* sayin' is the question. Make up your mind, brother. Does the truth anger the Shawnees or does a lie? You don't seem any too happy with either one. Tell me which'll please you best, and that's the one I'll give you."

The Indian studied him thoughtfully. "The Shawnees are lovers of truth. If there are no more skins in this camp of yours, then Wide Mouth shows honor as well." Captain Will showed him a grim, sinister smile. "It greatly pleases a man to find honor in another, Boone. Still, it would please me as much to find a liar with a great treasure of skins."

It was nearly dark when Daniel brought the Shawnee party through the low hills and down the hollow toward Station Camp Creek. Whatever happened now, he'd given Findley and the others a good head start. Findley knew Indians, and he'd know exactly what to do—start running, keep going, and don't look back. Even with the pack horses loaded up full, he would have a damn good chance of making it.

Daniel tried not to think about his own future.

The pack horses would leave heavy tracks and the Shawnees would read his lie in minutes. He had no idea what Captain Will would do when he found that the camp had been deserted only hours instead of weeks. The high scaffolds built all over camp would tell the Indian exactly how big a cache had slipped through his fingers. He wasn't going to like that. And before the braves took out after Findley, Captain Will might decide to do a little skinning of his own.

As the Shawnees climbed up the hollow to the outskirts of the camp, their high-pitched yells pierced the silence like arrows. Warriors broke from their column and thundered past Boone and Stewart into the woods.

"Maybe we ought to run for it now," Stewart said dismally. "They'll cut our throats for sure, Dan'l, when they find what you done to 'em."

"You chew this rope through, and I'm right behind you. I ain't got the teeth for it."

"Lord," groaned Stewart. "This is a sorry end for sure. I'll never get back home for any of those Christmas pies, Dan'l, or for any more lovin' from my Hannah." Stewart stopped and sat up straight. Terrible war whoops erupted from the woods, and the Shawnees began firing their rifles in the air. "Oh, Great Jesus!" Stewart stared wide-eyed at Boone. "They're comin' for us. You hear that? Oh, Jesus, *Jesus!*"

"For God's sake, shut up!" snapped Daniel.

Captain Will tore out of the brush straight for them, his heavy buffalo robe flapping at his shoulders, and his rifle raised high over his head. He was grinning from ear to ear and shouting at the sky. Jerking the pony up hard, he let out another yell, then trotted crazily around the pair in a circle. "Boone, you are a fine liar," he laughed. "It is a good joke you pull on Captain Will. A very good joke indeed!"

Daniel stared at him, then dug his heels hard into his horse's flanks dragging Stewart's mount along with him into the camp. He knew what he'd find there, but even when he saw it for himself, he couldn't let himself believe it. Findley and the others were gone, but everything was just as Daniel had left it a few days before—the pots, the pans, the blankets, the traps, even the horses and rifles and ammunition—everything, including the high scaffolds, covered solid with prime skins. Everything he owned and half a year's work. John Findley had run off and left it all for the Shawnees.

Chapter 13

As the Shawnees reveled in their find, a dark, killing rage began to smoulder inside Daniel. Stewart saw the fire in his brother-in-law's eyes and feared for his own life. He was certain Boone would go crazy and get them both slaughtered.

Daniel, though, wasn't thinking about killing Indians. He was thinking about killing Findley. How could he do this? How could he let such a thing happen!

Great God A'mighty, he'd had all the time in the world to get the damn skins out! Boone could understand Cooley and the others running scared. They were farmers, not woodsmen. But John Findley losing his nerve—that was a notion Daniel couldn't take to. Goddamn it—how could you be so wrong about a man?

Daniel was certain now that Captain Will would let them live. He understood the man and knew how his mind worked. In spite of what most folks thought,

129

Indians wouldn't kill you just for the hell of it. In Daniel's experience, they were no more savage or brutal than most white men. A lot less, maybe, if you got down to it. Will had a fine cache of pelts to take up the Ohio, and a great story to tell the braves back home. Had he not stripped the mighty Boone himself of his treasure? And better yet, left him alive to bear his shame? To the Shawnees, this would embellish Captain Will's deed in a way no mere scalp could ever hope to.

By the end of the second day, the Indians had everything worth taking from the camp loaded on pack horses. Daniel couldn't stand to watch. When the Indians saw this, they took every opportunity to taunt him.

Finally the Shawnees were ready to leave, and Captain Will cut the bonds from his prisoners, then walked alone with Daniel down through the hollow. There he gave him a single rifle and enough powder and shot to take game.

"Wide Mouth," he said gravely, "I know your thoughts. You believe I have taken these skins from you, but you are wrong. If I had truly taken the skins, then I would be a thief. It is you who are the thief, Wide Mouth. I merely take the skins back, for they have always belonged to my people. The white man keeps cows about his towns and farms. He kills these cows for food and skins. The game you take here is the cattle of my tribe. It does not belong to you, any more than the white man's cows belong to the Shawnees."

Will paused, and looked at Boone for a long moment. "I leave you with your life, and I tell you this. Go back where you came from. Do not rob the Shawnees again. If you return, my brother, you will find angry wasps waiting here to sting you."

Captain Will turned away, pulled the buffalo robe about him and gazed out at the hills. "Now I will speak of something else, Boone, because we are not true enemies. If we were, we would do each other honor in battle. Is this not so?"

"It's as true as it can be," Daniel agreed. "If we was to fight, there'd be pride in it for both of us."

Will nodded soberly. His dark eyes looked squarely at Boone. "I know of your fight with the Shawnees, Wide Mouth. Three were killed and one was not. It was a fair fight. I know about the girl, too. All this has been told to me." The Indian paused. "Where is the girl now, Boone?"

"I don't know where she is," Daniel said honestly. "She was here with the others. She's gone now."

Captain Will nodded thoughtfully. He knew it was true. He and Boone were not lying to one another now. "What I tell you is from my heart, Wide Mouth. Listen well. It is for your ears and not for another. The girl was taken by Shawnee warriors for Black Knife. The braves you killed belonged to him. This is why I have not taken your life. Black Knife's ways are not mine, though many Shawnees welcome him to their fires. I do not call him brother. I think this Black Knife shames his white father, and his red mother, too. That is much shame for a man to carry. Let him take revenge upon you if he wishes. There is no honor in it for me."

Captain Will looked steadily at Boone, his broad face showing no expression. "I have finished, Wide Mouth. You have heard my words." With that, Captain Will turned away and stalked back up the hollow to where a brave waited with his horse. Boone and Stewart stared at the low hills long after the Shawnees had disappeared. Finally, Daniel turned away and tossed a few sticks on the fire. The camp seemed dark and alien now. He was glad the night hid the sight of it from him so well.

"Well, they left us alive," sighed Stewart. "That's about all, Dan'l."

Daniel gave him a weary grin. "Ol' Will's a real sport, John. Damned if he ain't."

But Stewart knew as well as Daniel that the Indians had done them no great favor. They were stranded alone in some of the roughest country a man could imagine. And they were on foot in the dead of winter, with one rifle between them and enough powder to down maybe a deer and a jackrabbit. The Shawnees didn't have to kill them. With a little luck, nature would take care of that for thcm.

Stewart caught Boone's look and laughed out loud. "Hell, Dan'l, it's gettin' on toward supper. There's a pouchful of corn them Injuns dropped by the stump. Not enough for both of us, mind you, but I'll race you to the creek for it!"

That night, Stewart slept near the dying coals of the fire. Daniel took his own blanket and walked far across the hollow into the trees. John could do what he liked, but Daniel wasn't about to bed down in Station Camp. It wasn't his anymore. It was a lonely stretch of trees against the side of a hill.

He hadn't let himself think much about Flint. When the Indian told him the girl belonged to Black Knife, it took all of Daniel's control to mask his disgust. Damnation. No wonder the Shawnees hadn't raped her. They were saving that horror for Flint!

It was real peculiar if you thought about it, Daniel

132

decided. The whole thing had started with a woman—Becky's cousin Mindy. Then there had been Becky herself, and now, another woman was between him and Flint. The blood debts were piling up fast, Daniel thought. And there would be no end to it till one of them was cold and buried under the earth.

Daniel dreamed about Becky through most of the night. Then something began to intrude on his rest.

He was aware of the sound for a long time before it brought him fully awake. Opening his eyes, he lay perfectly still and listened. He knew it couldn't be an acorn because there weren't any about this time of year.

Daniel sat up slowly and waited. Someone was tossing little pebbles at him, and whoever it was was a friend. Indians didn't bother to wake you before they slit your throat.

"All right," he finally said, in a low, clear voice, "who's out there?"

"It's me, Wide Mouth," the small voice whispered.

"Blue Duck?" Daniel felt a quick surge of pleasure and relief. "Hell, girl, come on in here!" She was alive, then. He'd figured she would be, but how could you know for sure, the way things were going?

The girl slipped silently out of the brush and knelt down beside him. "I am glad you are safe, Boone. Everything happened so quickly, I could not know if . . ."

"Hush up and get on under here 'fore you freeze." Boone raised the buffalo robe, and the girl came eagerly to him. She was shaking uncontrollably and her skin was as cold as ice. Boone put his arms around her and pulled her close. "Blue Duck, is that goddamn doeskin dress all you have to wear?"

"Yes, that is all, Wide Mouth. I know it is foolish to have so little protection against the cold, but there was no time to take more."

Daniel's expression softened. She had run from the Shawnees, damn near frozen to death and then mustered the courage to come back to Boone. She couldn't have known what she'd find here—Black Knife's Shawnees might have been waiting. Yet, she had done it. She had come back looking for him.

He didn't talk to her. He held her tightly against him and let the warmth of his body flow into hers. She snuggled up to him like a child, moving her back against his chest and belly till they fit together like two spoons. He rubbed and kneaded the blood back into her arms and when she tucked her legs up to her stomach, he felt the chill in them and softly stroked her thighs.

It happened slowly, and ever so naturally. His hand was simply there, in the warmth between her thighs, right where it seemed to belong. The girl murmured at his touch, then twisted, turned to face him and came joyously into his arms. Her breath was hot against his throat; her mouth moved hungrily up to meet his. Silently, she slipped the buckskin over her shoulders and started to undo his shirt and trousers.

When he felt her nakedness against him, Boone nearly cried out, for the great and terrible emptiness within him seemed to fall away in her arms. The sorrow, the loss of everything he had worked for, was swept up in this greater need. They were alone together with little to keep them alive. But for this one moment, it didn't matter. Nothing did. The chilly wind swept across the blanket, but neither Boone nor Blue Duck felt the cold.

When Daniel walked in at dawn with Blue Duck trailing behind, Stewart said nothing at all. One look from Boone told him the wisdom of keeping his peace.

"Well, it's about like we figured," commented Daniel. "Blue Duck says Cooley came ridin' in hard with Holden on his heels, both of 'em screamin' bloody murder 'bout Indians. Findley and the whole bunch went runnin' for the woods."

Stewart shook his head. "It just don't seem like John Findley to run scared. Maybe he tried to stop 'em, Dan'l."

"If he did," Daniel said darkly, "he didn't try too damn hard!" He looked soberly at Stewart. "John, you know the truth as well as I do, and we'd best face it square. We got almost no chance of makin' it without horses."

"We got to. There ain't none to be had."

"Yeah, there are too," Daniel replied thoughtfully.

Stewart frowned, then opened his eyes wide. "Oh, now, come on, Dan'l!"

Boone grinned at his friend's expression. "You know of any closer? Besides, they're our own goddamn horses, and we're flat entitled to 'em!"

Stewart's mouth opened, but nothing came out.

"By the way, John," Daniel added, "Merry Christmas to you. Though I think it was maybe yesterday, or the day before that."

Chapter 14

"You will come back, Wide Mouth," Blue Duck commanded. "You will not get killed by the Shawnees and leave me here."

Daniel laughed. He wanted to take her slim figure in his arms and to crush her to him, but Stewart's presence held him back. "Hell yes, I'll come back, girl. With horses, too. I got no intention of walkin' 'round Kentucky all winter!"

"My heart and my body are yours," she proclaimed boldly. "You have taken much of me, but there is still much more to give. I will stay here, waiting under your blanket."

Daniel swallowed hard. "Goddamn, you aren't makin' it any easier to get out of here."

"Hah! Blue Duck's man is wise indeed," she grinned broadly. "I am not trying to make it easy!"

But Daniel gave her a teasing wink, turned away,

and trotted from the campsite into the woods with Stewart by his side.

Captain Will's party was simple to follow. The Shawnees weren't concerned with covering their trail. They were moving north at a leisurely pace, putting no strain on the heavily laden pack horses. On the second night out, Daniel and Stewart spotted their fires glowing by a shallow river sheltered under a high bluff. The horses, tied to a long rope stretched between two trees, were thirty yards downstream.

Daniel breathed a sigh of relief. He had half expected to find the mounts closely guarded, or so near camp that they would be hard to snatch without a fight. Boone wanted those horses, but the last thing he needed was blood between himself and Captain Will. Stealing was one thing, killing another. The Indians had taken everything he had, but they left him a fighting chance to survive. More than that, Will had done Boone a personal favor by letting him know about Flint. A man couldn't easily lay aside a debt like that.

While the Shawnees slept, Daniel and Stewart crept in and took five horses. It was as easy as taking foals out of a barn. They simply untied the five they wanted, walked them quietly along the bank a short distance, then mounted up and rode like hell.

By midnight the biting winds fell away and left the air brisk and invigorating. The sky was clear and a bright silver moon lit the cold, bleak landscape. Boone and Stewart took advantage of the light to ride fast, putting many miles behind them. They wasted no time covering their tracks. Only distance counted now. When the Shawnees woke at dawn, they would know the pair had a good six or seven hours head start. They would have to be good and mad to halt their trip north to take up a chase that could last for days and still yield them nothing.

Boone called a halt to rest the horses only twice during the night, and each stop lasted no more than six or seven minutes. He kept the pace hard, driving himself, Stewart and their mounts to their limit. Finally, when the sun came up over the hills, he pulled his horse to a stop and sprawled out on the ground.

"By God, we did it!" he laughed. "We did it and got clean away, John. We ain't licked yet!"

Even Stewart· was in high spirits as he limped wearily over to Daniel and leaned down to tighten a loose thong on his moccasin. "You think they'll follow or leave us alone? We're pretty far ahead of 'em."

"Can't tell for sure, but my guess is they'll call it a day. They got everythin' we own, and we sure ain't hurt their pride much takin' back a few horses. The Captain will be anxious to get his booty back to the Ohio, where he can show off his . . ." Daniel stopped and put his ear quickly to the ground. "Oh, Great Jesus!" he groaned.

Stewart's grin faded. He jerked up, stared past Daniel's shoulder and went white. Captain Will and his warriors topped the crest of the hill and thundered down upon them. Daniel came to his feet and grabbed for his reins, but a Shawnee pony hit him hard and sent him sprawling. The Indians yelped and pranced about in a circle, their horses churning up the dirt. Captain Will reined in and looked down at Boone, his features set in a stern, angry mask. Daniel faced him squarely, ignoring the half dozen weapons jabbing at his face.

Suddenly, the Indian's dark features split into a

smile, and Captain Will threw back his head and laughed. "Wide Mouth, you are very hard to say good-bye to. Did you miss your Shawnee brothers? Is this why we see your white face again?" He shook his head sadly, like a father chiding his son. "First a stealer of skins, and now a stealer of horses. You try your brother's patience, Boone!"

Will turned his head and barked a harsh command. A brave beside him screeched like a hawk and sprang to the ground. In seconds, every Shawnee in the band had spilled from his horse and crowded around Daniel and Stewart. The Indians pushed them roughly to the earth and lashed out viciously with their feet. Daniel fought back, but quickly went under. Stewart yelled and an Indian stilled him with the side of his tomahawk. A hand grasped Daniel's hair and jerked his neck back. Something tight cut into his throat and shut off his air.

Good God, he thought in terror, they're going to scalp me and strangle me both!

Then, as quickly as it had begun, the fracas was over. Boone dragged himself up onto all fours and shook his head. Bells seemed to tinkle in his ears. The Shawnees howled with laughter and made sounds like horses. Daniel reached up to touch his throat and felt the horse bells tied there. Anger started in his belly and he jerked up, feeling his face flush hot.

"Goddamn it, Will! You gone too far now and—ugh!" A rifle butt hit him solidly in the back and sent him sprawling. Captain Will kicked his pony and trotted up close. Daniel jerked his hands away from the dancing hooves.

"Stay down, Boone," Will said harshly. "Horses

do not stand like men. They gallop about on their hooves. They kick their feet in the air and shake their heads from side to side. Let us see how good a horse you can be, Wide Mouth."

"In a pig's eye, brother!" The rifle butt hit him again, splitting his face and nearly busting his jaw. Daniel coughed and spit blood. "Will, this ain't no way to treat an enemy you give honor to, much less a friend."

"You are right," Will said stiffly. "But where is this man of honor?" He craned his neck from side to side, making a show of searching the hills. "I am sorry, Wide Mouth. Your eyes are clearly sharper than mine. I see no one here but horse thieves. Not even thieves. Only horses. Do you think you can be a good horse, Boone? I ask you again."

Daniel glared and turned away from him. He knew he had to do it, just like Will wanted. If he balked again, Will would kill him. Maybe the Indian didn't want to, but he would have no choice.

Daniel couldn't remember a greater humiliation. He pranced about the ground and kicked up his heels until his limbs ached. He shook his head to make the bells ring, and pawed the air like a wild pony. The Shawnees doubled up with laughter. The great Boone Wide Mouth and his friend made fine horses. They were as good as any horses the Indians had ever seen!

Daniel didn't look at Stewart, as he was sure Stewart wouldn't look at him. That was something, anyway. They didn't have to see each other make damn fools of themselves.

When the Shawnees finally let them stop, Daniel was too tired to stand. Stewart lay sprawled nearby, his chest heaving as he gasped for breath. The Indians crowded around like taunting schoolboys and pulled them to their feet, shouting with glee and pounding their prisoners on the back. Then the same brave who had nearly fractured Daniel's skull embraced him like a brother and thrust water and jerky in his hands. Another took his own metal armpiece and clasped it over Boone's wrist. Finally, the Indians grew so pleased with the pair that they set them on the same horses they had stolen and let them ride back to the encampment in style.

Goddamn Indians, Boone thought darkly. Don't make any sense at all, even when you're sure you've got 'em figured.

Captain Will said nothing the rest of the day or that night. When the party started off the next morning, however, Daniel and Stewart were taken along. Daniel had been afraid of this since their first capture. The Shawnees had shown great patience in letting them live, but he was certain they had no intention of letting them go again.

To Daniel's great surprise, Will assured him this wasn't so. "You will have to go north with your Shawnee brothers, Wide Mouth, at least for a while. I freed you once, but you have shown you are not a man of reason. I am sorry this is so. In a few days, we will reach the Ohio and speak again. If wisdom has touched your head and you seem to be more a man than a horse, perhaps you will again see your home." His stern mouth eased into a grin. "If this comes about, brother, you will walk away on two legs. But you will not leave Captain Will again on a Shawnee pony!"

"Dan'l," Stewart asked later, "you believe that Injun or not? I sure as hell can't see him givin' us no big farewell party at the river. Them Shawnees get us that far, they're goin' to take us all the way, and that's the God's truth!"

"Maybe, and maybe not," Daniel remarked thoughtfully. "You know as well as I do that Indians got a whole lot more patience than most whites. Look what they let us get away with already." Daniel shook his head. "Hell's fire—I would've shot us dead a week ago, John."

Still, the more he thought about it, the more he agreed with Stewart's conclusions. Captain Will had been patient. He had been firm and hard only when he had to. Only, they couldn't really *know* what Will was planning until he did it. Daniel still wanted to believe the Indians would let them go. But if he guessed wrong, he and Stewart would be playing horsey for Shawnee children for a long time to come.

"I don't like it," he told Stewart finally. "I'm startin' to get itchy, and we're a long damn way from Station Camp."

Stewart gave him a pained look. They were close to four days from where they had stolen the Shawnee horses. The land was flattening out and the nights were getting colder. The Indians were riding steadily northeast through country neither he nor Boone had ever seen before.

"This just sorta come on you, Dan'l, or you been chewin' on it? I mean that's all I been sayin'—we're almost to the goddamn Ohio!"

"I know it, and right here's 'bout as close as I figure on getting."

143

"You talked to Captain Will about this?"

Daniel grinned. "Naw, I figure we already said good-bye 'bout as much as we need to."

Stewart started to speak, then pressed his lips tight. He glanced over at their ponies, all roped together. There were Shawnee braves ahead and behind. As always, three rifles were steadied on their backs. Boone grinned at Stewart's sour look.

Daniel said nothing more on the subject but he was keeping his eyes open. The next day, the trail snaked down to a broad, shallow river. Daniel figured that the Ohio lay just beyond the hills, past the grey and wintry horizon.

But it was an area along the south bank of the river that interested Daniel more. Around noon, the first patches of cane appeared. An hour later, a vast canebrake stretched out past the river as far as the eye could see. It grew right up to the Shawnees' trail, towering twelve or fifteen feet above the ground. Daniel guessed it might run ten or twenty miles to the west. He had seen more than one that size in Kentucky.

When the Shawnees made camp that evening, Daniel finished his supper and laid back easily, waiting till the Indians settled down. Finally, when the fire burned low, he spoke softly to Stewart. "John, don't look 'round or anythin', just listen. It's about time for us to go."

"Huh?" Stewart sat up straight.

"Relax, damn it!"

"Dan'l, I don't know what the hell you got in mind, but . . ."

"I got in mind to grab a couple of them rifles

144

stacked by that cottonwood and then to take a stroll into that cane. You ready?"

"You mean *now*?"

"Hell yes, now. You got somethin' more interestin' to do?" Daniel didn't wait for an answer. The Shawnees were drowsing by the fire. Springing to his feet he bounded for the tree, grabbed two rifles and crashed into the cane. Stewart, cursing Boone's hide with every name he could think of, stumbled along behind. The Shawnees began yelping and whooping their war cries, drowning out Stewart's voice. Daniel, laughing so hard that his sides hurt, ran blindly on through the thick forest of cane stalks.

Chapter 15

James hefted the pack onto his shoulders and headed down river. The sky was clear and blue with only the ragged tails of clouds floating off to the north. Cold still settled in the hollows, but it felt almost warm in the open—not bad, James thought, for the last day of December. With luck, the weather might hold till he reached the Yadkin. Counting off the miles in his head, James decided he'd make it right before dark, even carrying the deer.

The thought of home brought to his mind a flurry of pictures—his own bed, Ma, his brothers and sisters all about, a fine stew bubbling in the fireplace. The thoughts warmed him, and he quickened his step. Except that, when he considered for a moment, he wasn't nearly as eager to get back as he might have been. Now how could that be? he wondered. Of course he wanted to get home! And as quickly as he could. Everybody was supposed to feel that way.

The words came to him unbidden, and with them came a hot flush of shame. It was happening again—thoughts coming out of nowhere, and most of them bad thoughts, too. It scared him sometimes, because it felt like there was someone else inside, and not him at all.

Lately he had decided that maybe he was just growing up. Strange things were happening in him, for sure, things he couldn't tell anybody, not even Israel. Whatever it was, he hoped it would go away soon. He was getting mighty sick of feeling bad about everything. Why, he hadn't even liked Christmas! You had to be plain crazy to think like that! It hadn't been a bad day or anything. It just didn't seem like Christmas. Ma had been feeling poorly after giving birth to his new baby brother just two days before, but there was a present for everyone, and fresh pheasant and hot pies. Still it hadn't thrilled him as it used to. Maybe he was growing out of holidays, too.

Hauling the buck tired him out more than he had figured it would. By late afternoon he decided to camp another night and to go on in the morning. Ma wouldn't worry—she wasn't expecting him this soon.

As always, before bedding down, he packed his rifle the way his pa had taught him. A patch of linsey went over the muzzle to keep bugs out, even if there weren't many of the critters about at this time of year. He made certain his powder horn and bullet pouch were tied securely to his belt. Finally, he inspected the flash pan carefully, then covered it with doeskin to keep out the dew

Just before he set the rifle aside, James absently

ran his fingers over the stock. Then in a sudden flood of anger and shame he jerked his hand away. Jesus God, it happened again and again and again, and he couldn't stop it! No matter how hard he tried! He had to go and handle that stock with the wrong touch and the wrong thoughts. Now God might make all the bad things he had thought about Pa come true. He would die out there in Kentucky, and James would be the cause of it.

There wasn't anything wrong with the new stock. Pa had carved it out good, and it fit just fine. It didn't look like the old stock, the dark and oily wood that came with the rifle off the shelf. . . . It was just as good, though—it was! It truly was!

"You ought to be real proud, boy. This rifle cracked the hell out of a Shawnee skull. Saved my life and your ma's, too. We'd be meat for ol' Flint if I hadn't had it near!"

James remembered his father's words and broad grin. But more than that, he remembered seeing the rifle broken. He remembered how he had just sat there, staring at the ugly thing in his father's hands. Brand-spanking-new only the day before, now it was ugly, cracked and split off at the breech. It didn't even look like his rifle anymore. It looked like a long piece of iron with an open, bloody wound on the stub. He had not even wanted to touch it!

I never even fired it new, he thought as he lay in his bedroll, not at a deer or anything. Not before you broke it. It was mine to have and you took it and went after Ma without me. After we shook hands and everything, too! Like I was a man. Only I'm not, and you lied to say I was. I'm a boy or you would have taken me and not just my rifle! I don't want to be here and take care of Ma anymore. You hear me? That's what you're supposed to do! Goddamn you! I hope you die and don't ever come back!

The tears racked his body and tightened his throat until he could hardly breathe. He pounded his fists on the ground until they bled, until he could no longer feel the pain.

Oh, dear God, I don't mean it and you know that! Don't listen to anything I say! I love you, Pa. I truly do! Don't let anything happen to him, God. Please don't let anything happen to him.

Chapter 16

Daniel was greatly pleased with himself for outfoxing Captain Will. As he had figured they would, the Shawnees had wasted precious minutes covering their mounts, giving the pair the time they needed to lose themselves in the cane. The Indians yelled and thrashed about, but tracking men in a canebrake was like hunting the only two fleas on a horse. Finally, after making gruff noises and threats for the entire night and half the next day, Captain Will gave up and rode on.

Stewart had the shakes halfway back to Station Camp and grumbled continually. "You scared the hell out of me," he muttered darkly, "just pure scared the hell out of me. That was a damn fool stunt, and you know it!"

"Yeah, sure was," Daniel agreed.

"Well, what if we'd got caught? What do you think he'd have done to us then?"

"We didn't get caught, John. I thought you'd have noticed by now."

"Lord. He'd have scalped us for sure."

"Might have."

"Well, goddamn it, Dan'l. I mean—well, *goddamn*!"

Daniel laughed and shook his head. His thoughts were already a mile down the trail at Station Camp. Blue Duck would be there, waiting for him. He could still feel the heat of her, the taste and smell of her skin. The girl had a hunger as great as his own, and no shame at all about showing it. Lord, she was a fine one! Just thinking about her stirred his loins and quickened his step.

"We'd best take the girl and move right on," he told Stewart. "Captain Will ain't comin' back, but I don't like the idea of stayin' the night there anymore. The place is gettin' kinda tattered."

Stewart nodded. Station Camp was just beyond the draw now, past the shallow ridge of rock and into the trees. "How far you think Findley went? Reckon we'll be able to catch up?"

Daniel gave him a dark look. "He's likely in England or France by now, the way he was movin'. That son of a bitch sure lit out like a rabbit!"

"You're hittin' the man hard, Dan'l. You know that."

Daniel turned on him, his face like stone. "By God, John, how hard did that Injun hit you? Some of them skins was yours, son!"

"Yeah, you're right as you can be. I just . . ."

"Just nothin'," Daniel snapped. "You kiss that jackass on the cheek when you see him, but I'm damned if I will." Boone turned and stomped heavily down through the draw.

There was no wind. A wisp of smoke near as straight as a rule curled up to the bare branches over Station Camp. Daniel paused under a tall ash, then walked quietly into the clearing. The girl was gone, out gathering wood, maybe, or bringing up water. He motioned Stewart to stay where he was.

"Blue Duck?" Daniel stopped, sweeping his eyes over the clearing. "Blue Duck, you here?" he said softly. A motion caught his eye. He jerked around and saw the buffalo robe under a tree. He hesitated, then grinned and walked toward her.

"You sure are one lazy Cherokee gal, sleepin' in the middle of the . . ." He pulled the robe aside. Her wide, frightened eyes stared up at him. A cry stuck in his throat. Right away he saw the gag in her mouth, the tight cords about her arms and legs and the welts and dried blood steaking her naked body. He threw himself away from her, shouted to Stewart and came up running. Stewart's gun shattered the silence. The Shawnee came at Daniel's left. Boone turned and fired blindly, knew he had missed and never heard the Indian behind him. The blow glanced off his head, numbed his shoulder and brought him to the ground.

Stewart screamed, the cry tearing his throat, but Daniel couldn't help him. The darkness was coming over fast, and he was falling into it. He was grateful he couldn't feel the blows any longer. . . .

He awoke to a dark sky. There was a fire somewhere. He turned his head to see it. A sick wave of nausea rolled over him. Daniel choked back bile and swallowed. If he threw up now, he would strangle to death for certain.

He knew he had been there a while; the cold from the earth had seeped up into his body and left him numb. He tried his arms and legs—a little feeling, but not much. He was staked out flat on his back at the edge of the camp. They had nearly beaten him to death, but they had left him alive. Now that was bad news, for sure, he thought. Getting killed by Shawnees was one thing. *Not* getting killed was something else.

"Daniel?"

"John? My God, are you all right?"

"I'm alive, Dan. I . . ." Stewart's voice broke. "I wish to hell I wasn't!"

"Hang on, now. Don't give it up, boy."

"I can't help it, Dan."

"You can. You can if you try. You know what they done to Blue Duck? Is she still alive?"

"I don't know. They was—Ohhhh, *Jesus!*"

Daniel jerked at the terrible cry. Turning his head as far as he could, he saw the big Shawnee squatting down to his left. There was a grin on his face, and he was doing something to Stewart's belly.

"Bastard! Leave him alone!" Daniel shouted hoarsely. The Indian turned and gave him a curious look. Holding the knife up high, he made a jerky motion in the air, then reached down and grabbed his own genitals and grinned. Daniel got the picture. "You want to do some cutting," he yelled angrily, "just let me up off here and give me a knife! You and me'll go at it good!"

The Indian started to answer when a pair of

leather-clad legs stalked up next to his face. "Well now, Mr. Boone, it sure has been a while."

Daniel's heart came up in his throat. He stared up at the gaunt features of Henry Flint. All hope of dying easily faded fast. "You been a long time comin'," said Daniel. "I was afraid we was goin' to miss each other."

Flint spread his pale lips into an easy laugh. "By damn, I'm goin' to enjoy killin' you, Boone."

"Every dog's got his pleasures."

Flint's eyes clouded. He bent down close, till Daniel could smell the whiskey on his breath. "Guess you already know most of the tricks I got in mind, Boone, seein' as how you been around Indians a spell. You want to hear some of 'em, or just wait and get surprised?"

Daniel looked at him. "Flint, you'll do what you got to, an' there ain't much I can do about it. I'll ask you this. Is there some way I can talk you into killin' the girl and my friend here quick?"

Flint's eyes went hard and he spat in Daniel's face. "The girl was mine, Boone, you know that? Ol' Will tell you? I had my eyes on that one a long time. Watched her grow from a child. Came in and crossed the mountains special, just to see that pretty little body goin' naked in the creek." He paused, and his eyes seemed to flicker as they caught the light of the fire. "You know what I was thinkin' all that time. I'll wait, I said to myself. I'll just bide my time till that one gets ripe enough to pick. She's growin' pretty for Henry Flint, only she don't even know it."

Daniel felt a chill run up his spine. God A'mighty, Flint had forgotten Daniel was there! His eyes had no color at all—only the pale touch of a fire that raged in his soul.

"You ruined her for me, Boone. You know that?" Flint's face stretched into a mask. "You dirtied her up 'fore I could even touch her once! Goddamn! What you think I'm goin' to do to you for that?"

The poor bastard is crazy, thought Boone, just as crazy as a man could be. "We already talked 'bout that."

"No, you don't know," Flint said softly. "You think you do, but you don't. Not really . . ." Flint looked up suddenly, and Daniel saw the white, round little face at his shoulder. Billy Girt! He's still got Girt with him! The sight of the man startled him nearly as much as Flint had.

Billy Girt beamed. "Howdy, Dan'l. You feelin' all right?" He cackled and winked at Flint. Flint never took his eyes off Boone.

"You can do what I said, Billy. Just that, and nothin' more. You hear?"

"Yes, sir, Mr. Flint," Billy said quickly. "Won't do a thing more, cross my heart."

"Fine, then. Let's see if you do."

Girt walked out of sight and came back with a brand from the fire. The wood crackled orange and red. Billy puffed out his cheeks and carefully brought it back to a hot, glowing yellow. Then he squatted down and grinned at Daniel. "You kilt two of my brothers, Boone. I'm goin' to have your eyes for that. Mister Flint says I can."

"Not now," Flint corrected. "I didn't say right now."

Girt's face fell. "Like the man says, Dan'l. You

goin' to have to wait." Billy blew once more on the stick, then pulled up Daniel's shirt and calmly laid the brand on his chest.

Daniel didn't try to hold back. He screamed and howled and thrashed against the terrible, burning pain. The fire ate into him, blackened his flesh and drove its hot, searing agony through every fiber of his body. He knew he couldn't take it. One more awful second was more than he could bear. Still, the fire gnawed through him, starting a thousand new islands of pain wherever it touched.

Jesus God, he thought, it can't hurt more'n it does!

His thoughts blurred. There was nothing but pain. The hurt was everything. He let himself fall, drifting in the sweet, agonizing tide.

Flint cursed, shoved Girt aside and kicked the coals off Daniel's chest. "Goddamn fool!" he raged. "You kill him, and you'll take his place down there!" Girt whined and stumbled away; Flint cast a last look at Boone. "You get a good sleep, now. We got a right big day ahead."

Daniel had no way to know how long he'd been unconscious. But a terrified scream awoke him from his sleep.

There was no way to shut his ears to the sound. He knew what they were doing to her, knew the horrors that caused her ragged cries of pain. He knew every detail because Flint told him. "We're touching her here now, Boone . . . doing this to her now . . ."

Once, Flint had the Shawnees bring her up close. Girt held a torch so Daniel could watch, and Flint went to work on her. There was nothing Daniel could do but watch. When he tried to close his eyes, they only hurt her more.

The whiskey was making them careless, impatient, hurting her so much that she scarcely had the strength to cry out. Once, her voice stopped abruptly, and Daniel prayed they had killed her. Finally, though, Flint brought her around, and she screamed all the more.

Again Daniel drifted into unconsciousness. When he finally came to, his body was so cold he could barely feel the pain. The only sound was the sharp crack of an ember in the fire. Nothing else. He struggled against the dull press of cold that numbed his mind. Was it over? Was she dead? Squeezing his eyes, he brought the sky overhead into focus. There was a faint touch of color in the east. Good Lord, already? He strained to turn his head. There was nothing there. Nothing but darkness.

Slowly his head cleared and his mind chilled with a terrible, nameless fear. He searched about frantically for the nightmare that had trailed him up out of sleep. It was there, somewhere, above him, past his head. Inching up behind him was a soft, animal-scratching on the earth.

He nearly cried out when it touched him. He stiffened and tried to shrink back from it. It seemed to snake out blindly and find his arm. It stopped there, groped a moment, then slid coldly down to his hand.

When the blade touched the cords at his wrist, he strained up and saw her. Bile rose to his throat, and he bit his lips hard to keep from screaming. He turned away quickly, then forced his eyes back. He had to remember this. All of it. Everything they had done to her.

He wanted to hold her, let her cry the hurt away, but it was too late for that. The girl who had pressed her own warm body against his was no more. In her place was this ragged piece of meat.

Then, suddenly, all his feeling seemed to drain away. There was nothing to feel now. He was as dead and cold as Blue Duck. He felt neither anger nor hatred toward the sleeping figures. A great, soothing calm filled him. There was something he had to do. What he thought or felt didn't matter. Not now.

He took them one at a time. Moving quiet as death from one dark mound to the next. The first Shawnee was lying on his back with his mouth open. Daniel's blade whispered quickly across his throat. The second warrior opened his eyes, looked up drunkenly, and Daniel strangled him, crushing the man's throat with one quick, wrenching motion of his hands.

There were two, maybe three more Indians. He couldn't be sure. They were somewhere on the other side of the fire. Flint slept alone just beyond them. Boone crawled quickly around the circle on his belly. Daniel drove the knife into the first Shawnee's heart, abruptly stifling a loud snore.

"Huh? Wha . . . ?" Someone sat up straight and stared. Slipping a hand down hard over his mouth, Daniel swiftly drove him back to the ground. Billy Girt's eyes widened in terrible fear.

"You know who it is, don't you?" Daniel whispered. Billy nodded, and Daniel rested the blade on his chest, then pushed it in deep.

Girt's body stiffened, and he groaned against Daniel's hand. Then, a rifle cracked. A warrior cried out and jerked his hands up to his face. Stewart had taken the gun from one of Daniel's victims. The other Indian took one look and scrambled for the brush. Daniel sensed Flint coming and rolled just as a tomahawk dug the earth near his head. Daniel twisted, kicked out and sent the renegade sprawling. Springing to his feet, Flint whipped out his knife. But when he saw death all around him, he paled.

"I couldn't wait till morning," rasped Boone. "Let's get on with it now."

Flint feinted and Daniel lunged his blade, cutting a long arc in the air and forcing Flint hard against the trees. When Flint saw the line of blood on his chest, he cried out and staggered back. He knew then that Boone would kill him. Never had he feared a man he'd met, but this was not a man who faced him now. When Boone came at him again, Flint jabbed viciously with his knife, then turned on his heels and plunged into the trees.

Daniel went after him. But when the sun finally came up, whatever had kept him going abruptly left him. The pain and the cold rushed back and brought him to his knees. A cry squeezed from his lips. He stumbled through dead brush, every step an agony that threatened to drop him into darkness.

Flint was up there, moving fast and making no effort to cover his tracks. Daniel knew what his quarry was doing—choosing the roughest ground to travel on. If there was a flat place to run, Flint would choose a hill. When the woods grew thin, he would double back and tear through a dense and tangled thicket.

He's right, too, Daniel thought dully. I can't take a hell of a lot more of this.

The smart thing to do would be to go back, find

Stewart and take out after Flint on the Shawnee horses. There wasn't any way Flint could lose him then.

He's smart, though, Daniel thought. He's too damn smart, and I can't give him any more time.

The sun was up high, but it shed no warmth. A fierce wind had picked up in the mid-morning, and the cold was blowing in fast. Daniel couldn't feel his hands anymore. He held them up before his eyes. They were pale and crusted with blood. He peered at the top of the ridge, reached for the cold stone again and forced his body another foot.

It wasn't far to the ridge, just a few yards. He could get there and maybe get out of the wind and . . . rest a minute . . . just shut his eyes for a . . .

"No!" He bit his cheek until pain brought him fully awake. If he stopped now, even for a minute, he would go to sleep and freeze to death. He would likely die anyway, but not while Flint was alive.

With the last strength he could muster Daniel pulled himself over the lip of the ridge. The raw flesh of his chest scraped stone and he nearly passed out. "Can't . . . not yet . . ."

He raised his head, blinked, and stared wearily at the worn moccasins, the buckskin legs, the tall figure of Flint towering over him. Daniel's heart sank. He cried out, cursed his weakness, strained to start his limbs moving.

Flint laughed. "You sure are a hell of a climber, Boone. Damned if you're not. Didn't think you was ever goin' to make it."

"Didn't . . . think you was ever goin' to . . . stop runnin' 'way," gasped Daniel.

Flint kicked him solidly in the head. Moaning,

161

Daniel sprawled on his back. The renegade came down fast, straddling his chest and pinning his arms.

"Haven't got near as much time as I'd like," Flint said with a malicious grin, "but I reckon this'll do." He held the knife under Daniel's eye and flicked it. Daniel yelled as the blade opened his cheek. Flint's pale eyes went wide with pleasure. Reaching quickly with one hand, he grasped Daniel's hair and tugged. "I'm goin' to scalp you while you're still alive to feel it, Boone. Then we'll work our way down to your belly."

Flint shifted forward to bring the blade to Daniel's head, but when Boone felt the weight leave his arm, he jerked it hard and slammed his fist into Flint's mouth. Flint grunted. The knife clattered away. Then the renegade swept Daniel's hand aside and wrapped strong hands around his throat. Daniel clawed blindly for Flint's face. Then, as his vision faded under a veil of red, Daniel gasped, reached out blindly and jabbed hard.

Flint let out a ragged yell and fell away, one hand clasping a raw and bloody eye. Daniel gulped voraciously for air and again saw light. Flint raged and came at him.

Daniel stumbled back, caught himself, flailed the air as his foot came down on nothing. He heard his own cry in the wind and knew he was tumbling off the ridge through emptiness.

Chapter 17

Just before dark, Stewart found Daniel lying on the bank of a shallow stream, his head inches above the cold water. Stewart was certain he was dead until he noticed the slight heave of Daniel's chest. A big storm was blowing in fast, bringing frigid wind and rain from the north. Hefting Daniel on his shoulders, he searched out a limestone cave, built a fire, and stripped Boone naked. Throughout the night and the next day he fed wood to the fire and tried to rub the life back into his friend. Daniel was still alive the next evening, but Stewart was sure he wouldn't last through the night.

Early in the morning, Daniel began raving and thrashing about—a good sign, Stewart decided. Either that or the last throes of a dying man. He wrapped Boone in a buffalo blanket and tightly strapped him in with rawhide. He couldn't bear to look at the pale, drawn features under the heavy covers.

In the morning Daniel opened his eyes and looked at Stewart. "Did you bury her?" he asked weakly.

Stewart looked over at him, startled to find his friend still alive. "Dan'l, I would have," he said gently, "only I couldn't find her. Flint or one of the Shawnees must've hauled her off somewhere. I'm sorry."

Daniel sighed and closed his eyes. "They didn't leave me much, did they, John?"

"No. I guess they didn't."

Stewart kept him down for a whole week, feeding him broth a mouthful at a time, and later, as much meat as he could take. At least, Stewart decided, they both might make it now. He'd had the presence of mind to grab what he could from the camp, including a couple of long rifles and some lead and powder, without which, they couldn't survive. Game was getting scarce, and it was all a man could do to track it in the cold.

He wasn't worried any longer about Flint or the Shawnee. There was no sign around, and he was sure they had hightailed it north. With any luck, neither would reach home alive. He had taken their horses and guns. If the cold didn't kill them, starvation would, and Stewart didn't give a damn which.

It was difficult to even think about that terrible night—even harder to put it out of his mind. Daniel, he knew, thought of little else. Day after day he sat huddled by the fire under his robes, staring blankly into the distance. Stewart knew his friend was still back there, staked out on the ground, listening to the girl.

But Boone never spoke about that night, and Stewart was glad he didn't. He wondered if Daniel remembered what he had done, what he had turned into for a while in Station Camp.

When the weather cleared and Daniel's strength returned, they moved off southwest, away from Station Camp and below the Warrior's Path. There was no trail to follow, but Daniel insisted the others would come this way. Stewart was sure they had kept going, clear back through the gap to North Carolina.

"They're here," Daniel insisted. "They're still here somewhere."

Not if they got any sense, thought Stewart.

"What day you think it is?" asked Daniel. "I've plumb lost count."

"January somethin'," said Stewart. "Not much past the first of the year."

Daniel nodded silently. Peering about, he could see the far-off shadow of the Cumberlands, the Endless Mountains. From here they were a dark blur on the horizon, almost the same color as the winter sky. Stewart was right, he decided. The new year had come and gone, passed without his noticing. It was 1770 now, the year he had set aside for his own. He would come riding back to the Yadkin, pack horses straining under their load, and wipe out every goddamn debt he had. Lord, what a day! The skins, and one thing more—the fattest pelt of all hanging from his belt—the rich, vast land of Kentucky.

Daniel stirred in the saddle and the dream died, fading quickly into the bleak landscape. That was all gone now, dead and behind him. Kentucky had robbed him blind and nearly taken his life in the bargain. That, and more. It had ripped a piece of his soul with a cruel and bloody knife, leaving him cold and empty inside. The other wounds would heal, but that one would take awhile. Maybe, he thought, it would never go away.

Stewart saw the fire before he did, a small touch of light some two hundred yards up the hill, hidden by the bank of the river. He raised a hand and reined in fast. "Oh, Jesus—what if we'd come up the other way and rode right into it?"

Daniel looked past him. "We don't know it's Indians."

"You think it's Findley?" Stewart forced a laugh. "You know goddamn well it ain't!"

"Reckon we'll see."

"No, we won't. We can just . . ." Stewart stopped, and took a breath. "Yeah, we do, Dan'l. Sorry."

"Nothin' to be sorry for."

"I guess there is."

" 'Cause you're still scared to death, John?"

"Uh-huh."

"Good," Daniel said shortly. "I sure don't want no damn fool who ain't scared guardin' my back."

Stewart grinned, then looked past Daniel's shoulder. A figure came out of the trees by the ridge and started down the steep path to the water. The man carried a kettle, and squatted to dip it in the stream. Daniel hefted his rifle. The man by the stream looked up and saw them, dropped the kettle and scurried up the hill.

"Damn!" Stewart cried out. "He knows we're here now."

Daniel laughed for the first time in nearly a

month. "The cold's gettin' your eyes, John. That Injun looks a hell of a lot like my baby brother Squire!"

By the time Daniel and John reached the creek, Squire had run back down the hill, tossed the kettle behind him and sprinted across the flat to drag Daniel off his horse. When they met, they hugged and wept with joy like children. For Daniel, finding his brother was like rediscovering his life, his home back over the mountains. Squire was a strong, solid link with Becky, the children, everything he had nearly lost forever.

"I brought you plenty of salt, flour and ammunition, Daniel," Squire announced. "And I got another surprise for you."

"I'm in need of a good surprise, Squire."

"I got some friends of yours waitin' back at the camp—one of 'em name of Findley." Squire's broad grin disappeared as he saw the dark look that crossed his brother's face.

"Let's get goin' then," Daniel grumbled.

They were waiting at the campsite. Findley himself greeted Boone with the best smile he could muster. Cooley, Holden and Mooney stepped up to shake his hand. Daniel greeted each of them individually, but not one of the four could face him. Findley was the worst, shifting his feet and staring at the ground. He couldn't turn away from Daniel, and yet could hardly stay where he was. Daniel and the old man were both relieved when Squire interrupted and led his brother back to the fire.

By the time Findley came to him, Daniel was too weary to do anything but listen. Findley faced him, crossing his legs on the ground.

"Goddamn, I'm sorry!" he blurted out, his face

twisted in anguish. "I'm just as sorry as I can be, Dan'l. You got to know that!"

"John, I reckon I do. There's nothin' you have to say you don't want to."

"I got to, though." Findley shook his head and bit his lip hard. "You know that, Dan'l. Stewart just told me what happened to you. Jesus!" He paused a moment. "I—wish I could've done somethin' about the girl."

"I guess there wasn't much you could do."

"There was somethin'. Oh, there was somethin' I could've done, all right."

"I won't judge another man's actions," Daniel said evenly. "If that's what you want, John, I'm not goin' to give it to you. I can't."

"Yeah, I know that." Findley cleared his throat and sat up straight. "Cooley, Holden and Mooney ain't stayin', Dan'l. You likely guessed that."

"I did."

"I told 'em I'd lead 'em back, startin' in the mornin', if it's all right with you. I wouldn't let them go 'fore now, not till we found you, Dan'l, or knew you wasn't coming."

"I appreciate that."

Findley studied his hands. "It's just—well, Dan'l, the truth is, the years are gainin' on me an' I got no more stomach for this sort o' livin'. I truly don't. You can see that, can't you?"

Daniel looked at the man's hollow eyes and the deep, weary lines extending into the grizzled beard. He longed to reach out and comfort his old friend, to let him know he understood, but Boone knew it wouldn't help. "I can see it, John. I truly can," he said quietly, but taking the shame off Findley's shoulders was something he couldn't do. No one could do that.

At dawn, the four men headed off south down the hollow, then due east for the Yadkin. Daniel stood by Squire and Stewart and watched till they were out of sight.

"It wasn't the old man's fault," said Stewart. "Not all of it, Dan'l. Cooley came to me, though none of the others would. He said Findley cursed 'em all, damn near threatened to kill 'em if they ran off without packin' up the skins, but they was more scared of Injuns than Findley. Cooley flat out admitted it. Findley couldn't handle it hisself an' still get out with his own hide, so he just ran off with the rest. He told you that, I guess."

"No, he didn't tell me," replied Daniel. "I figured it, though."

Stewart looked relieved. "Well, you relieved him of the burden, then. That's good."

Daniel gave him a puzzled look. "No, I didn't, John. How could I? Findley's a man, and a damn good one. It was his job to get those skins out, and he knew it. He don't blame anyone but hisself, and that's the way it oughta be."

"Sometimes, Daniel, you can be a mighty hard man."

"We all got our burdens to carry, John. Findley's got his, I got mine."

Daniel's burden stayed with him throughout the winter. He still woke at night sometimes, the stink of his own fear upon him. For a terrible moment he would see himself again staked out at Station Camp, with Flint's grey eyes staring down at him and Billy Girt's brand on his chest.

But worst of all were the times he thought about the Indian girl. No matter how hard he tried, he couldn't hold a picture of her for long. Every time he nearly had it right, the picture shattered like ice on a river. The dark doe eyes, the golden skin and the soft, black hair turned abruptly into that other thing.

Sometimes the nightmares didn't come at all. When they left him for a day or so, he let himself believe there would be a time when he would be free of them for good. Not free of her, though. He didn't want that. All he wanted was an image of her whole in his mind again.

He also thought a lot about the renegade. He didn't want Henry Flint out of his mind, either. And though he knew it shamed every Quaker Boone who'd made it to Heaven, he fervently prayed that nothing would happen to Flint, that God would guard him well until he, Daniel Boone, could find him again.

Chapter 18

For his new campsite, Daniel chose a spot to the north and west of the old one, far from the Warrior's Path. It was on the bank of the great river he had come to know so well, a broad, coursing ribbon, big and bold enough to bear the name of Kentucky itself. Here, and in the tributary streams, beaver and otter were thick as gnats in the summer—a fat treasure of furs ripe for the taking.

Daniel threw himself into his work with a will. If the Indians had emptied his purse, then by God, Kentucky would fill it up again! The land was rich enough to make a man's fortune a thousand times over.

Boone was more cautious now, ever conscious of how quickly tragedy could overtake them. He continually drilled the same prudence into his friends. They could ill afford another encounter with the Shawnees.

Late in January, the winter skies turned a darker

shade of grey and punished the land with a steady, chilling rain. When the clouds moved on after a long, dreary week, the great river and its tributaries were left swollen with cold, raging waters.

"It's drainin' off some," said Stewart, gazing out over the rapid current. "I'd best take the boat and check the traps."

Boone looked at the frail canoe they had made and gauged it against the strength of the river. "I reckon it'll do, all right. Take a care, though."

Stewart grinned and dragged the canoe to the bank, then stepped out into the water. "God A'mighty, that's cold!" Daniel laughed, watching him dance about in the shallows.

"You ain't no beaver, John."

"I reckon not. Jesus!"

Daniel held the craft steady while Stewart got in, then handed over the long rifle and pack. Stewart studied the river a moment, then paddled away from shore. The current caught him quickly and shot the craft like an arrow into the quick, muddy water. Stewart wisely let the current have its way, keeping the bow steadily downstream with a touch of his paddle. Daniel loped along the bank, watching till Stewart beached the craft on the other shore. He waved. Stewart waved back, then disappeared into the woods.

Stewart didn't return that evening, or the day after. Daniel wasn't worried—camping overnight was nothing new. But one day stretched into another, and then a full week went by. There was no reason for Stewart to stay out this long, not in winter, not if he was just checking traps.

The river had by now spent its wrath, and early in

the morning Daniel crossed where it was shallow and picked up Stewart's path. For three days he tracked in cold forest. Once, he found a dead fire and the initials "J.S." on a tree. But the man himself was gone, swallowed up in the wilds.

The loss shook Daniel's spirit for a long time. A man would vanish at any moment in the wilderness. It had happened before, and it would happen again. It was a danger that Daniel and every man who dared tempt untamed country knowingly faced. But Stewart—Jesus, why him? Daniel asked himself painfully. They had been as close as two men could be. They had braved so much together, come out whole and alive, and now this. He kept his hopes up, thinking every day that Stewart might stalk grinning into camp with some wild, unlikely tale to explain his absence.

He knew, though, that the man was gone. Clearly, Daniel thought, Kentucky wasn't finished with him yet. Once again, the land had made him pay for what he took out of it.

At last, the dim winter sun began to grow brighter and warm the earth. As always, his spirits lightened when the world turned green, and animal life stirred lazily in the ground, then burst out to mate and nest.

On the first day of May, a year to the day since he had left the door of his cabin, Daniel helped Squire to load the pack horses, then bid his brother good-bye. There had been six of them in the beginning—later the number had grown to eight. Now, they were all gone, and he was alone.

Maybe, he thought, that was the way it was supposed to be. Maybe the land wanted to have him alone, to tell him something it couldn't say to the oth-

173

ers. There was no real reason to stay. Not now. It was too late for beaver, and he had barely enough powder to hunt for meat. Still, he had never given a thought to going back. In fact, he found that he relished Squire's going, eager to be rid of his last companion. Kentucky was his, now. It was a peculiar, almost mystical feeling, as though the land belonged to him, all of it. Now he didn't have to share it with anyone.

Great God A'mighty, he thought, as he shook his head to clear it. What kind of foolishness was that? Kentucky was as wide as the world, and he wanted it all to himself. And after his moccasins had found every inch of it, then what? He knew his hunger, knew his eyes devoured unexplored land like other men gobbled up food. There would be an end to Kentucky, a high hill that would look out on somewhere else he had never been. He knew it would happen, and it frightened him to think about it.

He set off north, letting the land guide his steps. Turning west to follow a narrow branch of the Kentucky, he came upon a wide bend in the river that struck his fancy. There was a great stretch of sycamore growing in a wide valley. Buffalo roamed the meadows, and deer darted through the woods. The land here would support settlers and livestock. Crops would spring up like weeds. By God, it was a spot especially made for Dick Henderson's settlement, and he vowed to stand on that very piece of land one day and show it to his friend.

Taking off north again, he discovered a new river that he named the Licking, and followed its course all the way up to the Ohio. There were Shawnees about, but he kept well out of sight. Sometimes he hid in canebrakes or caves along the river. More than once they found his fire, but never guessed he wasn't another Indian. One evening, returning to camp, he discovered they had left a drawing scratched in the dirt, telling him where they were. He was proud of that, and laughed out loud.

Several times he was certain that he had found traces of Henry Flint. He knew the man's print as well as his own. Each time he followed a trail, though, it wandered off and vanished. Daniel gave the man credit—he was a woodsman, and a good one.

Near the middle of summer Daniel ranged south again, nearly all the way back to where he and Squire had parted in the spring. Growing careless on familiar ground, he made a mistake that nearly cost him his life. Walking along a ridge above the river, he heard a noise behind him, and turned to see the face of Captain Will. One by one, braves appeared from the forest. There was no way back. The Indians had him cut off good, and there was nothing ahead but an awesome drop to the river. Captain Will raised his hand and whooped. The Shawnees poured down upon him. At first Daniel ran toward them a few yards, then turned and leaped as far as he could over the cliff. A great sugar maple reached up from the hollow and he stretched his arms to grab it. Limbs snapped beneath him, tumbling him through one layer of branches after another. Finally he stopped himself, nearly wrenching his arms out of their sockets, and made his way to the ground. Captain Will and his braves shouted and whooped from the ridge, and Daniel took time to wave before vanishing into the woods.

As the weeks went by, he carefully hoarded his

dwindling supply of shot and powder, often doing without meat and surviving on herbs and berries. Sometimes he saved ammunition by fishing and snaring small game. Only a fool could starve in a land like Kentucky—a man who hungered after meat pies and potatoes had no real business in the wilderness. But sometimes, even Daniel sorely missed salt and flour. Nevertheless, he could do without them. He had the whole world spread out before him. The land was his, every hill and tree and meadow.

In early July, he came upon a group of hunters ranging down the Green River from the Ohio. The Shawnees, they said, were raising a little hell to the north, and Henry Flint, Black Knife, was right in the middle of it, making a bloody name for himself among the settlers. Daniel shared a meal with them, then went on his solitary way.

In the last days of the month, he met Squire at the spot they had settled on, near the old site of Station Camp Creek. Squire brought fresh supplies and plenty of shot and powder. He also brought news from the Yadkin.

"You got a new man-child at home, Daniel. Born just 'fore Christmas last year."

"Well, I'll be damned!" Daniel exclaimed in delight. "What'd Becky call him?"

"Daniel Morgan Boone. An' he's a good-lookin' boy, too."

"Well, of course he's good lookin'. He's a Boone, ain't he?"

"And a Bryan, too," Squire reminded him. "That don't hurt any with looks."

"I can't deny that," said Daniel.

At the end of the summer, Squire once more made the trek back to the Yadkin with skins, and was back with provisions by December. When the cold set in, the pair made camp and began ranging the rivers where they set their traps for beaver. The catch was enormous, better than the year before, better than Daniel had ever imagined.

Finally, there would be money enough to satisfy every creditor who might crawl out of the woodwork—and then some, by God. He would ride home as he had dreamed, and when he again returned to Kentucky, he would have Dick Henderson and every family he could muster at his back.

He thought about that lush green valley, and the great sycamores that spread their branches over the river. Becky would like that, he decided. She would like that fine. And it wouldn't be any few acres down in a hollow, either. The Boones would be landed folk. Every hill and valley they could see would be theirs for the asking.

Winter passed quickly and spring returned to the land. In March of 1771, Daniel and Squire loaded up their treasures and started home. In the first few days of April, they passed once more through the high gap of the Cumberlands and started across the broad valley to the Warrior's Path. In spite of all the wonders he had seen, the raw beauty of this wild and untamed country with its tall peaks and broad valleys and mighty rivers, still took his breath away.

In Powell's Valley, with the Cumberlands at their back and the familiar Clinch Mountains ahead, Daniel and Squire camped for the night. In the morning they would pass Martin's Station, then turn southeast down the Watauga toward home.

Just as Daniel was settling back with a piece of venison, he looked up suddenly and froze. Eight Cherokee braves stood at the edge of the clearing.

Squire started to reach for his gun, but Daniel reached out a hand to stop him. Putting on his best smile, he stood and asked the Indians to join them for supper. The warriors looked him over, studied the camp, then stalked into the clearing. With the grin still stretching his mouth, Daniel caught Squire out of the corner of his eye.

"Just smile, little brother," he mumbled, "smile and watch 'em close."

The Indians squatted by the fire, tearing quick bites of venison with their teeth. Their dark eyes wandered over everything in camp. Daniel knew they had spotted the bundles of pelts. Wherever else their gazes rested, they soon returned to the furs.

Finally, as the warriors belched appreciatively and stood to leave, their leader turned and spoke.

"We thank you for the meal. We have nothing to give in return. I am sorrowed at this."

"The company of my Cherokee brothers is a fine gift," said Boone.

The Indian grunted. "Still, we should make notice of our meeting. It was a fine meal." He made a big show of cocking his head and giving the matter thought. Suddenly he grinned. "Let us trade rifles, as a bond of friendship between us."

Daniel looked at the Indians' rifles. They were old and falling apart. His and Squire's were new and clean, as pampered as a baby's bottom. The Cherokees knew he wasn't stupid. They would like the rifles, but they wanted a bigger prize.

Daniel kept his smile. "These rifles are precious to me, friend, or I'd give 'em to you sure. They've got my medicine on 'em. They wouldn't be much use to you."

The Indian stiffened. "We have good rifles," he said evenly, shaking his head insistently at Boone. "You take these and give us yours. It would be better to do this, brother."

Daniel caught the warning in his eyes as the other Indians drifted around the fire toward Squire. Squire jerked up, dove for his weapon. The Indians shouted and swarmed all over him. Daniel grabbed his own rifle and rammed the butt in the leader's belly. The Indian gasped and folded. His friends grabbed Boone and dragged him to the ground. Daniel kicked and flailed against them, spitting the worst Cherokee curses he knew.

The leader rubbed his stomach and glared. "You will leave with your hair if you shut your mouth now!" he said darkly. "You have angered me, brother. Do not anger me more."

Jerking his head at his companions, he pointed toward the forest. The Cherokees dragged the two Boones out of the clearing and brandished their tomahawks threateningly. Their message was clear—leave, or stay here and die. Daniel was black with rage. He yelled and cursed at the Indians and would have taken them on barehanded if Squire hadn't held him back.

When Daniel quieted, he set his brother running to Martin's Station while he trailed the thieves. Squire brought armed settlers to take up the chase, by noon the next day, it was plain that a whole war party was in the area. Giving chase would be suicidal.

Daniel was stunned in his defeat. Everything he had was gone: the furs, the horses, his rifles—everything. Two goddamn years in Kentucky had slipped from his hands in a few short minutes. The skins he had sent back earlier in the season had made him some profit, but that money had already been shelled out to creditors and put back in the pot for powder and lead. Hell, he didn't even have a knife to slit his own throat.

Chapter 19

Daniel stalked out of Dick Henderson's office, then stormed past the stables and across the street. A rugged old wagoner had to pull his team up short to avoid running Boone down. The old man shook his fist and shouted. Daniel didn't notice. He was trying hard to still the rage and frustration seething inside him.

Damnation but he felt like a fool! Why did he keep coming back? Dick wasn't about to budge—not now and not ever! Talking to the man was like butting your head against a tree.

He was a damn fool, he decided, but the fault wasn't all on his side, not by a long shot. What more did the man want? Daniel had brought the whole land of Kentucky back in his pocket and laid it out plain. Here's the route we'll take, right here's where the settlement will be. He had given Henderson everything he needed, right down to a layout of the town.

That had been five months ago. He had gotten back in April, and here it was halfway through August. Still, Dick sat there calmly behind his desk. "Wait, Daniel. Have a little patience. It's not the right time, Daniel."

Time? Great God A'mighty, time was eating him up. He would be an old man in a rocker before Dick Henderson thought it was time!

James and Israel spotted him a block from the store and ran down to meet him. By God, the boys were growing like weeds! Israel twelve now, James fourteen, and both showing stubble on their chins. He saw their smiles fade and their steps slow as they neared him. They had already caught his mood. Daniel tried hard to force a grin. There were times when he didn't even act civilly toward his family. They weren't the cause of his anger, but they caught the brunt of it. And they deserved more than that.

"Where's your ma?" he asked, lying his hands on their shoulders. "Still in the store?"

"Yes, sir," Israel replied soberly. "Reckon she's fair buyin' up the place."

"She ain't either, Israel," James disagreed shortly.

Daniel laughed. "I don't imagine she is, boy, 'less she struck gold somewhere." A lump swelled in his throat and a new surge of anger overwhelmed him. Salt and sugar, and maybe a little strip of ribbon for the girls. If Becky had more than that on her list, he would be mighty surprised.

It was late afternoon before he drove the team out of town and started north for the Yadkin. Becky rode beside him and the boys trotted out ahead on their horses. The air was thick and humid. The boughs of the trees met overhead to offer shade, but there was no cooling breeze. Only the locusts chattered loudly in the brush to break the heavy silence. Even the crows were stilled by the heat.

The minute he walked in the store, Rebecca knew, but she swallowed her comforting words and said nothing. Talk wouldn't help. More likely, it would only anger him more.

She had never cared much for Dick Henderson's fancy ways. Now, she was growing to hate him. Every time Daniel came back from one of their meetings, he looked like Israel running home after the Cully boy had licked him again.

Rebecca sighed and wiped her brow. It looked like God and the Devil had both been at work in Kentucky. The man who came back to her wasn't the man who had left. He was a man both blessed and cursed. And it was difficult to say which force would have him in the end.

He said nothing to her until they were on their way home.

"You ain't asked me 'bout Dick."

Rebecca looked straight down the road. "Figured you'd say if there was anythin' to tell."

"Well, there ain't," he said shortly. "Not a damn thing, Becky." When she didn't reply, he continued mockingly. "Take your time, Daniel. It'll happen, you'll see." Daniel snorted in disgust. "Time, my ass! It sure wasn't like this before, I'll tell you. Two years ago, he could fairly taste Kentucky, had it all plotted and parcelled out in his head." Daniel turned and looked at her candidly. "He ain't the same man, Becky."

"Men change for better or worse."

"Not like this. Not the way Dick has."

"It appears they do, Daniel."

"Humph!" Daniel snorted. He turned back to the team, letting the heavy silence hang between them.

Rebecca didn't have to ask about Salisbury. She had heard the story before a dozen times. Dick Henderson was hedging, approaching a Kentucky land deal with a lawyer's natural caution, a quality that tried Daniel's patience to the limit. Henderson had said he would move with the strength of the law behind him. In his present position, that was anything but easy. He was an associate justice now, a post that put him squarely in the limelight. The Royal Governors of North Carolina and Virginia had little patience with the speculators and land companies straining to open the West. What would they say if a member of the colony's highest court struck out openly across Indian lands? He was taking a big chance as it was, sending Daniel out to talk to the Cherokees.

"They'll sell their claim," Daniel reported earnestly. "Make the pot big enough, and you'll see. You'll get clear and legal title to Kentucky!"

"Let the chiefs know we mean business," Henderson advised. "Talk to them."

"They do," Daniel said testily. "There ain't anythin' more to say. I've done all the talkin' I can."

"Then talk to them some more," said Henderson.

"What the hell for?"

"So they won't forget what you said the first time."

"Indians ain't feeble-minded, Dick."

"I know they're not," Henderson said patiently. "But they are greatly inclined to best remember only the last white man who talked to them."

Daniel could have refuted that, but he didn't. He journeyed again and again to the Cherokee encampments, hunting, talking and keeping a smile on his face. It was something to do, anyway, even if he had already done it a dozen times over.

Sometimes, when talking to the Indians, he wondered if he was sitting down to supper with Blue Duck's father, or maybe one of her brothers. Perhaps the tall, slender woman gathering wood, the one with the dark and somber eyes, was the girl's mother. He longed to ask some of the braves he knew, but never did. In spite of what Henderson thought he knew about Indians—which in Boone's opinion was about as much as Daniel knew about the law—they were as smart as anyone else. If you asked them a question, they would want to know why you asked it. Why did Wide Mouth wish to know about the daughter who had vanished from sight and brought sorrow to her parents? It was a question Daniel didn't care to answer just yet.

"Daniel," Rebecca said when they had nearly reached the Yadkin, "are you just goin' to keep at it with Dick? You mind if I ask that?"

For a while he didn't answer. "Becky, what else am I s'posed to do? I ain't likely goin' to open up Kentucky without him."

"No, I s'pose not."

"There's hardly any s'posin' to it," he said bluntly. "Ridin' and huntin' alone is one thing. Takin' families in to settle is somethin' else. That takes money, which you might have noticed we don't have much of."

"Is it money, Daniel? Really? Is that what it takes to get there?"

He looked at her curiously. "Becky . . ."

"No. Listen. You get mad as you like at me for sayin' so, Daniel, but I'm bound to say it anyway. You've got used to thinkin' Dick Henderson's money gives him some special kind of magic. It doesn't, Dan. It buys things, and that's all. That's no little thing, now, when you haven't got it—but it doesn't lay the hand of God on a man. And that's flat where you've let your head get to."

"Becky, you're not makin' a damn bit of sense," he said flatly.

"Oh?" Rebecca's dark eyes flashed. "And what kind of sense are you makin', Dan Boone? S'pose Dick Henderson gave every family in North Carolina a sack of gold and a wagonload of goods? You think they'd all follow him into Kentucky? You been out there. You ever kill a Shawnee by throwin' coins in his face?"

Daniel's puzzled look split into a grin, then he laughed like a man set free. Leaning over, he kissed his wife soundly. "Lord, God, what a woman you are, Rebecca Boone!"

Rebecca pushed him off and clamped her lips tight. "Don't honey up to me," she said stiffly. "You just listen to what I'm sayin'. There isn't a family in this colony wouldn't follow you stark naked clear to the Ohio if you asked 'em to, so don't go shavin' inches off yourself to make Mr. Richard Henderson look taller. The man needs you, Daniel, a hell of a lot more than you need him."

Daniel stared at her. "Becky, there's more to it than that. You can't just decide to go, then up and do it."

"If six or eight men can, then fifty families, or maybe a hundred, can too."

Daniel grinned. "Not stark naked, they can't."

"I got a wagon and a team, Daniel, and a cow to tie on behind. I reckon there might be other folks who've got the same. And most all of 'em got clear to North Carolina without Dick Henderson."

Daniel stared at her in disbelief. It was the most ridiculous bit of talking he had ever heard. Becky had no idea what it would take to make a toehold in Kentucky. Why, she made no sense at all. As if you just took off and . . . it was just plain silly.

Becky said nothing else about the matter for the rest of the summer. Instead she bit her tongue and watched him work out his anger in the only way he knew. His half-hearted tries at farming ended quickly, and he was soon roaming far from home again, hunting, exploring, or simply walking from one end of the land to the other.

Summer slid into fall, and he went after skins, sometimes taking James and Israel with him. Winter brought the trapping season again and he made a little money on beaver, though all the nearby streams were trapped clean. The land was worked out of game; Daniel had been saying it for years.

Rebecca knew his mind. She saw the hunger in his eyes again, as he spent the long grey days sniffing the air for spring. Only during the Christmas season did she, for a few happy days, see him revel in the joy of his family. Still, nothing had really changed. March was barely off the calendar before he was gone again.

With a neighbor he crossed back into Kentucky, roaming the mountains with bear-hunting dogs and returning home with a pack horse full of dark, heavy skins. On another trip, he journeyed farther down the Cumberland than he had ever before, going so far west that he met some Frenchmen from the Mississippi coming east.

Becky wasn't surprised when he suggested they leave the Yadkin and move closer to Kentucky. She had seen it coming and had shut it out of her mind.

If they moved, he argued, he could travel more easily and still have more time with her and the children. There was a place they could live in Sapling Grove, deep in the Watauga Valley. It wouldn't have all the conveniences they had grown used to, but they would at least have more time together. And of course, they could always come back if she really didn't take to the place.

Rebecca hid her sorrow and said nothing. They would never come back, not ever, though Daniel didn't even know that himself. When the wagons were loaded and they moved off down the hollow with nearly all they owned, she stared straight ahead and refused to look back at the home she was leaving.

It was September, the time of the year she loved most. It saddened her to know she would never enjoy that season again on the Yadkin. And only weeks before, she had learned she was carrying another child. The baby would be born in a place she had never seen before. That was a sadness, too.

Maybe this'll teach you to keep your thoughts to

yourself, she thought darkly. You told him he was man enough, that he didn't have to wait for Dick Henderson. Well, he's not waiting. He's fair straining at the bit to get there.

PART TWO
1773–1775

Chapter 20

Ben Cutbirth urged his horse on down the ridge toward the settlement. Daniel hung back a moment, drinking in the vast expanse of land that lay at his feet. The mountains stretched away on either side, dark and somber peaks disappearing in a mist. These were the moments he relished. You could stand in a place like this and believe that you were the only man in the world, and that the land you saw would stay as it was forever.

It wouldn't, though, he knew. It was changing faster every day. Lord God, how the time went by! It was March already, 1773—nearly four years since the first time he had left the Yadkin with Findley and the others and set out for Kentucky. It seemed like a century ago, and yet, like no time at all. John Stewart was back there somewhere, dead in the wilderness, and Blue Duck, as well. He had heard John Findley was gone too, dead just a year after his family had gotten slaughtered by Senecas on Buffalo Creek. Daniel wondered if it was true.

So many had died in the past few years. Still, nature replaced its own, bringing new crops of trees, deer and even people to replace the ones it took. He would have a new child in his family by May. Damnation, he thought, that would make eight. He and Becky were sure doing their part to keep things going.

Ben was waiting for him at the bottom of the ridge and they rode together into Castle's Woods. It was a small settlement, perched in the valley between two high mountain ranges and the headwaters of the Clinch. Daniel already knew most of the people there; they had been his neighbors on the Yadkin before they fled to the West from debts they couldn't pay and taxes they couldn't meet. More and more now, the old-timers moved on to find breathing room, leaving the crowded land to newcomers, folks who seemed to relish living right in their neighbors' laps.

Boone and Cutbirth cleaned up at the home of a friend, and Ben walked on to the tavern. By the time Daniel arrived, Ben had made a place for himself at a table full of strangers. Daniel spotted Ben's freckled face and thatch of red hair halfway across the room. Ben waved him over with a grin and introduced him to the man beside him. "Daniel, here's a fellow wants to meet you. I told him you two ought to get your heads together. Cap'n Russell, this is Dan Boone."

The man stuck out his hand and Daniel gripped it. "Will Russell? Well, by God, for once Ben's right. I been hopin' our trails would cross some day."

Russell grinned. "I guess that day is here, Boone."

Daniel liked the man immediately. William Russell was a tall, quiet-spoken man around Boone's own age. His dark hair was worn long and loose over his shoulders, and his open, friendly eyes were sun-creased at the corners. His mouth was set in a firm line, and when he spoke, Daniel knew he could believe what he said. Russell's life nearly mirrored Daniel's. He had made a name for himself in the French and Indian War, then helped to lead the settling of the Clinch. Like Boone, he was a man thoroughly at home in the wilderness.

The pair wasted no time getting acquainted. Finding a table in a far corner of the tavern, they sat down over sipping whiskey and traded wilderness tales. Russell had already heard about Daniel's treks to Kentucky and was eager to learn more.

"Me and Ben just got back," Daniel explained. "We did some huntin' and roamin' 'round the old caves. There's some big herds of shaggies, but they're too far west right now, and there's too many Shawnees 'round this time of year." Daniel grinned. "I already learnt that."

Russell nodded and filled his cup again. "You see any white men?"

"Yeah, a couple." Daniel made a face and leaned toward the man earnestly. "And if we seen a couple in country that big, you know there's more around. Hell, four years ago, there wasn't hardly anyone but me. Now, they're movin' in fast."

"It's fair comin'," Russell agreed. "And soon, too. A fellow was through here in the fall and said he run into surveyors comin' down south from the Ohio. Whole party of 'em."

"In Kentucky?"

"In Kentucky. Down the Licking, I think."

"Yeah." Boone frowned and made circles on the table with his cup. "I been there. It's a good way in. Ain't a bad place, if you don't mind Indians up your ass."

Russell shook his head. "You know the Shawnees, Boone, as well as anybody. They'll be warmin' up to those surveyin' parties and generally be real helpful. Get their trade goods now and steal 'em blind when they get into the country."

Daniel was silent for a moment. "I'm goin' to do it, Russell. I fair got to. I been back two years and that's too damn long. If folks are goin' in now, what do you think it'll be like in another couple of years?"

"You already know that."

"I do for certain," Daniel said grimly.

After another whiskey and more talk of the wonders of Kentucky, Russell asked Daniel to step outside. As they sauntered down the dusty road, Will stopped Boone and faced him. "Daniel," he said evenly, "if you aim to go, I want to go with you."

Daniel stared at him and clasped the man's arm. "Well, by God, Will! You mean that?"

"I do," Russell said firmly. "I made up my mind soon as we started talkin'. And there's plenty of families here on the Clinch and all down the valley that'll join us."

Blood raced through Daniel's veins and warmed his face to a flush. Here was a man who would stand by him, a man who could be depended upon, who would not falter. "Then it's settled, Will." He offered his hand and Russell gripped it hard.

"It sure as hell is, Daniel."

When Daniel told Rebecca he wanted to sell the house on the Yadkin, she quietly agreed. "If you think it's the thing to do, Daniel."

"It is Becky," he said firmly. "Our life in these parts is dead, just like the land is. Kentucky's a place a man can build a proper home. Remember the meadow I told you about?" His eyes flashed when he spoke. "The one right off Otter Creek with the sycamores that come straight down to the river? That's where we belong, you an' me an' the children—all the children." He grinned and patted her swollen belly.

As ever, pride and sadness struggled for a place in her heart—sadness that she would once again leave so much behind, and pride that Daniel would do what he had always dreamed of without Dick Henderson or anyone else. "When you're ready," she said gently, "I'll be right beside you, Dan Boone. I told you I got a wagon and a cow."

Daniel soon got word that James and Robert McAfee had taken a party into Kentucky down the Kanawha off the Ohio, some fifty miles north of the Big Sandy. On the Kanawha they had come across James Harrod leading his own group, and the two parties had traveled together into Kentucky. Daniel's heart climbed to his throat at the news. He knew the area well. It was a different path than he had taken, but it led right to the heartland of Kentucky.

He had already made one trip to the Yadkin, and now he took James and prepared to hurry back there again to recruit families for the trip. They would have to be ready to leave by fall. He would make that clear if he hadn't already. There could be no delays now. Not any.

As if providence were blessing his plans, just before Daniel left, baby Jesse was born.

In Salisbury, Dick Henderson hailed Boone and waved him down. "I've heard the news, Daniel. I'm glad you're going. Unofficially glad, of course." Henderson's grin changed quickly to a sober look. "Dan, you don't have to say it. I'll say it myself. I've let you down, and I know it. You—ah, know my position. I hope to hell you understand it."

"You got to do what you think's right, Dick. I don't fault you for that and never have."

Henderson studied him closely. "Is that true, Daniel? I value your friendship greatly. You know that."

"It's true, Dick."

Henderson seemed to relax at the reassurance. "I hope so. I want it to be. It's the damn legalities, Daniel. The Crown's clamping down hard on speculators, and so are the colonies. You're breaking the law, you know."

"I got me near fifty families ready to go west, Dick, and the damn English law is one of their reasons for goin'. No offense, of course, but some of us have had about all of the law we can stomach. An' the taxes to go with it."

"I know that," said Henderson. He frowned and clamped his lips together. "Don't blame you a bit. As a Court Justice, I'm obliged to enforce those bloody laws, and some of them don't go down my throat any easier than they do yours."

Daniel knew he meant what he said. Whatever else he was, Dick Henderson was an honest and compassionate man. Sending debtors off to prison gave him no pleasure. Boone reached out his hand and Dick grasped it warmly.

"My heart goes with you, Dan. By God, you ought to know that."

"I reckon I do."

Henderson hesitated. "If there's anything you need . . . from me, personally, I mean—money for supplies, that sort of thing . . ."

Daniel couldn't help stiffening at the offer.

"Damn it," Henderson flushed, "I owe you that much and you know it. You've done more than enough for me. All your work with the Cherokees alone, Daniel . . ."

"You paid me for my work, Dick. I ain't forgot you got me to Kentucky in the first place."

"Well," Henderson fumbled, "well, goddamn it anyway, I don't feel right about this!"

"Hell," Daniel replied easily. "There'll be another time. An' I'm obliged. You don't owe me a thing."

Just saying the words seemed to lift a great load off Daniel's shoulders. Hell yes, he needed help! Selling his farm on the Yadkin had only made a dent in his expenses. But he was going, he and Will Russell and the others. By the skin of their teeth, maybe, but they were going. And if the King himself didn't like it, then he could by God get himself a horse and ride into Kentucky and say so!

Chapter 21

It wasn't the biggest expedition ever mounted, but he couldn't have felt prouder if he had been leading a whole regiment of British Regulars. Five families from the Yadkin were gathered and ready to go—children, pack horses, livestock and all. A troop of Bryans would join the train later, when Daniel's group met Will Russell's at Castle's Woods. All together they would count nearly two hundred. Not many, he thought, but enough. Others would soon follow, and the time wouldn't be long coming when a real town would spring up in that meadow by the river.

Followers and well-wishers remained with them nearly the entire morning, leaving them finally at the river. It was almost as if everyone in the valley wanted to feel they had played a part in the adventure, as if, in a way, they were going, too.

At the crossing, Daniel swept his eyes along the

small column of buckskin, blue linsey and homespun grey waiting for his word. Finally, he gathered the men from his party and directed them in firing a salute to the neighbors who had seen them off. The guns cracked in a ragged volley, smoke billowed over the water and everyone cheered. James and some of the other young men urged stragglers into line and chased a pack of squealing pigs out of the brush. In moments, the whole party was out of sight, lost in the bright autumn foliage of the forest.

Daniel rode up to James and slowed his horse. "By God, son, we're going," he said joyously. "All the way this time, clear across Kentucky."

James grinned back at him. "You said we would, Pa. You sure did."

"Well, I did, didn't I?"

The boyish grin faded, and Daniel saw in the firm, determined features and deep blue eyes someone he hardly knew. And he found himself shocked at the sight, as if, in a blink, a child had simply vanished and a man had appeared. God A'mighty, he thought wondrously, the boy's nearly seventeen now. He just grew up, and I didn't even see it!

"You remember when we talked, right before I went West the first time?" he asked James.

"Yes, sir. I remember," nodded James. "I ain't likely to forget, Pa." He gazed straight at Daniel, his sharp eyes proud and clear. "You said we'd get there, an' when we did, I'd be ridin' right beside you."

"Well, James, it took a while, but here we are." He glanced at the rifle cradled in his son's arms. "That piece of yours brings back a few memories. That was a day I won't forget too quick. It still shoot good?"

"Better'n ever," James commented easily. He smiled and looked at his father, then patted the stock. "You recall how it veered 'bout a hair up left?"

"I do for sure," said Daniel.

"Well, it don't no more. That Shawnee's head knocked it right back in line."

Daniel stared at the boy's sober look, then burst out laughing. "Jesus, boy, you spin a tale tall as your pa!"

James smiled, but held silent. He couldn't tell his father what he was thinking—that it wasn't exactly a yarn. Pa wouldn't understand. But James knew there was magic in the rifle, and his father had put it there. It lay in the stock Pa had carved and fitted after he had shattered the first one saving his mother. James had hardly been twelve, then, and hadn't understood the wonder of the thing. He remembered dark thoughts that had scared him plenty, not realizing then that he carried a powerful piece of his father's love locked in that oily piece of wood. James grinned at the thought and shook his head. Damnation, kids sure didn't know much. There was a lot you had to learn in the world.

The party moved north into Virginia, then curved up west through the mountains to Castle's Woods, where Daniel expected no trouble with Indians. Still, that was just when you got trouble, he knew. Throughout the trip he kept sharp-eyed riflemen on the flanks of the party, and his best woodsmen ranging through the forests and over ridges ahead. The Indians weren't as likely to come near if all the men were armed, but the women, children, pack horses and livestock put the party in a vulnerable position. A dozen Shawnees could scatter horses, cattle and screaming kids over half the Blue Ridge Mountains.

Will Russell was waiting below the last ridge before Castle's Woods. When Daniel saw the party gathered below, he threw his hat in the air, gave a loud whoop, and plunged his horse down to meet them. Russell grinned and pounded him on the back as Daniel marveled at the size of his group.

"Thirty folks at least," smiled Will. "More'n that, with the pigs."

Daniel laughed, heard a cheer from Will's group, and saw Squire leading his own party into the clearing. Soon, the two groups mixed easily with one another, scaring the stock and creating havoc for James and the other herders.

Daniel found himself surrounded by old companions, some he hadn't laid eyes on for ages. Stout, red-faced Michael Stoner was there, his thick Pennsylvania Dutch accent so smothered by corn whiskey that Daniel could hardly understand him. It looked to Boone like every frontiersman worth his salt was right here, ready and eager to range down the Clinch.

"I ain't lookin' for any trouble," he told Will Russell, "but we can likely handle what comes with men like these."

"The McAfees and their party came through from the west last month," said Will. "Both the Shawnees and the Delawares was quiet."

"We didn't move none too soon, friend. Every man in the colonies is headin' for Kentucky." Daniel shook his head in wonder. "Damned, if they ain't."

Russell, laughing indulgently, dropped an arm over Daniel's shoulder and led him toward the tavern. "Now it ain't that bad, friend."

Michael Stoner peered past Russell and fixed a bleary eye on Daniel. "It is true, Will. When Boone sees three men together, he thinks it is a village."

"I seen him run from a group of four, once," Russell said solemnly. "Thought it was a war breakin' out."

Stoner wheezed and patted his belly. "Is true, is true!"

"You boys laugh all you like," Daniel grumbled. "When we get there and find some fellow from Massachusetts sellin' rides on a buffalo, don't come hollerin' to me."

As the men joked and baited each other, the women were also getting acquainted. Rebecca liked Mary, Will's wife, right off. She was a practical, straightforward woman with no frills about her, someone you could talk to without being careful of what you said.

"Guess I better sit down on a seat that doesn't move while I have the chance," said Becky, resting on a large rock. "Be a while 'fore we get another chance."

"Isn't that the truth!" sighed Mary. "Lordy, Rebecca, looks like we could've picked us some nice, quiet store clerks for husbands, don't it? Someone who'd stay in one place more'n a minute."

"Does, doesn't it?" said Becky. She looked at the other woman's grin and let her own laughter burst out into the open. "What the hell you figure we'd do with men like that?"

The party moved out south and west, through the

narrow passes of the Clinch and the broad valley of the Powell River, where the Bryan families were waiting. Becky greeted her relatives as if she had never seen them before, giving them all a laugh, for it hadn't been a month since they had joined together on the Yadkin to plan the trip. Her brother James was there with his family, and so was Dan's sister Elizabeth and her husband. Becky was proud of all the Boones and Bryans who had come along.

Now the expedition party was complete. Daniel and Russell decided to break it into three detachments for the trip to the gap.

"Watching after everybody at once is too big a job," explained Boone. "If folks travel with people they know, they'll notice real quick if a child wanders off from its ma."

Russell agreed. He took a post at the rear with the Clinch settlers and a few experienced woodsmen. In front of him were the pack horses and provisions. The livestock was herded by a group that included James and Russell's son Henry—a job James and his new friend resented. They could both shoot well, knew the woods, and figured they ought to be out in the brush looking for Indians. Besides, Captain Russell's two slaves could handle this job on their own.

Daniel took the lead with his party, including the Bryans behind him. Some families had complained when Boone and Russell sternly forbade wagons on the trip and insisted that whatever they took to Kentucky would be carried on pack horses. Now the travelers knew why. Past the Powell River, the land turned steep and rugged, thick with trees and rough, stony ridges. Beyond that grew high patches of nearly impenetrable cane, the terrain so wild that even walking was a challenge. Some families had hedged the rules and brought small carts pulled by oxen, but these few soon wished they had never thought of the idea.

"Where the hell'd they figure we was goin'?" Daniel grumbled to Squire.

"Boston, I reckon. Or maybe Philadelphia."

"Well, we ain't. There sure are some fine wheels back there for the Cherokees."

"An' about a dozen good porkers runnin' wild. And a couple of fat cows."

Daniel turned to make sure his son was guarding the livestock, then frowned. "Tell James and the Russell boy to quit huntin' Shawnees and watch those goddamn animals," he growled.

Squire grinned and turned his horse back along the column.

Daniel brought his party to a halt on the slopes of Wallen's Ridge. They were making good time. With any luck at all, he would lead them through the gap on the next day. Sitting his horse, he squinted west into the fading sun. Just across the valley, the high peaks of the Cumberlands seemed to drip gold down their sides. Tomorrow he would be there, with Becky, the children, and all the rest. The sight sent a familiar rush of excitement through his bones. I've got you, Kentucky, he thought. I by God bought and paid for you, but I got you sure.

He stopped a moment to figure the date. They had left the Yadkin for the Clinch on the twenty-sixth. Which meant today was October ninth. The tenth, then, would be the day to remember. He might forget his birthday. But he sure as hell wouldn't forget the tenth.

After Daniel helped Becky and the children settle in for the night, he rode back along the trail a few miles until he found where James had stopped to quarter the animals. He looked the site over and nodded his approval. The boys had picked a steep-sided hollow with a creek, a place where the stock could get water and yet not wander off.

James left his companions about the fire and walked over to his father. "Everything all right, Pa?"

"Sure is, son." Daniel slid off his horse and laid a hand on the boy's shoulder. "I just wanted to ride back and have a talk with you. Figured now would be a good time to do it. You want to walk over here a ways?"

When they had gone a few yards from the little camp, Daniel stopped and faced his son. "You remember what I said about Kentucky, James, how you and me was goin' to ride through that gap together some day? Well, tomorrow's it, and I want you up front with me. So when we start goin' through, you by God hitch your mount up fast. I sure don't figure on ridin' into Kentucky again without you!"

James's face filled with pride. "We shook on it once, Pa. Mind if we do again?"

"I'd be proud to," said Daniel.

"Then I'll by God be there for certain, Pa!"

Chapter 22

James walked back to the fire as proud as he could be. Every one of his companions, even Captain Russell's two slaves, knew who his pa was. When Daniel left the camp, they all looked after him, then glanced reverently at James himself. It was as though his pa had suddenly rubbed off on him, and he felt another foot taller.

James was near bursting to tell Henry Russell what Pa had said about the following day, but he didn't, even though it nearly killed him to hold his tongue. His father wouldn't stand for such showing off.

The more James got to know Henry, the more he liked him. They were the same age, and Henry was the only person James had ever met who reminded him of himself. They had grown up knowing all the same lore about hunting and shooting and camping in the woods. In the few days they had been together, they had told each other nearly everything each had ever done, and then made plans for what they would do when they made it to Kentucky. The only difference James could see between them was that Henry's Pa wasn't poor. He figured that wasn't so important, though, and Henry never mentioned it.

The other folks looking after the stock were all right, but James could never think of much to say to them. Dick and James Mendenhall were younger than he and Henry. Henry said their folks came from the Clinch, but their pa wasn't a woodsman—probably a storekeeper or something. James had figured as much right off. Both boys were nearly scared out of their wits to be camping out, and neither knew one end of a rifle from another.

Old Isaac Crabtree and Bob Drake were hired hands who kept pretty much to themselves. Crabtree was a scarred veteran of the frontiers, a man with rheumy eyes and curly white hair. Drake was a gaunt man with a hangdog look. If he spoke at all, James never heard him. James didn't know what to make of the two Negroes, though. He had once seen some in Salisbury, but he had never talked to one. Henry called them Adam and Charles. He said they didn't have last names.

"Why's that?" James asked. "Everybody's got more than one name—everybody I ever knew, anyway."

Henry shrugged. "I don't know. They just don't."

"Well, it looks like they ought to, don't it?"

"Slaves ain't like other folk," Henry explained.

It wasn't much of an answer, but James didn't

pursue it. He didn't understand about slaves, anyhow. Henry said Adam and Charles had been around nearly as long as he could remember, and that they had come from a place called Africa.

"That's why they're black," said Henry.

"Where's Africa? I never even heard of it."

"It's up around Europe and England somewhere."

"Oh. Is that where your pa got 'em?"

"Naw. He ain't never been to Europe. He bought 'em in Virginia and brung 'em out here."

James frowned at that. "Bought 'em? What do you mean, Henry?"

Henry laughed. "James, that's how you get slaves. You find one you want, and you buy him."

"From who?"

"From whoever owns him."

James scratched his head. He was sure his friend wasn't lying, but he couldn't figure how you would just go out and buy someone. He decided to ask his father in the morning. Pa would know the answer, and he wouldn't have to ask Henry, who was beginning to treat James like a five-year-old.

That night, right after they had all pulled their blankets about them and settled down to sleep, a wolf up the hill began to howl. The Mendenhall boys nearly jumped out of their skins and wanted to put more wood on the fire.

"Goddamn, just go back to sleep, boys," grumbled Isaac Crabtree. "Them wolves ain't goin' to eat you."

"They sound kinda close," said Dick Mendenhall, who was trembling and growing pale.

"They are," said Crabtree. "An' that's as close as

they're goin' to get." He sat up and rubbed the stubble on his chin. "If those wolves bother you, you're sure goin' to have a time of it when you get to Kentucky. They ain't near as dangerous as them hollow-bellied bufflers."

"What's that?" asked one of the boys.

Crabtree raised a brow. "You never heard of 'em? Lord God, I thought everybody had. They're just like your ordinary buffler, 'cept they got these big hollow bellies. When they get riled up or somethin' they stand 'round breathin' real hard till their bellies are pumped clean full of air, and that's when they get dangerous."

"How come?" asked young Dick.

"Well," Crabtree explained, "if they get enough air in their bellies, they can just float off the ground and drift 'round the countryside. No harm in that, of course, 'less one of 'em happens to fart. Then he falls just like a rock an' crushes the hell out of some tow-headed chile who happens to be sleepin' 'round a fire."

Everyone in camp roared as Crabtree finished his tale. The Mendenhall boys turned beet-red and James felt sorry for them. He was sure they would have dreams about flying buffalo the rest of the night.

James himself had a dream that night. He was riding beside his father through the pines and out of the valley at the bottom of Wallen's Ridge, when his father grinned and pointed up ahead. James looked up and saw a great wall of naked white granite reaching up and into the sky.

"That's it, boy," said Pa, "the Cumberland Gap. And you and me are goin' to be the first ones through."

James stared, struck by the majestic sweep of that

212

great rift in the mountains. He had never imagined it would be so high! Why it just kept rising, stretching up through the clouds, and no matter how far you craned your neck, it never seemed to . . .

James sat up straight. His heart pounded hard against his chest. He turned, peering keenly through the murky grey dawn to find the source of the sound. Suddenly James froze, eyes wide with horror. Standing at the edge of the clearing were four Shawnee braves wearing loincloths and war paint.

"Henry!" James bellowed, reaching for his rifle. Then a sound like a whole nest of wasps buzzed in his ears. Pain slammed him flat on his back. He gaped at the arrow in his thigh. God, it hurt awful! The Shawnees, brandishing their tomahawks, yelled and ripped through the camp. Out of the corner of his eye, James saw Henry sprawled beside him, two arrows in his hip. One of the Mendenhall boys screamed. He saw the other lying still, his face white and his eyes wide open. When James tried to sit up, one of the Indians turned and kicked him in the chest.

"Goddamn you!" he shouted. The Indian grinned and kicked him again. He couldn't see Crabtree or Drake. Maybe they had gotten away. The cattle were crashing in a panic through the brush.

"Oh, Jesus Lord, no!" the voice cried out.

James turned around and saw Charles, terror in his face, breaking for the woods. A big Indian stepped right in front of him and cleaved his head in two with a tomahawk. James choked and vomited.

"James, you all right?" Henry called weakly.

"I guess so. God, what are we goin' to do, Henry!"

A Shawnee squatted down beside him. The Indian was so close, James could see the fine coat of sweat on his bare skull, smell the rancid grease in his dark scalp lock, and see the wet sheen of war paint streaking his broad features. The Indian jerked up his knife and slashed it across James' chest again and again.

James screamed.

Chapter 23

Rebecca knew. She knew the moment the rider came plunging out of the trees, shouting for Daniel. She saw Daniel's face when the man told him, saw his features go slack, then twist in a terrible mask of pain. Her heart felt as if it had been touched by a cold hand. Then Daniel's eyes met hers, and she was running across the camp and moving blindly into his arms.

"Oh, God, Daniel—oh, dear God, don't tell me, please don't tell me!"

Daniel drew her to him and held her. "He's gone, Becky."

"No, no!"

"James is dead," he said woodenly. "He's dead and already in heaven, Becky. Our boy is gone."

Rebecca pulled her head back and looked at him. "I want to see him. I want to see him, Daniel."

"You can't Becky. Not the way he is."

"I will, Dan. I will see my son!" Tears scalded her cheeks and clouded her eyes.

"No." He pulled her gently away. Squire was running toward him. Others from the column followed. "I'll see to him now. I'll see to our boy. I promise you."

Becky began to protest, then saw his eyes shut coldly against the world. He wouldn't hear her now, wouldn't know what she was saying. He turned and left her, and she looked back to her gathered children, pale and frightened. God in heaven, what am I going to say? What am I going to tell them?

Daniel waited till they had herded the women and children down to the creek, set the pack horses in a circle around them, and posted guards. The killings were only a few hours old; the Shawnees might still be about. They might be part of a larger war party that planned to hit them later. He wanted to assemble the three detachments together to marshal their strength. Squire told him firmly that he would handle that himself, that Daniel wasn't to worry about it now.

Halfway back to Wallen's Ridge, Daniel met David Gass, a man from Russell's party, coming up to meet him. Gass stood his horse on the narrow path, blocking Boone's way.

"Dan'l," he said grimly, "how much did the runner tell you?"

"That they were killed, Dave, that's all."

Gass set his jaw and stood his ground. "I want you to know before you see him. He ain't just killed. I'm trying to say that there ain't much left of him. Someone had to tell you."

Somehow, Daniel had already known what was

waiting for him. He closed his eyes a moment. "I'm grateful to you, Dave."

Gass nodded, pulled his mount aside and followed Daniel down the path.

The warning had been meant to steel Daniel against what he would see, but nothing anyone could have said could have prepared him for the sight that awaited him. His whole life seemed to shatter and fall apart in an instant. His legs began to buckle, but he caught himself and forced himself to stand firm.

Jesus God, James, he thought, you look like you've never been alive. . . . Not ever. . . .

The pain had lasted a long time. There was no use putting that aside. The two boys had suffered horribly. The Indians had kept them alive, in pain, as long as they could. Their scalps were gone. All of their fingernails had been pulled out one at a time. There was nothing left of their faces. Every inch of their bodies had been cut and gouged and most of their blood had soaked into the soil.

Daniel's mind roiled: James cried out, screamed and begged to die. . . . He called for me to come and help him, I know that for certain. . . . I'm sorry, son. . . . God, I'm sorry I couldn't get here . . . !

When Daniel stood up from touching his son's cold face, he met Will Russell's eyes and went to him. The two men silently held each other for a long moment. They knew instinctively that if they spoke, or looked at each other for too long, the strength that kept them standing would leave them.

The men buried James and Henry together, wrapping them tight in a fine linen sheet Rebecca had sent with Daniel. They dug the grave deep, set the bodies in gently and placed the soil back tight. They offered to finish the rest without Boone and Russell, but the two men shook their heads and waited. Neither turned away until a high mound of stone was set atop the grave to keep out the wolves.

There were other bodies to bury, but Daniel didn't wait to watch. He heard part of the story from Gass, and the rest later. Dave told him that the Mendenhall boys, Drake, and Charles, the Negro slave, had been killed outright. Isaac Crabtree had been hit in the back with an arrow, but fled into the brush, finally staggering into Russell's camp with the news.

"We found this," said David, and showed him the war club the Shawnees had left at the massacre.

Daniel nodded. "It's a challenge—their idea of spittin' in your face an' darin' you to spit back."

"Yeah, I've seen 'em before."

"David, they'll likely be back. I'd be obliged if you'd help Squire get everyone together as quick as you can. Russell ain't up to it, an' I guess I ain't either, but it's gotta be done. We're naked as we can be, spread out like this."

"I'll do it, then." Gass looked at Boone and frowned. "Dan'l where you goin' now? Or do I already know?"

Daniel gazed past him into the trees. "Where'd you be goin' if you were in my shoes, Dave?"

Gass nodded and watched him disappear into the brush.

Boone followed the tracks down the creek, with the flank of Wallen's Ridge at his back. The livestock had trampled all over the place, obliterating the trail in spots, but he picked it up again quickly at the edge of the woods. There were four of them, running quickly to the west. After a few minutes he found where they had left their horses. He followed the tracks a short way to be certain, but he knew where they were going—across the valley to the Cumberlands. There were others waiting there, Daniel was certain of that. He hoped Gass and Squire were organizing defenses quickly. If the three detachments weren't forted up in one place by nightfall, the settlers wouldn't stand a chance.

Daniel stopped. Something lay in the path just before him. He walked over, stared at it and sank to his knees. The Indians had been riding fast and dropped some of their booty. There was a small sack of salt and jerky, and a rifle. Daniel picked up the weapon and ran his hand over the familiar stock. His arms shook uncontrollably, and his eyes clouded. For a long time he lay there in the forest, grasping the cold wood to his cheek, letting the pain and the tears rack his body.

Squire, Gass and the others had run themselves ragged, but by nightfall they had rounded up the frightened members of the party into a single defensible position. It hadn't been easy. In spite of their fears, many of the families were hell-bent on chasing through the woods after a lost pig or a milk cow. It was all the veteran woodsmen could do to convince them that a porker wasn't worth their scalps.

When Daniel returned to camp, he learned that Adam, the second slave, had escaped unharmed, hiding the whole time in the thick brush by the creek. He had lain there and watched in terror, witnessing the massacre from only a few yards away, wondering when the

Shawnees would sniff him out. When it was over, he had bolted for the woods and gotten lost. Nearly the whole day passed before some men from the Clinch brought him in.

When Daniel returned to camp, he immediately sought out his wife.

"Are the children all right?" Daniel asked her. "Lord, I reckon it was terrible hard on 'em, 'specially the young ones."

"No, not the young ones. It was bad for them, Daniel, but they don't truly understand what happened. It's Jemima and Susannah who took it worst. They're old enough to know. And Israel." Becky sobbed and leaned against him. "Oh, Lord, Daniel, they loved each other so. Poor Israel! He's just shrunk back and gotten smaller all day, like he was dryin' up inside."

"I know." Daniel held her close and looked past the fire at the dark shapes of his children under their blankets.

"I talked to Mary Russell some," said Becky. "She's doin' all right. Same as me, I guess." She looked up at Daniel, and the tears welled in her dark eyes. "She and Will's got other children like we do, and that's a blessin'. But there's never children to spare, Daniel. I've lost one, and now I feel like I've lost 'em all!" She buried her head in his shoulder and let her tears flow freely.

"It'll be better, someday," he assured her. "Better than this, Becky. I promise. It won't hurt as much." He said it because it was the thing to say, but he knew it wasn't so. With James gone, it would never be the same, not ever.

*   *   *

Just before midnight, Michael Stoner, the Pennsylvania Dutchman, edged up to him and shook him awake. Stoner held up a hand and motioned him away from Becky. "They are out there, Dan'l, the Shawnees. Gass and another man have seen them."

"How many, you think? Any way to tell?"

Stoner set his jaw. "There is no way to say, Boone. Enough, I imagine, ja?"

"Yeah, enough."

Daniel followed him quietly down to the edge of the encampment. Squire, Gass, Russell and the others were waiting. The place had been well chosen. The sheer rock cliff bowed out over their backs and sheltered the women and children. A rough cropping of waist-high stone made a natural wall in front, an obstacle to every approach to the camp.

"You seen 'em?" asked Daniel.

"I did," grunted Squire. "And they been practicin' owl talk 'bout the last ten minutes."

"They're trying to spook us," said Daniel. "Draw a little fire." He turned to Stoner. "Pass the word on down the line, Michael. We'll shoot in two volleys. Everybody keep their heads and let 'em come in close. If we don't start shootin', they'll have to make their play." Stoner nodded and melted into the shadows.

"Nothin' personal," Squire spoke softly, "but if there's any farmers up on the line, I'd like to get 'em off, Daniel, 'fore they start shootin' at trees, or somethin'."

"Good idea," put in Russell. "I'll send a man around. Tell 'em we need men back close with the women."

"They won't believe that."

"Don't give a damn if they don't," Russell shot back fiercely. "Dan's right. I want those devils to get in close!"

Lying quiet against the cold stone boulders, Daniel listened to the sound of a hundred owls talking at once. The Indians were moving all over the place, trying to swell their number. If they really had that many braves, Daniel knew they wouldn't be playing games. They would be right here on top of them.

It happened quickly.

War cries split the night, and the Shawnees were upon them. Daniel smiled grimly and raised his son's rifle to his shoulder.

"Fine. Just fine, you savages," he murmured under his breath.

They had waited for the Indians and forced them in close. Now they were no more than fifteen yards away.

There were more than he had guessed, maybe forty or fifty. But they made good targets against the dark, and the men beading down on their chests remained cool-headed, firing and reloading quickly, methodically while the second volley thundered. It was over before it started. The surviving Indians melted away into the woods.

Stoner jammed a rod down his barrel with a satisfied grin. "That was fast and easy, Dan'l. They will not come back, I think."

"They won't. They'll keep us up all night, likely, but they won't come back."

At full light, Daniel and five others snaked down the hill to check the night's damage. There were no dead Indians, but there was plenty of blood on the ground.

"We got some," Will Russell said darkly. "They dragged 'em off in the night."

"Yeah, that's what they did," said Daniel. Leaving Russell and Stoner to study the high ground, he wandered off alone past the creek. There were plenty of clear tracks in the wet soil. Going down on his hands and knees, he studied the ground a long time. There were so many prints there, one on top of the other, it was hard to tell them apart. But he was only looking for one, one he would know for certain if he found it. If you followed a man's moccasins long enough, they became as familiar as his face.

Finally, he stood and crossed the creek again, circling out wide until he was sure there were no more tracks. If Flint had been there, he had kept to his horse. There was no reason to think he was involved with the massacre, but the idea pestered at the edge of his mind. The Indians had found and killed someone he cared for—again. It was hard to think about that without thinking about Black Knife.

When he returned to camp, he discovered many of the settlers preparing to go back home.

He stood beside Becky at the head of the valley, watching the party gather for the return trip. The clouds had parted early, letting the sun break through to sweep the mist off the mountains. In the sudden light, the trees burst red and yellow, as though the whole forest was aflame. Squire came up and stood with Daniel and Becky.

"You can't blame 'em," Squire said. "They're

scared out of their wits, Daniel, every damn one of 'em."

"By God," Boone replied angrily, "they haven't lost nothin' but a couple of pigs. I lost a son!"

"They figure they'll lose the same, Dan," Becky whispered sadly, "you know that. And you can't say they're wrong. The Shawnees haven't gone back home. They'll be waiting somewhere past the gap."

"I know they will. They're always goin' to be there. It ain't nothin' new."

Squire held his gaze a long moment. "You're not the same as those folks, Daniel."

No, Daniel thought bitterly, I know I'm not. I'm not the same as anyone. But I wish sometimes that I was.

"Dave Gass says we can stay in his cabin at Castle's Woods," he told Becky. "I guess I'll have to take him up on it. We got nowhere else to go."

"I guess, Daniel."

He took her shoulders and turned her around to face him. "Becky, if you hate me for what I've done, I won't blame you for it. I sold everything we had for this. Took your home from you and everything in it. And by God, I killed your son, Becky. Just as sure as if I'd done it myself!"

She saw the lost, terrible look in his eyes and held him to her. Squire looked away. The column began moving down the valley, the outriders shouting for everyone to take their places and not to wander off. Still, she held him there against her, afraid to let him go. Oh, Lord, Daniel, she thought desperately, I'll try to take the hurt away. I'll try as hard as I can.

Chapter 24

Sometimes a hunter would see him, a lone figure against the bleak winter sky, or a trapper on the Holston or the Clinch might catch a glimpse of a tall figure in black deerskin, whose hair was clubbed and plaited at the neck. He spent the long, cold days that way, staying to himself and putting meat on the table for his family. Dave Gass or Will Russell would come to see him when he was home, but their visits were always short. If Daniel had been a solitary man before, he was even more so now.

He tried hard to let the wounds heal, to make the hurt go away. The children needed him, and so did Becky. He tried to reach out to them, but there was nothing in him to give anymore. James' death had left an emptiness that Daniel could find nothing to fill.

Christmas was an agony, more than he could bear. He left the house on Christmas Day and roamed alone in the hills for a month before coming back home. When he finally returned, Becky said nothing. It hurt her that he would take neither her love nor her comforting. In time he would, she knew, but there was little she could do to hurry that time along.

Two nights after he came back, Daniel went to her and brought her into his arms. Rebecca nearly cried out with joy. It had been so long. Lord, how she needed him. It had been so very, very long!

Then, Daniel abruptly pulled away from her and stared deeply into her eyes. Becky could only look back, puzzled.

"There's somethin' I got to say," he said quietly. "Somethin' I got to tell you, Becky."

"Then do it, Daniel."

He shook his head and turned away. "Maybe I can, an' maybe I can't. It's got to be done, though."

She listened quietly. He told her about the Indian girl, about how he had found her and what had happened between them. It took him a long time to tell it all. When he finished, she held his face affectionately between her hands. "Daniel, you didn't have to tell me. It doesn't hurt the love between us any. You know that, don't you? Oh, God, Daniel, what a terrible agony for you. And that poor girl. I'm so sorry!"

"Becky . . ." He stared at her in wonder. "Can you really understand? Can you, truly?"

"Of course, Daniel. Of course I can. That's all of it now 'cause, it's over."

"No!" He jerked away from her and hid his face in his hands. "It's not, Becky. Oh, God, I wish it was!"

She came to him quickly, tried to pull his hands away and stop the racking sobs.

"Don't you see?" he said. "I don't know, Becky. I don't know if it was Flint who got my boy. If it was, it was me who brought him to kill our James!"

It was a bad night, one of the worst she could remember, but when it was over, she knew something had changed in him, some of the darkness had drained out of him. It would take a while, but he would heal. And when he did, she could heal, too.

Spring brought plenty of news to Castle's Woods, but none of it was good. The massacre at Wallen's Ridge had only been the beginning, a pebble dropped in a bloody pond, and the ripples were spreading wider every day. Isaac Crabtree, who had taken an arrow the night James died, had recently walked up and shot a Cherokee at a horse race on the Watauga. The Indian had done nothing to deserve it, but he was an Indian, and that was enough for Crabtree. The Royal Governor set up a reward for anyone who would bring in the murderer, but no one was interested. Folks said it would be easier to find a regiment of men who would hide him than to scare up a dozen who would turn him in.

Then Daniel Greathouse, a thief and a ne'er-do-well, committed an act that set the frontier aflame. One night Greathouse murdered the family of a Mingo chief named Tahgahjute, a long-time friend of the settlers whom they had nicknamed Logan. Greathouse found the Indians camped on Yellow Creek, not far from the Ohio River, got them drunk on whiskey, and slaughtered them all. Among the victims were Logan's brother and sister-in-law, heavy with child. Not content with the killings, Greathouse had then scalped the male corpses and taken the unborn child from its mother's womb. The warriors who came on the scene after found the child impaled on a stake.

"It sure isn't all on the Indians' side now," Russell remarked soberly to Boone. "Now they got an axe to grind, and matters are going to get hot."

Russell was right, Daniel knew. Only the week before, Michael Stoner had ridden back from North Carolina with the story that two Shawnee chiefs had been caught and executed for taking part in the business at Wallen's Ridge. But so were a couple of Cherokees, who were made to pay whether they had had anything to do with the incident or not.

The storm spread quickly. Word reached Daniel that the Shawnees and Mingos in Kentucky had put aside their differences and gone on the warpath against the whites together. Settlements all along the Ohio were in flames. The river itself had been effectively closed to boat traffic by Shawnee war parties.

Then James Harrod had taken thirty-one men deep into Kentucky, staking out settlements on Indian lands. Surveyors were streaming in from the north in spite of the Shawnees, and what the Indians had feared most was coming to pass. Watching from the hills, they saw white men laying out plots of land right in the middle of their hunting grounds. Daniel knew what they were thinking: if we don't stop the white man now, we'll never stop him at all.

In spite of the danger, Daniel rode out to visit his son's grave in May. Wolves had been there and scraped some of the stones away, but Daniel piled them high again. In the night, he heard Indians about and led his horse quietly back down the valley. He didn't tell Becky where he had been, but Becky knew. When she saw the look on his face, she didn't have to ask.

A month after Daniel's trip to Wallen's Ridge, Will Russell stopped by. Accepting a cup of whiskey, he drank it in one swallow, then got to his subject. "Governor Dunmore's real itchy about this Indian business, Dan'l. It's gettin' out of hand, and more so every day. Now, he's afraid Chief Logan's goin' to start his own little war."

Daniel nodded. "Don't hardly blame him. I reckon I would, too."

"There's truth in that, but it isn't going to solve anythin'."

"Well, it had to happen." Daniel refilled Russell's cup to the brim. "We been steppin' on their toes and them on ours from the beginning. God knows you and me have got enough bad juice in our craws to hate Indians, but I can't bring myself to go killin' 'em. Hell, I know 'em too well."

Russell let out a breath. "You're right, friend. You're right as you can be." He set down his cup and looked squarely at Daniel. "The governor asked Colonel Preston up in Fincastle to get me to help settle the matter. I'm comin' to you to see if you'll lend me a hand." Daniel waited, and Russell went on. "Dunmore's worried about those surveyors runnin' loose in Kentucky. He thinks they're likely to get themselves killed if nobody warns 'em what's comin'."

Daniel made a face. "Hell, Will, it was Preston sent 'em in there in the first place."

"I know that."

"Now he wants someone to bail 'em out."

"For more than one reason," Will explained firmly, "an' this is Dunmore's thinkin', not Preston's. The governor'd like to see 'em come out alive not just for their own sakes, but also for the sake of the frontier and what's likely to happen to it. The more people get killed—Indian or white—the worse this thing's goin' to get."

"Will, it's goin' to happen anyway. It's gone too far to stop."

"Maybe." Russell held up a hand. "Maybe not."

Daniel leaned back and looked into his cup. "What you want me to do, Will?"

"Go in and bring 'em out if you can. You and Mike Stoner."

"Good man."

"That he is. And you're another one."

"Where exactly are these surveyors s'posed to be?"

Russell cleared his throat. "That's, ah—kind of the problem, Dan'l. They were makin' surveys up at Ohio Falls, down in the valley and on the Licking, too. And along the Cumberland, if they could."

Daniel stared. "Goddamn, Will—that about takes in all Kentucky!"

Russell gave him a painful grin. "Sort of does, doesn't it? Why d'you think I came to you?"

Chapter 25

Daniel and Mike Stoner left Castle's Woods on June 27 and crossed the Cumberlands into Kentucky. The land lay full and lush before them. The trees were bursting with green, and Daniel swore he could feel the grass growing under his feet. Somehow, though, this familiar beauty brought him little pleasure, a lack of feeling that troubled him greatly. For the first time, he felt no joy in this land. It wasn't his alone anymore. Men were crawling over it like fleas on a dog, men who didn't know it or understand it and who had no business being there—men like the surveyors he and Stoner were after—damn fools who had hiked into Kentucky with no idea what they would find there. He couldn't help hating them for even setting foot there.

"What we should have done was to bring Lord Dunmore with us," Stoner said dryly. "We could use a good coon dog, ja?"

Daniel snorted in disgust. "Yeah, that'd be a help. Dunmore's like all the rest of them politicians that tell other folks where to go. Likely he figures Kentucky's laid out like London."

Neither of the two discussed the enormity of their task. They were both experienced woodsmen and there was no need to belabor the point. It was dangerous for a white man to set foot in Kentucky right now, no matter how well he knew the land. The Shawnees and Mingos were madder than stirred-up cottonmouths. Daniel and Stoner saw sign behind every bush, even before they crossed the mountains. The days when a man could wander safely about the country, if he watched his step, were over. Now, Indian war parties looking for blood sniffed out every river and stream.

Daniel headed away from the mountains for the north fork of the Kentucky River. If the surveyors had come down the Licking, he and Stoner would likely pick up their trail somewhere north or west—unless they had gone farther east, he thought darkly.

From the start, the two men made small fires or no fires at all. They were well aware of the Indians almost always nearby. At night, Daniel and Stoner ate their jerky and corn sitting back to back in case a war party came down upon them.

As they traveled past the Kentucky up to the Licking River, Boone grew more cautious than ever. The Ohio wasn't far off, and the Shawnees were everywhere hereabout. One morning in early July, Stoner crept back into camp, soaked to the skin and stinking to high heaven. Daniel started to comment, but Stoner waved him off.

"Don't say nothing, Daniel. I can smell it worse than you can."

Daniel held back a grin. "What the hell you been doin', son?"

"Crawling on my belly in a swamp," Stoner grumbled. "For three miles, maybe four. There were a hundred Shawnees in the valley by the river. I have to get past them and this is the only way." He gave Daniel a grave look. "They have a white man, Daniel, maybe one of the fellows we look for."

Daniel frowned. "Is he alive?"

"Ja, alive."

"Damn."

Stoner got out of his clothes and began to disassemble his rifle to clean it.

"Reckon I'll go take a look," Daniel said, and started gathering up his powder horn and pouch.

Stoner guessed his thoughts. "Flint is not with them, Daniel. I looked for him."

"Uh-huh. I'll just mosey up, anyhow. Give you a chance to get yourself smellin' better."

"You find a better way to get up there than the swamp, I will be glad to hear it."

"I will, for certain. Rather run a foot race with the Indians than stink like that."

He knew Stoner was right, the swamp was safer, but Daniel risked the more open path along the limestone ridges over the river. The Shawnees were camped in the valley under a high bluff where the water snaked into the trees. Just as Stoner had reported, there were close to a hundred of them, all mounted, armed and streaked with paint. A full-scale war party on the move. Daniel guessed they were ranging due south, crisscrossing the rivers to see what they could find—which was exactly what he and Stoner were doing.

A damn fool business, he told himself. The Indians will find the surveyors before we do, and we'll be lucky to get back with our scalps.

There was little left of the man they had captured. He was either dead or close to it. They had skinned him alive and rubbed dirt and salt all over him, then tied him to a spit over slow-burning coals. With any luck, he was too far gone to know what was happening to him. Daniel knew he didn't dare risk burying the poor bastard after the Shawnees left. If they came back and saw that other white men had been there, they would turn the country upside down until they found them.

After a few minutes, Daniel recognized an old friend among the Shawnees. There was no mistaking the broad, stocky figure of Captain Will, sitting straight and stern on his spotted pony. The red jacket was a little dirtier now, but it was Will for certain. With a last look at the charred body over the fire, Boone bellied down the ridge and made his way back to Stoner.

Daniel decided they were advancing too far north. Another two days up the Licking would take them right to the Ohio. If any surveyors had come this far, they were already dead. It was time to turn southwest, toward the Kentucky River.

That afternoon, the pair rode over a low hill and came upon an enormous salt lick just north of the river. A small herd of buffalo was roaming about, rooting in the ground for salt. It was an old lick, a place in which the animals, after centuries of use, had worn a maze of deep trenches that riddled the earth for nearly a mile.

Stoner, when he saw the trenches, grinned and dismounted.

"What the hell you fixin' to do?" asked Daniel.

"You watch. You watch and see, Dan'l."

"Yeah, I'll do that."

Stoner scurried down into the nearest gully and followed the maze for twenty or thirty yards. In a minute, Daniel understood what the man was doing. Stoner crept up quietly on a large bull buffalo that was pushing its nose into the trench dust, waved his cap around a sharp corner that hid him from the animal and shouted. The buffalo jerked up, started to bolt, then changed its mind. Instead of running like it was supposed to, it turned and drove its head through the wall of dirt and came after Stoner. Stoner raced through the trenches, a foot ahead of shaggy's horns.

"Goddamn, Dan'l!" he shouted. "Shoot him! Shoot him!"

Daniel threw back his head and laughed. In a moment, Stoner leaped out of the gully, got to his feet, and, while brushing dirt off his clothes, cursed like a madman.

"You didn't shoot!"

"Figured you'd make it."

Stoner glared. "Ja? You figured better than I did."

"Well, at least you don't smell like a swamp anymore. Now you smell like buffalo dung. I reckon that's a damn sight better."

A day and a half after Stoner's adventure at the

lick, the pair passed Otter Creek and the stand of sycamores that spread out into the valley. The sight made Daniel's stomach knot. Here was the place he had set out for nine months before, with his own family and the other settlers behind him. By now, he and James and Israel would have built a fine cabin here. They would have survived through a winter, done some hunting and planted crops over past the meadow. Daniel set his jaw and turned away. Stoner, saying nothing, followed him.

The next day at noon, they crossed the Kentucky River and found James Harrod's settlement. Daniel was amazed to see how much they had done in so little time. A few crude cabins were already built and others nearly finished. Tracts of land had been plotted, parceled out, and fenced in all up and down the river.

"Real nice," he told Stoner. "I wonder where the hell everybody went?"

A note nailed to a tree at the river's landing gave the answer. "Company attacked by Shawnees. Two men killed. We are going down the river." Hastily scribbled in another hand at the bottom was this: "We have followed." It was signed in a name Boone couldn't read.

"Well, what you make of that?" asked Stoner. "Harrod's people have gone, but who is this other?"

"Some of the folks we're lookin' for, maybe."

"Maybe. I don't know who else it could be."

Daniel squinted his deep blue eyes and looked out over the river. "What I figure is, some of the surveyors was workin' out of Harrod's place. When they came back and saw what happened, they took off. Guess we better go see."

That night Boone and Stoner camped well away from the settlement, then rode on to the falls of the Ohio the next morning, but they found no signs that anyone had passed that way. The pair turned back and began the slow and dangerous task of ranging up and down the great river, searching out the dozens of streams that fed its flow, and the hundreds of smaller creeks that wormed through the surrounding wooded hollows. It was a nerve-racking business, even for experienced woodsmen. Three times Daniel and Stoner saw Shawnee and Mingo war parties searching the same streams.

Once the two of them followed a fresh Indian trail for miles before it suddenly dawned on them that the Indians were also following *their* sign—the tracks they had made themselves less than an hour before. Both parties were going around in a circle, after each other. The red hairs on Daniel's nape bristled at the thought.

"This here's not much fun anymore," he told Stoner. "I stopped feelin' lucky 'bout ten minutes ago."

Stoner's mouth was grimly set. "Dan'l, I think you are wrong by maybe nine minutes. Let's get the hell out of here *now*."

They stopped worrying about how close the Shawnees were. They were damn sure close enough. Crashing through the trees, they rode away from the river as fast as they could.

Three days later, circling back to the river from the north, Boone and Stoner splashed through a wide creek and found seven of the lost surveyors huddled along a limestone bluff. Daniel knew he and Stoner had been damn lucky these men had been too terrified to raise their rifles. If one of the party had kept his courage, they would both be dead.

When the party saw two whites on horseback, they threw up their hats and ran shouting glory to salvation across the stream. Stoner ordered them to keep their voices down, or he would personally scalp every last one of them.

Daniel glanced distastefully at the pale, haunted faces. He had to feel sorry for them, no matter how much he disliked them. They had been through plenty of trials and were frightened to death. "How the hell did you get down here?" he asked a man named Douglas. "When did you leave Harrod's place?"

The man looked at him blankly. "Why, we haven't been near Harrod's. We was way east of there."

Daniel looked at Stoner. "Damnation, we still got another bunch out there somewhere."

The men explained how they had been going about their business, making their way from one site to another in canoes on the Kentucky River to save traveling overland. The Indians had fired on them from the bank, killing one of their number and wounding their leader, Hancock Taylor.

"He died," said Douglas, " 'bout two days later. We left the damn boats and took off into the forest." He looked lamely at Boone. "I don't guess that was a good idea."

"It wasn't," Boone said flatly. "Not any time 'cept this one. If you'd kept to the river, they'd have had you sure."

Daniel considered giving up on the others, and

Stoner agreed. They had best take what they had and make tracks for the Cumberland. As it was, they were long overdue for getting their hair lifted.

"We been lucky," said Stoner, "just damn lucky."

Chapter 26

In the months Boone and Stoner had been gone, war had come to Castle's Woods and the whole Clinch Valley. Chief Logan had not forgiven Daniel Greathouse's atrocities. War parties ranged up and down the river, taking an eye for an eye and then some. Rumor had it that Logan gave special honors to warriors who brought in white women swollen with child.

"Goddamn it," Will Russell raged, "you know good and well Tahgahjute likely never said any such thing! Not that it makes any difference if he did. The settlers believe it, and that's what counts."

Daniel followed Russell's gaze past the porch of his cabin. Two more families were gathered before the stockade, ready to head back East. Teams and wagons were piled high with household goods and howling children. A milk cow and a train of pack horses were strung along behind.

"That's the fifth family in two days," scowled Russell. He shook his head at Boone. "They got about a fifty-fifty chance of making it on their own. There's nobody to watch out for 'em 'cept their own menfolk. We can't spare anyone from here. They're leavin' the only protection they got, but they won't believe it from me."

"Can't make folks do what they don't want to," replied Daniel.

Frustrated and angry, Russell sat down and looked at his friend. "You think we can hold out here, Dan'l?"

"Sure we can. We can fort up like we done before. We'll see it through if enough people stay to man the walls."

"They'll stay." Russell gave him an easy grin. "A lot of people here believe in you, Dan'l."

Daniel frowned. "What have I got to do with it?"

"Major Campbell's ordered me to present you with a lieutenant's commission in the Virginia Militia. He wants you to command the defense at Moore's Fort. It's where Logan's hittin' hardest."

Daniel looked thoughtful. "I'll take up a gun, Will, you know that, but I don't know about runnin' the damn fort."

"I do," Russell said firmly. He leaned across the table on his hands. "Look, I'm not goin' to make a big speech, but I want you to hear this. For now, politics doesn't hit us as hard out here as it does back East, but it's soon goin' to. It's goin' on right now in Boston and New York and a dozen other places. There's a powder keg burnin' back there, and it's goin' to go off one of these days. The damn King's pushed folks too far with laws and taxes, and I don't have to tell you what's likely to happen."

"No, I reckon you don't."

"All right." Russell nodded and let out a breath. "When it happens, we're goin' to be left on our own out here. Maybe we'll have British troops *and* Indians against us outside these walls."

Daniel raised a brow.

"You think it couldn't happen?" Will asked fiercely.

"I know there's goin' to be trouble."

"You're damn right there is. This year or the next. Daniel, our little piece of militia ain't goin' to make much difference if it comes to an all-out fight with the British, but maybe it's better than nothin'. We're goin' to be all alone out here one day soon, with no help from the colonies back East."

"Hell," said Daniel. "We've always been alone out here."

Daniel knew Russell was right. An organized militia might serve the frontier well in times of trouble, but frontiersmen didn't take much to soldiering. They were independent cusses, and used to taking care of themselves. They didn't put much stock in carrying out orders, even if the orders came from Lieutenant Dan Boone.

Daniel knew he was in for a difficult time even before he started. The hastily formed Moore's Fort detachment was at best a ragtag collection of farmers, hunters and trappers. At worst, it was an unruly mob, more interested in fighting each other than the Indians.

Twenty families, including his own, moved into the fort with all their belongings. Daniel set up a guard

roster and led regular patrols of the surrounding countryside, a practice, he learned, no one else had thought
of. The other Forts stayed shut tight, with families and
militia packed inside. Two weeks after he received his
commission as lieutenant, the people at Blackmore's
Fort and Russell's Fort demanded Daniel be promoted
to Captain and put in charge of all three forts. When
Dave Gass told him, Daniel threw back his head and
laughed.

"Hell, Dave, it don't take much to rise up in this
man's army, does it? If one of Becky's pigs bit Logan
in the ass, they'd make him a goddamn colonel!"

"Maybe not," mused Gass. "Maybe only a major."

"You are right," chimed in Stoner. "I say Becky's
pig is no better soldier than Preston, and he is a
colonel, too. The pig will have to rise on his own mer-
its, ja? This is fair, I think."

Daniel now had fifty-six militiamen under his
command, hardly enough for three forts spread miles
apart up and down the valley. And, in spite of everything Daniel could do, they would never be more than
Sunday soldiers.

"I don't think I'm cut out to be a military man,"
Daniel told Becky. He sat back on the bed and ran a
hand over his brow. "Lord God, I spent an hour tellin'
some fool why you're supposed to stay awake when
you're standin' guard." He stared wide-eyed at Becky.
"Now wouldn't you think a feller'd know why?"

Rebecca sat down beside him. "Now they can't all
be Captain Boones," she teased. "Don't expect that."

Daniel muttered to himself and pulled her to him.
"We ain't had much time together, have we? I'm sorry,

244

Becky. I'm not even sure where I am from one day to the next."

"Oh, I don't know, 'bout that." Becky stuck her tongue in her cheek and looked at the ceiling. "You must have been home some since you got back. I think there's another Boone gettin' ready to make an appearance."

"Huh?" Daniel sat up straight. "Becky—oh, Becky are you sure? A new little 'un?" He took her in his arms and joyously held her.

Rebecca laughed against his shoulder and pushed him back to see his eyes. "I don't know why you're all that surprised, Dan Boone. All you got to do is look at me and . . ." she snapped her fingers in his face, "I'm with child just like that."

"It takes more'n just lookin', Becky."

"Oh? What you think's causin' it?"

"You got a minute?"

"I better have more than that."

Daniel kissed her pale, slender throat. "You ever get less than you wanted, lady?"

"My, my, you sure are gettin' cocky since your promotion, Captain Boone." She pulled her dress off and faced him. "I don't have to salute, or anythin', do I?" She looked down and her dark eyes flashed. "My Lord, Dan, looks like you're the one doin' the salutin'!"

In late September, Will Russell rode into Moore's Fort with Major Campbell and Colonel Preston. Daniel thought Campbell a dependable man, but he had little use for Preston, whom everyone knew had sent the surveyors into Kentucky at Lord Dunmore's direction. In public, Dunmore had always decried promotors and speculators who lusted after Indian lands. In private, however, he had his own finger in the pie and was determined to grab all he could. Some people in Virginia even believed Dunmore was doing his best to encourage war with the Indians.

When Campbell and Preston mounted up to leave, Russell hung back a moment. "They were impressed, Dan. You're doin' a first-rate job here, and they know it." Will looked over his shoulder. "And thanks for the other thing, too."

"What's that?"

"Not hittin' Preston in the teeth. I appreciate it."

"Just don't count on me again, Russ, if you bring that son of a bitch back here," Daniel said darkly.

Russell grinned. "I never press my luck with a friend."

"Give my best to Mary."

"I'll do that." Russell moved up close, and spoke under his breath. "Hold out a little longer," he said quietly. "Looks like somethin's brewin' up on the Kanawha. I got a feelin' all this fuss ain't gonna last much longer."

Daniel wanted to know more, but Russell would say nothing.

If the fighting was easing up some, Daniel decided the Shawnees and Mingos hadn't heard about it. Dave Gass found him after supper and asked him to step outside. Daniel followed his friend to the far wall of the fort, where Mike Stoner was waiting in the shadows.

"I thought you should know," reported Stoner. "I took scouts down to Russell's Fort. On the way back, we met with a war party. No one is hurt bad—a boy got hit in the leg is all." Stoner paused and looked down at his feet. "I think I saw Flint, Dan'l. There were six, maybe seven Shawnees and this tall man in buckskin who is not all Indian. He has a patch over his eye."

Daniel clenched his jaw.

"I didn't know if we ought to tell you about him or not," Gass muttered. "Still—well, you got a right, I guess."

"Yeah, I guess I do," Daniel said quietly. "My thanks to you both." Nodding, he turned and walked back to his cabin.

"I ain't sure we done right," said Gass. "He wouldn't have ever known a thing, Mike."

Stoner leaned on his rifle. "He would know, David. No one has to tell him about Henry Flint, I think."

Gass shivered. "You're gettin' spooky now, Dutchman. All I say is, if ol' Dan'l leaves this fort, one of us is damn sure goin' with him."

"Fine. You don't want to miss him, you better sit right here by the gate, ja?"

Rebecca found the length of thread she was after and started back for her cabin. Instead of heading straight across the yard, she turned off abruptly and walked toward the gate. Pausing a moment, she remembered the children were by themselves. Good Lord, she told herself, they can sure do without you a minute, Rebecca Boone. Isn't going to hurt you or them to have a moment to yourself. The warm October sun felt good on her shoulders, a welcome relief after the damp confines of the cabin.

It'd sure be good to breathe your own air again, she thought. The war wasn't a month old, and it seemed like they had been shut up forever. There were twenty families crammed in under the walls, and there just wasn't enough space to go around. She wondered if the cabin at Castle's Woods had been burnt to the ground like so many others had. She shook the thought away. Like Daniel said, you could always fell another tree, and build another.

Rebecca stopped and stared past the gate outside. Why, damn you all! she thought furiously. The men were just lolling about on the grass, rifles cast carelessly aside. Daniel's out of sight one minute and the whole place falls apart. If the Shawnees caught them like that. . . . Coarse laughter caught her attention, and she walked a step further. Lord! They were swimming in the creek, splashing about like they hadn't a care in the world!

Appalled, Becky turned stiffly and walked back to the compound. There, she gathered some of the other women together.

"Rebecca, you sure this is all right?" Marcy Williams said nervously. She was a slight, frizzy-haired woman who reminded Becky of a squirrel.

"Just do it," Mrs. Waller said grimly. "Becky's right, Marcy. Those men are shameful, just shameful."

"They ain't goin' to like it," said Marcy.

"Don't have to like it," Rebecca snapped. "Now, we got 'em done? Fine."

Becky inspected the rifles and handed one to each woman. The weapons were loaded with light charges, just like the Shawnees used. With a few whoops and hollers thrown in, the women ought to sound like right respectable Indians.

Becky led her troopers to the far wall of the fort. "All right. Ready? Fire!" The weapons discharged in a ragged volley. The women cupped their hands and tried hard to sound like Indians.

"All right, that's enough. Let's go!" Following Rebecca's command, the women ran from the far wall to the front of the fort and quickly slammed the gate closed. Howls erupted from the men outside. Peering through chinks in the wall, the women saw the surprised militiamen running in circles, yelling at each other for help. A few remembered to pick up their rifles, but most let them lie and beat frantically on the gate. Some, Becky noted with pleasure, dove in the creek fully clothed and started paddling for the other shore.

When the gates were opened, nearly everyone in the fort lined up to laugh at the ashen-faced men. A big, bearish fellow, dripping wet, stalked in and scowled at Rebecca.

"By God," he said, shaking a fist in her direction, "you ought to be whipped for a trick like that, woman!"

"By God," Rebecca replied evenly, raising her rifle to her shoulder, "you ought to try it."

Chapter 27

Near the second week of October, a rider burst through the gate of Moore's Fort bearing news that set the haggard settlers cheering. A few days before, on the tenth of the month, General Andrew Lewis had soundly whipped Chief Cornstalk at Point Pleasant on the Kanawha River. The war was over.

The rider who brought the news had witnessed the battle and was eager to tell his story. Cornstalk had amassed more Shawnees than a man could count, and Lewis had met him with more than a thousand colonial troopers. "The Injuns came at us in the mornin'," recounted the rider. "We fought 'em with rifles and bayonets the whole day long and into the afternoon 'fore they run off. I don't know how many was killed. We lost plenty of good boys and so did the redskins. Cornstalk wanted to keep on fightin', using women and kids to go at it till every Injun was dead, only his men

251

wouldn't have it. They forced ol' Cornstalk hisself to come and make peace."

Daniel studied the man carefully. "Peace is a big word, friend. Is that really what we got here, or do we just quit fightin' awhile?" Some of the men who were crowded around nodded at the question.

"Oh, they're finished for certain," the man answered. "They got to give back everythin' they took—horses, guns, prisoners, everythin'." The man grinned. "An' best of all, they ain't even allowed to set foot south of the Ohio River."

The crowd cheered and pounded the man on the back until Daniel raised a hand to quiet them. "Kentucky's their huntin' grounds," he said evenly. "Does Lewis believe they're gonna quit eatin'?"

The man glared, deeply offended. "Well, hell, they'll have to hunt somewhere else, won't they? I know what I'm talkin' about. I was there!" And everyone was anxious to hear more. But as the messenger plowed back into his story, Daniel stalked away.

"If that ain't the biggest pile of buffalo chips I ever heard," he later told Stoner and Gass, "you show me one bigger."

Gass agreed. "They'll ease up for awhile, but that don't mean nothin'."

"I didn't hear anythin' about Logan at that peace treaty," added Daniel. "You can bet he wasn't there and that he don't give a damn about it."

"People think what they want to think," shrugged Stoner. The big Dutchman hitched up his trousers and grinned. "Maybe we should go out and kiss a few Shawnee brothers, ja?"

"You go out and find Logan," Daniel said grimly. "He'll show you somethin' to kiss all right."

Everyone in the fort wanted to make the tenth of October, the day Lewis had beaten the Indians a regular holiday in the Clinch. Daniel figured he would remember it all right, but not for the same reason. It was a year to the day since James had been tortured and killed on Wallen's Ridge. Daniel spent his fortieth birthday in the cramped cabin at Moore's Fort. Rebecca managed to scrape up berries and flour enough to bake a pie. On the twentieth of November, he was discharged from the militia with a note of thanks from Colonel Preston. He cursed at the note and threw it in the fire.

Everyone was eager to get out of the fort and to go back home, but Daniel couldn't see much reason to celebrate. Nearly all the houses on the Clinch, including his own, had been cleaned out and burned. Winter was coming on, there were no crops or stores of food, and it was a bad time to begin building cabins.

But there was nothing else to do. He led his family back to Castle's Woods and began to construct a new roof over their heads. Boone, Russell, Gass and some of the others worked out a schedule of hunting and building so that no man would have to do the same task all the time.

At least for the time being, it was safe to travel between the Clinch and North Carolina and Virginia again. Before the month was out, teams and wagons began arriving from the East with sorely needed goods. Frontier wives broke out in tears at the sight of sugar and flour and a few sacks of potatoes. Maybe it would be a Christmas to celebrate after all.

But the approaching holiday season only added to Daniel's dark mood, though he tried hard to mask his feelings. Becky and the children had been through enough hardship. They didn't need to see his sour face now.

What was ahead for him? he wondered. He was poorer than ever, with little hope of ever seeing better days. There were still suits against him in Salisbury—the papers were probably growing beards by now. How was he ever going to begin paying them off?

More than anything else, he was angry at the senseless war he had just fought, and the suffering it had caused them all. And why? So that Lord Dunmore could grab Kentucky? Is that why he had played soldier on the Clinch, so that one of the King's fancy boot-lickers could put a little more gold in his own pocket?

Goddamn, Daniel raged, I didn't fight so you could get there first, you British idiot!

His grim thoughts plagued him more and more every day. Four days before Christmas, two more wagons arrived from the East. Driving one team was a young wagoner who worked for Dick Henderson. He had for Daniel and his family a large wooden box in which were fine gun tools and bullet molding equipment, French lace and bolts of cloth finer than Becky had ever seen, and candy and sweetmeats for the children. The wagoner also carried a sealed letter, to be delivered into Daniel's hands only. Daniel read it quickly, gave a yell and shouted for Becky. The letter was from Henderson. It read:

My dearest friend Daniel Boone,

    In greatest confidence I inform you that I am now prepared to purchase a considerable amount of land in Kentucky, and open such properties to interested buyers. I eagerly await your presence here in Salisbury regarding this venture.

    Daniel, I know you have waited long and patiently for my action in this matter of mutual interest. Wait no longer, my good friend. If all goes well, you will be a holder of great property in Kentucky by the spring.

Your obedient servant,
Richard Henderson

Becky forced a smile. "That's real fine, Dan."

"Fine?" Daniel affectionately grabbed her shoulder and laughed out loud. "Damnation, Becky, didn't you listen?"

"I listened, Daniel."

"Well?" He caught the cynical look in her eyes and clamped a hand to his brow. "All right. I reckon you're gonna start in on Dick Henderson again, is that it?"

"Start in?" Rebecca stiffened and glared at him. "No, Daniel. I'm not going to start in on Dick Henderson. Not Daniel Boone's good friend Dick Henderson."

"All right, Becky."

"All right, yourself!" she snapped. He tried to walk around her, but she stood her ground in his path. "Oh, God, Daniel, don't you see what he's doing? The same thing he's been doing for near ten years! And what's it ever come to? Nothin'. Nothin' at all!"

"Times are different now," muttered Daniel.

"Oh, well, of course."

"They are, Becky. He acts slow, I know it—God knows I do. But Kentucky's his dream, too."

"He's got money in the bank," she shouted. "He can afford to dream. You can't, Daniel. You've got nothin'!"

She caught herself the minute she spoke and saw the hurt look in his eyes. She wished could bite off her tongue. "Oh, God, Daniel, I didn't mean that."

"Don't be apologizin'," he told her. "I reckon I know what I've got and haven't got. Nothin's real close to the truth."

"Daniel, please!"

He looked at her a long moment, thinking of the shame she had tossed in his face and almost hating her for it. The hate wasn't real, and he knew it—there wasn't a way in the world he could feel like that about her—but the shame was there all the same. And the worst of it was that she was right. He would go chasing after Dick if there was a chance in hell of going to Kentucky. I'm not much better than a man who's a slave to whiskey, he thought miserably. One more swallow's 'bout all that makes it better.

Henderson studied the golden liquid in his glass and raised a toast to Daniel. "To us, my friend. To a new year, 1775, and to the success of our venture." Daniel, expecting whiskey, felt a different kind of heat slide smoothly down his throat. Henderson saw his puzzled look and smiled. "It's brandy, Daniel. French brandy. Near the last bottle, too, and likely the last we'll see for a while if things get worse."

"You think they will?"

"Oh, yes. Indeed I do." Henderson nodded gravely. "Have to. Too much bad blood between us and our British cousins. Some's bound to get spilled before it's over."

"Yep, that's what Will Russell thinks."

"Russell is right. I do not hold with revolution, mind you, but we're being pushed to the wall. King George and that idiot North will not see reason." Henderson shook his head and filled their glasses, then gave Boone a sly wink. "Still, though I don't ask for trouble, trouble will favor us if it comes, Daniel. Our Royal Governors are soon going to be too busy to concern themselves with Kentucky."

Daniel frowned. "Dunmore's going to pounce on you for sure."

"Yes, the old hypocrite's lost his chance in Kentucky, and he'll rail righteously against anyone else who tries to settle there, but the times are against him, friend. He has an angry nest of bees to tend to, now. Last fall, while you were holed up in that fort, a Continental Congress met openly back East. You heard, I imagine. Well they're not about to sit still and see their grievances ignored."

Daniel couldn't help but note the change in his friend. Henderson had never been especially resentful of the British, but he was clearly a rebel now. With his term of office behind him, he had thrown caution to the wind. Instead of hiding his plans to settle Kentucky, he flaunted them boldly. His Transylvania Company was already inviting settlers to new lands in the West. Henderson excitedly showed Daniel several drafts of handbills and newspaper ads, but so far, Daniel knew, Henderson didn't own one square inch of the lands he was now eager to sell.

That, said Henderson, was where Daniel came in. It was perfectly legal, he explained, to buy lands from "Indian Princes or Governments" through agreements or grants—without consent of the King.

"Of course," Henderson said blandly, "that law originally applied to the natives of India, but it doesn't say American Indians are excluded."

Daniel laughed out loud. "By God, Dick, I reckon a lawyer could sell hell to the Devil and make a profit!"

"I suspect it's been tried, Daniel. At any rate, the next step in this venture is up to you." He looked squarely at Boone. "You're about to renew your friendship with the Cherokees, Daniel. Because we want to buy twenty million acres of land from them." He stood and gripped his friend's hand warmly. "I told you you'd become a landowner, and so you will, Mr. Boone."

Daniel took Stoner along on his trips to the Cherokees, for company more than anything else. He had been to these villages a dozen times before and was expecting no trouble. The Indians there knew and welcomed him. Daniel decided Dick had been right—the friends he had made before were showing their value now.

It was hard to keep himself from looking for Blue Duck's family. He thought he saw her in every other face, now—in grown women who laughed a certain way, in ten-year-old girls with soft doe eyes and gangly frames who were just about to blossom.

I'm going to ask, he told himself. I just got to. But the time never seemed to be right.

In late February, Boone and Stoner camped in a dry cave on the bank of the Holston and roasted a haunch of venison. They had visited two villages in the past three days, inviting chiefs and elders to a meeting at Sycamore Shoals, and promising that fine goods would be on hand for Wide Mouth's Cherokee brothers.

"I ain't sure I like this business too well," said Daniel over the fire. "It ain't goin' down my craw real good."

Stoner wiped his mouth. "Visiting Indians, ja?"

"Naw," grumbled Daniel. "Buyin' Kentucky from 'em, an' tellin' em what a fine deal they're gettin' from Henderson." He looked up at Stoner. "You've seen Kentucky. How many blankets and beads you figure it's worth?"

Mike nodded slowly. He stood and ran his hands over his trousers and peered out at the dark. "Why not, Dan'l? They will get little from the bargain, it is true. But if they do not sell, Henderson or someone else will get it anyway. If not now, maybe sometime later."

"Yeah. I reckon that's what the Cherokees are thinkin', too."

Stoner sat back and chewed a blade of grass. "My friend," he said, "can I ask someting?"

"Ask away."

"Did you find him, Dan'l? I have wondered about it."

Daniel looked up. "Find who?"

"Flint. You looked for him. Gass and I know."

Daniel grinned slightly. "I know you do. I seen you doggin' my tracks." Daniel shook his head. "Yeah, I found him, Mike. He'd been just where you said. He left his tracks plain, knowin' you'd seen him an' certain you'd tell me about it. There'll be another time. We ain't through with each other."

Stoner said nothing, and Daniel busied himself cleaning his rifle. There was more to the story, but he couldn't tell it to Stoner or anyone. Flint had left him a little leather pouch hanging from a limb where he knew Daniel would find it. The sack was stiff with blood. So were the objects inside, but Daniel could tell what they were—the fingernails the Shawnees had pulled off his son and Henry Russell.

Chapter 28

It was the tenth day of March, a pause between winter and spring. The night had been cool enough for blankets, but the day promised a warm sun in a sky without clouds. Morning burned the frost off the grass, and the Watauga River shone like polished steel. Daniel stood on a low hill over the valley waiting for Stoner. Smoke from the Cherokee lodges formed a haze in the trees; women, children and Indian dogs wandered about, while the braves clustered in tight little groups.

As usual, a crowd was forming about the six cabins built along the shore. In a moment, Henderson's men would open the wide doors and let the Cherokees peek inside. The doors would stay open that way all day, and the Indians would stand around until nightfall, earnestly admiring the treasures.

Henderson knew exactly what he was doing, thought Daniel. He had waited till the Indians began to arrive in force at Sycamore Shoals before bringing in the goods. Arriving with great fanfare, six heavy wagons loaded with blankets, bolts of cloth, tools, beads, pots and pans, skinning knives, guns and clothing had rolled into the site. Most of the clothing was used, but nearly every item was brightly colored. And if the long rifles weren't the latest and best available, they were at least in working condition. Daniel had warned Dick about that: "You give these braves guns that go off in their faces, an' they'll club you to death with 'em for sure."

The contents of the wagons filled six cabins to the rafters, and the Cherokees could clearly see everything they were getting. They had agreed to the cost: goods worth eight thousand pounds sterling, and another two thousand in cash. That was the price of Kentucky. Daniel doubted that the goods were worth anywhere near that much, but he wasn't about to take Henderson to task. Dick had already convinced himself the Cherokees were getting more than a fair trade.

Stoner waved at Daniel, and Daniel sauntered down to meet him. In spite of the moderate weather, the big Dutchman was soaked in sweat. Stepping down off his horse, he wiped a hand across his brow and spit on the ground. "Goddamn," he said tightly, "we are going to have to horsewhip some fellers sure, Dan'l. I send two wagons back already this morning. You know what they are bringing? Whiskey! Fifty barrels of bad rum from Virginia!"

Daniel shook his head. "Well, that's sure all we need, ain't it? I don't want nobody shot or nothin', Mike, so you better tell the other boys. This ain't no county fair."

Right from the start, it had been clear to Daniel that the treaty signing could turn into something neither Henderson nor anyone else had bargained for. The Royal Governors of North Carolina and Virginia wanted the sale of Kentucky stopped. They protested that the whole business was fraudulent, and that every debtor in the colonies would run off to Kentucky. The land would become a haven for the dregs of the land. Besides, a separate treaty with the Indians was against the King's law.

Now crowds were fighting to get into Sycamore Shoals just to watch. Men, women and children were flooding in from all over. Worse still, every merchant who had bad stock to sell saw a golden opportunity to unload his wares.

Daniel wasn't having any of it. Everyone who didn't have good reason to be there was stopped at the head of the valley and sent on his way. In a day or so there would be fifteen hundred Cherokees in the encampment. If one drunken Indian or white decided to have at it, there would be a fair-sized massacre on the Watauga.

"Dave Gass and your brother are here," reported Stoner. "I met them up the valley. Squire says Dick Henderson is behind him. They will be here in the morning." Mike led his horse down to the river, and Daniel walked along.

"That's just fine. I want Dick to get used to the Indians." He grinned at Stoner. "And them to him. Old Attakullaculla himself is here now, and Draggin' Canoe too. I know 'em both, and Draggin' Canoe's a mean one."

"You think there will be trouble?"

"Not from the old man. But his son don't care much for beads, especially when they come from whites."

"That's fine," Stoner said lightly. "Dick Henderson does not like Indians. They will make a fine match."

Daniel made a face. "Sure glad you're along, Mike. Makes me feel warm all over."

"Ja, I am a fine fellow for sure."

The next day, Dick Henderson and his partners rode into the valley at noon on pure-bred horses, dressed from head to toe like English lords. Henderson might not care for Indians, but he knew what turned their heads. The great chiefs of the Cherokees would not be dishonored here. They would know they were dealing with men of high station.

Daniel introduced Henderson to Attakullaculla, Dragging Canoe, and the other chiefs. Dick played his part like a professional on stage, treating the Cherokee leaders with the deference and respect due great leaders. He said nothing at all about the treaty, but invited them all to a feast that evening. Daniel caught the looks that passed among the Indians. This white man was in no hurry to do business. He was not a merchant selling blankets; he would honor his guests before mentioning serious matters.

Henderson had made certain the feast would be the best. He had hired several families who lived along the Watauga to prepare the finest foods available— venison, buffalo, beefsteak, pigeon, wild turkey and pork. There were vegetables and cornbread, and even delicacies like pies and candies, which few of the Indians had ever tasted. By nightfall the valley was heavy with rich and succulent smells. As Dave Gass put it, "You give them Indians a pen right now an' they'll sell you everything from here to the Pacific Ocean, whether they own it or not!"

After dinner, the Indians danced around the bonfires blazing along the shore, and Henderson provided a foot-stomping fiddle band that at first perplexed, then delighted the Cherokees.

When it was over, Henderson asked Daniel to his tent for a nip of brandy. The lawyer's fine silk jacket was set aside, and a determined frown replaced his diplomat's smile. "Well," he asked evenly, "are they happy?"

"Sure they are," said Boone. "Indians are always happy after a feast."

Henderson hid his impatience. "You know what I'm asking. Will they be ready to sign tomorrow?"

"I reckon so. They wouldn't be here if they weren't. Indians are serious folks, and they take a pride in their word, Dick. They made an agreement, and they'll stick by it if they can."

Henderson raised a brow. "What do you mean, if they *can*?"

"Just what I said. There's goin' to be speech-makin' and solemn noddin' and a lot of gruntin' and thinkin'. But you get impatient, Dick, or even look like you are, and these ol' boys'll have you for breakfast."

"Yes, yes, so you told me," Henderson remarked irritably. He lit a clay pipe and gave Daniel a half smile. "I'll try to behave, Daniel."

"Good. You aren't dealin' with no Royal Governors or judges, friend. These here are high-class folks."

265

Henderson looked at him curiously, but Boone kept a straight face.

The Indians sat on their robes, their rigidly straight backs to the thick grove of sycamores. Dick Henderson tried hard to match his own expression to their grave, wooden faces. He opened the ceremony with great praise for the Cherokee people, honoring their bravery, wisdom, prowess as hunters—damn near everything, thought Daniel, except their cooking pots and dogs. Finally, he made an exaggerated show of respect for the Cherokees' sovereignty in Kentucky. He told how the Iroquois had relinquished their claims to the area in 1768 at Fort Stanwix, and noted that the great British King himself had recognized the Cherokees' ownership just five years before.

"Here," he said, presenting to the chiefs the map Boone had drawn, "is the land of Kentucky. It is this land I wish to buy from the Cherokees—the mountains, trees and valleys west of the Endless Mountains, where the waters of the Cumberland and Kentucky Rivers flow."

The chiefs studied the map thoughtfully, passing it from one to the other, and finally to their own white attorney hired for the occasion. He was a pompous little man who irked Dick Henderson no end. Who the hell ever heard of Indians have attorneys?

Finally, Attakullaculla gathered his heavy buffalo robe about his square frame and stood to say his piece. Daniel had figured the old man would make the final decision. He was greatly respected by the Cherokees, and he knew the white men well. When he was young-

266

er, he had traveled to England and even dined with the King.

"It is good that we meet here," he said slowly. "The Cherokee people welcome their brothers, and thank them for the honor they have shown, and for the great feast they have given us. . . ."

The speech went on for nearly an hour, and Attakullaculla stopped frequently for his words to be translated into English. In the end, he made it clear that the Cherokees approved of the treaty, and praised the quality of the goods Henderson had promised in trade.

Henderson relaxed when the old man sat down. The whole business was going well. Only the signing of the treaty and delivering of the goods in exchange remained to be accomplished.

Then, Attakullaculla's son turned to his father and asked to speak. Henderson glanced at Daniel, who quickly glanced up at the sky. Dragging Canoe looked nothing like his father. He was a large, heavily muscled warrior with a furrowed brow and piercing eyes.

"I honor my father and his words," said the Indian. "Attakullaculla is wise. He says what is in his heart. He speaks as the spirits guide him, and he has great love for his people." Dragging Canoe looked at his father and the other chiefs, then turned his dark eyes on Henderson. "Now I, Dragging Canoe, Tsiyugunsini, would speak. I, too, say what is in my heart. I also love the Cherokee people. And I would tell you this, my brothers. What we do here is unwise. The white men have already gone beyond the Endless Mountains and into the Cherokees' lands. Now, they ask us here to sign a treaty. They give us a great feast

267

and promise many things. If you wish to give up your lands, you will do so. But what, my brothers, will happen when the white man wants more land? Do you truly think Kentucky will be enough for him? Where will he tell the Cherokees to go next?"

Dragging Canoe turned quickly and thrust his finger at Henderson. "I tell you now what he will do. He will push our people farther and farther away until there is no place left for us, until the Cherokee tribe is strangled and dead! That is the end the white man sees for us! This treaty we speak of is for men too old and weak to pull a bow or shoot a rifle. I am not an old man, and neither are my warriors. I say we must keep our lands. I say we must fight for them if we have to!"

Dragging Canoe stomped out of the clearing and disappeared into the woods. The Indians and whites stared after him. The chiefs then began mumbling among themselves and many nodded approval of his words. Dick Henderson was stunned. Great God, the whole business was falling apart before his eyes! Everything had been just fine until this—this hulking savage put his two pennies in! Turning desperately to Boone, he found the frontiersman already on his feet and talking to Attakullaculla. The old man listened gravely. Then Daniel came back to Henderson.

"I've gotten him to call a recess," he said. "That's the best we can do right now."

"What happens next? My God, Daniel . . ."

Boone shot him a warning look. "Relax, damn it! You want 'em to see you're worried? Get back to your camp and stay there. I'm goin' to see what I can do."

Henderson shook his head. "I thought the fellow was going to go for our scalps right here!"

"Don't be a fool," Daniel remarked soberly. "He ain't goin' to scalp anyone at a talkin'. That ain't good manners. If he's planning on liftin' your wig, he'll wait till the meetin's over."

Henderson waited for Boone to smile, but Daniel never blinked.

Mike Stoner, Ben Cutbirth and Squire Boone were waiting for Daniel by the Watauga, away from the fires. "You think there will be trouble?" asked Mike. "Me, I don't think so."

"No, not if you mean fightin' trouble," Daniel told him. "I'm goin' to have me a little talk-fest with Draggin' Canoe an' see if we can pull this thing out of the fire."

"Well, at least we don't have to worry if there *is* trouble," Cutbirth said stoically. "Fifty whites fightin' a thousand Indians ain't goin' to take that long."

Daniel and the others joined in the laughter. "Damn sure won't," said Daniel. "Poor ol' Dick thought he was goin' to be the first to go." He turned, glanced over his shoulder, then faced the others. "I don't have to tell you boys to keep your eyes open, just in case. These aren't the first Indians you ever seen."

"No, just the most at one time," Squire said dryly.

Cutbirth grinned. "You just give the word, and we'll start runnin' for Boston, Dan."

"Anyone starts runnin' is goin' to see my backside right ahead of 'im. I'll be the one 'bout two miles behind Dick Henderson."

Dim light from the Cherokee lodges guided Daniel up the hill through the sycamores. He stopped twice to

269

ask the way before he finally found the camp of Dragging Canoe. Squatting outside over a low fire were two warriors who glanced up as Daniel approached. One returned his greeting and looked away. The other stared at him defiantly. Daniel's eyes went wide and the muscles in his shoulders knotted hard. He recognized the man, and he had to force himself to swallow the anger that rose up to choke him as he met the warrior's gaze. "Evening, brother," he said lightly, and stooped to enter the lodge.

Daniel knew where he'd seen the Indian before. It wasn't a face he'd likely forget. Four years before, on another spring night that same Cherokee had walked into camp with some friends and shared venison with Daniel and Squire. When Daniel refused to trade his own good rifles for the Indians' relics, the Cherokees had turned on them. Then they had stolen everything the Boones were bringing back from Kentucky.

Chapter 29

Dragging Canoe sat in the low, red light cast by the dying coals of his fire. Daniel saw neither warmth nor hostility in the Indian's eyes, only a curious mixture of caution and understanding.

"Wide Mouth, I know why you come," he said solemnly. "Now I would know who you are. Is it Boone, the friend of the Cherokee, who talks, or Boone, the servant of Henderson? With whose mouth do you now speak?"

Daniel boldly met the Indian's gaze and spoke with the stiff formality of the Cherokee tongue. "I am no man's servant. Tsiyu-gunsini knows this and does me no honor with his question."

Dragging Canoe nodded imperceptibly. "Perhaps this is so. Perhaps Boone's anger answers Tsiyu-gunsini's question." The Cherokee motioned to the silent old woman in the rear of his lodge. The woman pulled herself up and brought him a pipe and a leather pouch. Dragging Canoe spent a long time tamping tobacco into the bowl and lighting it from the fire. He puffed on it hard, then passed it to Daniel. Daniel drew in the acrid fumes and passed it back.

"You know the white man well," Boone said quietly. "He is crossing the mountains, my brother. His numbers are small, now, but soon they will grow so great that the Cherokees will be unable to count them. I do not say this is good—I only say it is true."

Dragging Canoe frowned thoughtfully. "If you think it is wrong for the whites to live on the Cherokees' land, how can you then come to the Watauga and ask them to sell it? Your heart says one thing, while your tongue speaks another."

"Part of my heart is the Indian's heart," said Daniel. "It says the Cherokees must fight the white man and drive him back. Fight even if you die, and your women and children along with you. This is your land, and he does not belong here. These are also the thoughts in your head, Tsiyu-gunsini. I understand them. But my Indian heart also says that the Cherokee people have other land on which to hunt and fish, other land on which to build their lodges. Is it not far wiser to sell this land than go into battle and die for it so that the whites will steal it anyway? The Cherokees are great fighters. Everyone knows this. Still, when a storm comes over the mountains, does a warrior fire his arrow at the rain? Can he stop the storm this way?"

When Daniel finished, Dragging Canoe stared into the fire, his dark eyes gazing deep into the hypnotic flames. When he looked up again, Daniel knew what the man had seen, all the pain and sorrow of his people was mirrored in his eyes. "The things you say are true," he said.

"Yes, my brother. They are true."

The Indian shook his head. "It would be good if you were a Cherokee, Boone. Your heart would hurt more, but it would be a whole heart."

Dragging Canoe turned away. Daniel pulled himself up quietly and left the lodge.

Henderson saw him walking past the fires to the shore and ran down to meet him. "Daniel! I thought you were going to be in there all night. How'd it go?"

"He'll do it," Daniel told him absently. "You got your treaty."

"Marvelous!" Henderson beamed and clapped Daniel on the back. "By God, I knew you could . . ."

"Damn it, Dick!" Daniel shook his hand off and turned on him angrily. "You got what you want, now leave me the hell alone!" He stomped off down the shore into the darkness, Henderson staring in confusion after him.

In the morning, the talks began again. Henderson's people sat on one side of the circle, the solemn Cherokee chiefs on the other. Once more, Attakullaculla rose to speak for his people. His speech was short. He told the white men that the Cherokees had listened carefully to the words of Henderson, and decided the trade was fair and good. They were prepared to sign the agreement.

Dick Henderson held back his excitement. He rose from his place and stood before the chiefs, resplendent in a blue silk jacket and breeches he had saved for the occasion. "I am grateful for the wise decision of the Cherokees," he said. "Still, I am deeply troubled. You have shown me great honor, and I cannot, in my heart, repay that honor with disrespect. You have sold me the land of Kentucky. Yet, I have no way to reach that place without crossing land that still belongs to the Cherokees. I would not insult my brothers by walking over their land. I ask you now to sell me a roadway into Kentucky. For this, I will be pleased to add even more fine rifles and other goods to the price we've already agreed upon."

When these words were translated, Dragging Canoe jerked to his feet, his dark face trembling with rage. "You see, my brothers? Is it not as I have said? The white man eats and eats, but he is never full. He has swallowed Kentucky, and he is still hungry!"

Daniel translated quickly and shot Henderson a look of warning. He stood again and spread his hands openly to the angry Indian. "Dragging Canoe, I have no wish to take more. My only desire is to respect the rights of the Cherokees. Please understand this!"

"Respect!" spat the chief. "Your respect will kill my people, Henderson."

Attakullaculla held up a hand. "What is it you wish, Henderson? I would hear it."

"Only a narrow path to Kentucky," said Dick. "A road from the Watauga to the gap in the Cumberland."

Attakullaculla glanced up at his son. Silent words passed between them. Dragging Canoe clenched his teeth and stomped his foot on the ground. "It is yours," he said tightly. "From this spot to the mountains!" He turned, then, and took his place by his father. The anger in him had cooled. Now, his eyes were dark and empty.

*   *   *

There was still much to be done. The Great Grant and Henderson's new Path Deed had to be written, the land meticulously mapped and copies translated into Cherokee. Henderson left that job to his employees. The treaty had been accomplished and his mind was on other matters. "We'll be at this eight or ten days," he told Daniel. "There's no use your wasting time around here. We've a road to build, my friend."

"You ain't signed any treaty yet," Daniel reminded him.

"That's a detail, Daniel, a detail. It's as good as done."

Daniel shrugged. Leaving early was fine with him. He had no more heart for the Watauga. "I'll send Squire and Ben and Gass. They'll find me some good men, and I'll go on with Stoner."

"Fine, fine. It's finished, then," said Henderson. He gave Daniel a quick smile and hurried away.

Daniel looked after him, then stared over the bright waters of the river. He could leave tomorrow, put this place behind him. A few days after that he would be blazing a trail toward his own piece of Kentucky. I ought to feel good about that, he told himself, but somehow, he didn't. He couldn't forget Dragging Canoe's speech about the white man's hunger. His own bite of Kentucky was already tasting bitter in his mouth.

Dragging Canoe sought him out in the late afternoon and asked him to come for a walk in the woods. "You have gained a good land," he told Daniel. "The Cherokees will honor this agreement, and we will not trouble the white man in his new country. But the Cherokees cannot speak for other tribes. You have

caught a fat wolf in your trap. I think you will get bit-
ten badly when you try to take it out."

Boone looked at him. The Indian turned and
gazed into the west, toward the Endless Mountains.
"There is a black cloud over this land of yours. It casts
a shadow on the earth, and makes the ground dark and
bloody."

"I've been there," Daniel said quietly. "You're as
right as you can be, Tsiyu-gunsini. The land's rich, but
there's much blood in it."

"Not as much as there will be," said the
Cherokee. His face grew more animated, and he turned
to Daniel. "Now, come. We are finished with this, and
there is one here who would speak with you."

Daniel gave him a puzzled look, but the Indian
moved away and motioned for him to follow. Dragging
Canoe walked far into the sycamores, past the last of
the lodges. The woods were thick and dark here. Each
great trunk competing with every other to thrust its
branches to the sky. A small creek, no wider than a
step, snaked down the hill toward the Watauga.

Dragging Canoe stopped by the creek, and an Indian woman stepped into the open. Daniel was startled
by her appearance. She was about thirty, tall, a strik-
ingly beautiful woman with long black hair and high
cheekbones. Only the sorrow in her eyes disturbed her
beauty.

"This is Flower-by-the-Rock," said Dragging
Canoe. "It is she who would speak to you." He nodded
at Boone and was gone.

The woman looked at him curiously. "You are
Wide Mouth."

"I am, yes."

276

"Come. Please?" She turned, and Daniel followed her through the trees to a small lodge hidden by the stream. The woman turned then, and faced him. "Boone, I am the mother of Blue Duck."

Daniel was surprised only for a moment. "Yes. I see that you are. You look much alike."

"She is here, Boone."

Daniel stared. "What!? You mean she's—alive?"

"She is alive." The woman lowered her eyes. "That is her curse."

"I got to see her." Boone started past her for the lodge.

"No." The woman held up her hand. "Hear me, Boone. My husband died of the sickness last winter. I have no one now, but Tsiyu-gunsini is a great and kind chief. He cares for the families of his braves." She nodded toward the lodge. "Blue Duck was returned to us four years ago. We were camped to the south, far below the Catawba. The Shawnees brought her back, but not as a kindness. They left her here in the brush for us to find, with a war club beside her. My husband and Tsiyu-gunsini rode after the Shawnees, but they found only one, whose horse had hurt his leg. Before my husband was through with him, he told us many things. I know all that happened to Blue Duck. I know about you, Boone, and I know of the man called Black Knife." She stopped, searching Daniel's face with eyes he had seen before. "Was there love between you and my daughter?"

Daniel swallowed hard. "Yes. There was love between us."

"Good. Tsiyu-gunsini says you are a man of honor. He says it is possible for a white man to show honor, though such a thing is rare. I ask a favor of honor from you now. I think you will want to hear it."

Stooping into the lodge, she came back quickly with a knife in a deerhide sheath. Drawing the knife, she handed it to Daniel. It was a fine blade, sharp and free of rust, the handle, made of polished bone. The handle was wound tightly with dark strands of hair. The butt had been carved in the shape of a buffalo's head.

"This knife belonged to my husband," said the woman. "It is to cut only once. The sickness took him before he could find the man he sought. If you take the knife, you take his debt of honor."

Daniel thrust the blade into its sheath. "You don't have to ask me, Flower-by-the-Rock. The debt is already mine."

"Tsiyu-gunsini said this was so." She looked at him a long moment. "Place it where it belongs, Wide Mouth. And place it slowly."

"You got my word on that," he told her. He glanced at the lodge, then back to the woman. "Look. I gotta ask you . . ."

"No." Flower-by-the-Rock caught his eyes and held them. "She is no longer a human being. She is less than a child. She does not know me, and she would not know you. She is my daughter, but my shame is that I cannot look upon her face. There is no face there, Wide Mouth." Tears welled in her eyes and she set her lips tightly. "Do you think Black Knife would have brought her to me if she was a person still?"

Daniel didn't answer. He gazed at the lodge once more, thrust the knife into his belt and walked away through the forest.

The Agreement of Sycamore Shoals was signed on March 17, 1775. By then, Daniel was some fifty miles west on the Holston with thirty experienced woodsmen, already blazing a trail to Kentucky.

There was great feasting on the Watauga. Dick Henderson broke out the rum he had been saving for the Indians until the treaty was safely signed. The six cabins, where the payment of goods and weapons was stored, were opened, and the price of Kentucky was presented to the Cherokees. Not everyone was happy with his share. The treasure looked inexhaustible in the cabins, but seemed a great deal smaller shared among fifteen hundred men, women and children.

One brave complained loudly about the single worn shirt he received. He stalked up and down before the white man's camp, shouting that he could take enough skins in Kentucky in a single day to buy a dozen such shirts.

Attakullaculla got two rifles, a red blanket, and a blue coat, which, he thought, looked almost as good as Henderson's.

Dragging Canoe took nothing.

Chapter 30

When Daniel and Mike Stoner saw the tall plume of
smoke rising from the river, they exchanged quick
smiles and kicked their mounts into a gallop. Rounding
the bend of the Holston, they whooped and hollered as
the green tip of Long Island came into sight. At the
same time, the men on shore saw them. Rifle shots
cracked in the air and a ragged volley of cheers echoed
through the valley. Stirred by the sight of his friends,
Daniel splashed across the narrows, waving his hat.
Squire, Ben Cutbirth and a dozen others waded out to
meet him. In a moment they were all crowded about,
shouting, laughing and pounding Daniel and Stoner on
their backs. Dave Gass passed them a jug of whiskey
and Daniel raised it to his mouth, letting the fiery liquid burn his belly and run down his cheeks. The men
roared and Daniel passed the jug to Stoner.

"Don't give it to the Dutchman," Gass shouted in alarm. "I've seen him take a swallow before!"

"You are about to see another," Mike told him flatly and nearly emptied the jug before Gass could jerk it away.

Daniel looked around at the thirty men who had gathered to follow him west. He had picked them all himself and they were the best on the frontier. Squire, Stoner, Gass, Cutbirth, Dick Callaway, Will Twitty, Felix Walker and young Will Hays, who'd just married Daniel's daughter Susannah. Lord God, he thought in wonder, she would be fifteen in the fall. It seemed like only yesterday she had been toddlin' around in the yard.

Boone's heart swelled with pride. "Damnation," he grinned, "if I'd have had you boys in '69, we'd have likely settled China by now!" The woodsmen cheered him again and Daniel grabbed the jug back from Gass, but when he turned it upside down, only a single drop fell to the ground. Again the men cheered.

"Dan'l," said his new son-in-law, "tell us what's happening at the Shoals. How long we goin' to have to sit here?"

"Will, we ain't goin' to sit here at all. We're goin' now! First thing in the morning, by damn!" It would be at least a week before Henderson and the Indians quit fussing with the treaty, but Daniel was here, and the men were ready. By God, it didn't make sense to sit around and wait. Nothing could stop them now!

At noon the first day out, Ben Cutbirth shot a bear on the Holston. Every man on the trek said it was a sure omen of a good beginning. The cooking fires sizzled with succulent red meat that night.

Then, leaving the Holston behind, Boone led his woodsmen overland toward the Clinch. The country was rough and tangled, crowded with tall trees and dense thickets. Rugged mountains loomed on every side. Sometimes traveling would be easier through a valley meadow, and all the cutters had to do was mark an occasional tree for the settlers to follow. A few yards farther, however, and they would inevitably run into heavy forest or a dense field of cane. Then, the air would echo with the sharp ring of axes and loud curses.

Daniel figured Castle's Woods was still some forty-odd miles to the northeast. Another day or so and they could turn due north to cross the Clinch. Then the traveling would go a little easier for a while.

That evening, Captain Will Twitty sought out Daniel and took him aside. Twitty was a great hulk of a fellow, built more like a bear than a man, and Daniel liked him. Twitty had brought seven good woodsmen from North Carolina, a slave named Sam, and ever at Twitty's side, the meanest yellow bulldog Daniel had ever seen. Stoner said that if they met any Indians, all twenty-nine of the party could hide in the brush and let Twitty and his dog do all the fighting.

"I ain't a man to carry tales," Twitty said gruffly, "but I thought you ought to know, Dan'l. That goddamn Callaway's shootin' off his mouth more'n he ought to. He told my man Walker we could make better time movin' north right now, 'stead of plowin' down the valley. He's full of crap an' everybody knows it, but he's gettin' folks irritated."

Daniel nodded. Callaway was a good frontiersman from the Yadkin but a little puffed up with his own importance. He had once been a colonel in the Virginia

Militia. "I appreciate it, Will. Dick's likely feeling his oats some."

"Yeah?" Twitty shot a fierce look over his shoulder. "Well, he better feel 'em somewhere I can't hear it. I'll have my dog chew his behind off."

Daniel grinned.

At Moccasin Gap, Boone's party crossed the awesome Clinch Mountains and began working their way northwest toward Wallen's Ridge. James was buried there, only a few miles away, but Daniel didn't visit the grave. James wasn't lying in the ground. He was riding right there beside him. Daniel could feel his presence every mile of the way. We'll go through the Cumberland together this time, he said silently. We shook on it, son, and we'll do it.

Just this side of the Clinch River he found what he was looking for—the familiar track of the Warrior's Path. The men were cheered, for now the work would go faster. The Warrior's Path was no post road, but it was less difficult than an unmarked wilderness.

After they crossed the Clinch, Daniel sent scouts ahead and to the rear at either flank. Some of the men made light of his cautiousness, but Daniel didn't waver. "I don't recall no Shawnees at Sycamore Shoals," he said dryly. "I figure they ain't too interested in Dick Henderson's deed to Kentucky."

"I wouldn't worry," Dick Callaway said absently. "We made short work of the Shawnees at Point Pleasant, Boone. They'll give us no more trouble, I assure you."

"That sure makes my scalp feel better," said

Gass. Callaway shot him a withering look and whipped his horse away.

Following the Warrior's Path over the Powell Mountains, the woodsmen wound down into the valley to Martin's Station. The Indians had burned Martin out, but he was stubbornly rebuilding.

Now the great range of the Cumberlands, the awesome white giant to the West, marked their way. Boone and his men covered the miles quickly. Then one bright spring morning, he reined in his horse and stared at the sight ahead. The mountains rose over a thousand feet toward the clear blue sky. The yawning gap in the Cumberlands was so bright in the sun it hurt Daniel's eyes to look at it.

"It's the same every time," Squire said by his side. "If I came here every day, I don't think I'd ever get used to it."

The party snaked through the green valley and climbed the slope to the top, where Daniel sat for a long moment looking down on Kentucky. He stayed there, waiting until the others started down, then got off his horse and led it to the side of the gap. Peering upward, he studied the sheer white wall thrusting out of the earth at his feet. Finally, he found what he was looking for—a fault in the stone where a man could make his way up. Strapping James' rifle to his shoulder, he started his climb. He scraped the calloused palms of his hands as he held tight to the rock, and he cut his knee twice. In less than a hundred feet the fault closed up and he could go no higher. Hugging the wall as best he could, he took James' rifle from his shoulder and jammed it into the rock. It held better than he had hoped, wedged securely up to the breech. It would stay there, he knew, until the long years rusted and flaked the barrel down to powder. Maybe part of it would last forever.

Wrapping his arm about the stock, he pulled the short hatchet from his belt and began to laboriously scrape at the hard granite face of the mountain. It took nearly an hour to get the inscription the way he wanted it, and when he was through, the hatchet was dulled to worthlessness. Still, the words were there, and he nodded his head in satisfaction. No one would ever climb up there and see it, but Daniel hadn't done it for other eyes to see.

"All right, son," he said softly, "you made it, now. Can't anyone pass through without you knowin'."

His eyes clouded, and he made his way slowly back down the wall, leaving the rifle wedged in stone, and the legend he had carved beside it:

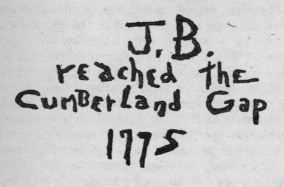

The way stretched clear from the eastern foothills to the broad lands watered by the Cumberland River. Ahead lay more miles of steep hills, dense forests and stretches of choking cane. The way behind was smooth compared to what they would face to the west. His cutters would earn their pay and then some. There were a hundred creeks to cross and dark, swampy ground, where a man sank in up to his knees and came out smelling like thousand-year-old mud.

"Where's all this goddamn beautiful country we been hearin' about?" Cutbirth called out cheerfully. "I sure hope this ain't my piece of land that I'm right now clearing."

"Naw, you're workin' on Stoner's place right now," Daniel joked. "Mike's goin' to build a cabin right here an' go into gator farmin'. Bringin' a whole herd of 'em up from Florida. Goin' to teach 'em to hunt buffalo."

The woodsmen whooped and jeered and Mike Stoner told them all what they could do with their comments.

More canebrakes faced the party, and though Daniel had a special feeling for the tough, fibrous growth that grew thick as a man's leg, his woodsmen cursed every mile of it. They grew tired of Boone saying what a fine place it was to hide from Indians and threatened to scalp him themselves if he spoke of it again.

Finally they reached Big Hill, the summit Daniel had climbed on his first trip west, and the men stopped grumbling. Rolling meadows and lush fields of new bluegrass stretched out before them. They had nearly worn their axes to nubs, but it was worth it to them. This was what the money they would make for this trip would buy them—over four hundred prime acres in the heart of Kentucky.

"Well, there's the bluegrass you been belly-achin'

about," Daniel told Cutbirth. "Pick you out a piece 'fore it's all gone."

Ben Cutbirth whistled softly and shook his head. "Dan, there's enough here for everybody. Strike me dead if there ain't."

"You think so, hah?" Stoner said warily. "You wait, Ben. Dick Henderson is coming over those mountains in a couple of weeks with half the goddamn country."

"Mike, not everyone wants to live in Kentucky."

Stoner scratched his chin. "Ja, you are right, there is one, I hear. King George, he is not coming. He does not like white Americans, much less red ones."

Daniel laughed. "He's put his finger on it, Ben. I ain't heard of anyone else stayin' home."

"Damn," Ben said glumly. "What's west of Kentucky, Dan'l?"

Two nights later, on March 24, Boone's party made camp at Taylor's Fork. There were low hills to their back, and a gentle slope to the river. High fires lit the night, and Dave Gass broke out the last jug of whiskey he had squireled away for the occasion.

Daniel walked down to the river and gazed north. Otter Creek was no more than a dozen miles away. He would be there before the next day was halfway done. He could already see the place clearly—the great stand of sycamores, the green meadows where he and Rebecca would build their home and plant crops. After all the years, all the pain and sorrow, the dream was now only a day away. They would put up a fort and start laying out cabins, and when things got going, he would return home for Becky and the children. His share for cutting the road through the wilderness was two thousand acres. And he would get even more in the end. Henderson had promised him that, and by God he would take what he could. He had damn sure paid out enough to earn some back.

The celebration lasted into the night. Daniel posted guards, but no one took his duties too seriously. They had cut their way through nearly two hundred and fifty miles, from the Holston to the belly of Kentucky, in fifteen days. On this night, they felt no less than lords of the land.

And they slept so soundly when the celebration was finished that no one heard the crackling of twigs and rustling of brush in the forest, alien sounds in the tranquil night.

Chapter 31

Daniel jerked up quickly. Rifle fire lit the clearing and a bullet chunked wood at his head. He grabbed his weapon, rolled to one side and got off a shot. Cries of alarm mixed with the howls of Shawnee braves. Twitty's dog barked and Boone heard a man scream. Scuttling back in the brush, he bumped into Squire.

"Grabbed my goddamn shirt 'stead of my pouch," Squire cursed. "Give me some fixin's, Daniel!" Daniel tossed his horn and pouch and bellied up to a tree. The clearing was quiet. Then, gunfire cracked from behind. One woodsman, then another and another poured lead into the woods. An Indian yelped. Daniel saw him stagger and drag himself off. Horses hooves made a sudden, fluttering beat into the shadows.

"They're gone" Stoner said quietly. He was a few yards to the left somewhere. Daniel stood up slowly, grabbed his horn and pouch from Squire and reloaded.

The pale grey of dawn filtered through the branches. As he walked into the clearing, Stoner moved up beside him. "Squire, get the boys back in here and set out guards. Take a look at the horses. I think they took a couple."

"Daniel . . ."

Boone peered through the half-light, saw Captain Twitty and rushed to him. Twitty's face grimaced in pain. "Got me in the knees," he said tightly. "Damn— both of 'em, I guess."

"Take it easy, Will. Couple of bullets can't hurt a man your size." Tearing the man's trousers, he saw Twitty was right. The wounds were bad. One knee was open clear to the shattered bone. The other wasn't much better, and both were bleeding fast. Daniel started ripping cloth and tying the legs up tight.

"You know what?" Twitty said feebly. "That worthless dog of mine saved my hide. Would've lost my hair, but that little devil run 'em off!" He grinned beneath the pain. "Can you believe that?"

Men were moving back into camp. Daniel, after calling one of them over to finish with Twitty, searched out Gass. "Well, what's it look like?"

"Better'n it could have been. Twitty's slave caught it. Dead back there in the brush. Felix Walker's got a bullet in his ass, but it ain't too bad. Look at that, Dan'l." He nodded to the right. Daniel saw Twitty's bulldog, a tomahawk buried in his head.

"Will's right. Fiesty little bastard. The captain's in bad shape, Dave. Wounds like that ain't good out here."

"Uh-huh. But we was lucky as hell. I saw them bastards. Wasn't more than six."

"Six Shawnees is 'bout enough," said Daniel.

Squire reported four horses and one man, Lew Draper, missing—likely the Indians had gotten them all. Daniel was angry, but mostly at himself. He had known the guards weren't taking their jobs seriously, but he hadn't pushed them.

Dick Callaway took the incident in stride. He had brought his own black slave along to cook, a gaunt, taciturn woman named Lucy, and while the others were still burying Twitty's man Sam, Callaway sat calmly down to breakfast. Daniel heard he had remarked that Taylor's Fork was obviously a bad location for a campsite. Mike Stoner's Dutch temper turned him red when he heard that, and he threatened to teach Callaway a lesson, but Boone told him to leave the man alone. "You can't stop a fellow from bein' miserable," he said. "Dick's got a natural bent for it."

"A good bent is what I would give him," muttered Stoner. "I would shut that fool up for sure!"

Daniel was anxious to move on to Otter Creek. The Shawnees would be back, and next time he knew they would bring reinforcements. They would soon have to begin building a fort for their own safety, and for Henderson's folks, who would be coming through the gap in the next few months.

With a sudden chill, he realized that the whole dream could end right here—could have ended last night, for that matter. The words of Dragging Canoe came back to him. "A storm over Kentucky—a dark and bloody ground . . ." He couldn't let that happen. Not now, not half a day south of the goal he had worked for, ached for in his heart since that night so long ago when Findley had spun tales of a new garden of Eden. God A'mighty, how long had it been? Twenty years since they had followed Braddock's army to Duquesne? Sometimes, it felt like only yesterday, but right now, it seemed much more than a lifetime away.

By the end of the day, it was clear there was no chance of moving north, not with Will Twitty fading fast. A late winter storm was forming in the north, and Daniel had trees cut and stacked to shelter both Twitty and Walker, who seemed to be holding his own.

The second day, Twitty grew feverish, then cold again. On the night of the twenty-seventh, he died in his sleep. A light, unseasonal snow fell around midnight, swirling in eddies about the camp.

"He was a good man," Dave Gass said solemnly. "We could use more like him in Kentucky."

"Yeah, we could." Daniel huddled in his blanket against a tree, staring at the snow. "How soon can we move Walker? I don't like hangin' around here, Dave. It ain't good for the rest of 'em either."

"We can take him in a couple of days. Have to carry him, though. He won't be walkin' for a while."

We've got to get out of here, and soon thought Daniel as he lay back later, trying to sleep. By God, if it wasn't snowing and cold, I'd move 'em right now, right in the middle of the night.

He woke to a woman's screams, sat up and saw Callaway's slave Lucy running frantically around the fire screaming her lungs out.

"Oh, Lord, Indians!" she moaned. "Thousands of 'em!" She pointed shakily toward the trees, then dropped in a faint.

The camp came alive as the woodsmen grabbed their rifles. Daniel went to his knees and aimed into the forest. This is it, he thought numbly. They've got us in the light of the fire and it's over. "Hold fast," he said evenly to the others. "Take as many as you can!"

The fire crackled and something moved in the brush. "Jesus, don't kill me!" shouted a voice. "I'm a white man!"

The figure walked out of the forest, his eyes wide with fear. Daniel stared and lowered his rifle. It was Lew Draper, the man who had disappeared the night of the ambush. One of the men laughed, and the others joined in, breaking the tension. Daniel stalked up to Draper. "What the hell you been doin' out there, man?"

"I don't know," he stammered. "I thought maybe you was all dead."

"Well, we ain't," Daniel said shortly. "But you just now come damn close to it yourself." Cursing to himself, he wandered back to his bedroll in disgust.

In the morning, Daniel tended Felix Walker. Walker claimed he was feeling fine, but he still looked weak. They would wait another day, but no more. After that, he wouldn't risk staying at Taylor's Fork. The threat of an attack by the Shawnees had made the tension in the camp unbearable. The cutters quarreled over trivial annoyances. Who had tended the fire last, and who hadn't. Who hadn't taken night guard duty lately. When they could find nothing more to fight about, Dick Callaway helped them out. There was a better way to post guards, he said. Anyone who had served in the militia as long as he had would know that. Daniel ignored him until the man started changing the roster around to suit himself. Then Boone took Callaway aside and walked him down to the river.

"I'm glad you're here, Dick, and I count you a good man," began Daniel. "But I'll tell you this straight. We got enough trouble around here, and I don't intend to take on more."

Callaway looked puzzled. "Why, you're as right as you can be, Dan'l. What's that got to do with me?"

Daniel studied the man's full, pink cheeks and the slight touch of amusement at the corner of his mouth. "You know what I'm tellin' you, Dick. I ain't runnin' no army here, and you ain't no colonel in Kentucky. You got suggestions, fine, but you make 'em to me."

Callaway's color rose, but he swallowed his anger and smiled. "Why, certainly, Dan'l. I have no desire to offend you. I hope you know that."

"I'm sure glad to hear it," said Boone.

Callaway took a deep breath, set his chin and marched back to the camp. Daniel gazed after him. Stoner was likely right. Dick Callaway was a born troublemaker, but they were stuck with him now.

Daniel sent Gass and Ben Cutbirth out the next morning to scout for game. Before the day was half over they were back, galloping fast down the river, digging up muddy puffs of snow. As Gass swung off his horse, Daniel saw a small boy sitting the saddle behind him. Cutbirth lifted him off and took him to the fire, and Dave stalked over to Boone.

"Found him in a camp 'bout eight miles out," he said tightly. "Says his pa's named Sam Tate. They was hit by Indians last night. Likely the same ones that found us."

"Where's his pa now?"

"Don't know," Ben shook his head. "The boy saw two men drop. He thinks his pa got away with some of the others, but he ain't sure. He was too scared to look."

"What the hell was they doin' out here, anyway?"

"Boy says they were on their way to Harrodsburg."

"Goddamn." Daniel spat into the fire. Just what we need, he thought.

Daniel had heard James Harrod was again trying to get a settlement started, but this was the first real news he'd had. Dick Henderson'll have a fit, he decided. James Harrod was a strong-willed man and wouldn't much care whether a Salisbury judge thought he owned all Kentucky.

Posting extra guards around the camp, Daniel took Squire and Cutbirth back to the creek where the boy had been found. There were two men dead, shot through the chest and scalped. Ben and Squire dug holes while Daniel searched the area for fresh sign.

Tracking was easy over the light coating of snow. Five men had escaped and scattered down the creek. One was bleeding, but not badly. Two had doubled back to check the camp, then rejoined the others. All the tracks led off northwest toward Harrodsburg. Daniel shook his head. It was only twenty miles or so, and they would make it easily unless the Shawnees found them again. There was no use worrying about them now—whatever was going to happen had happened already.

Daniel took a long, careful look at the tracks of the Indians. There had been about a dozen. If this was the same party that had attacked Boone's camp, they had picked up some friends. They had come in from the north, left their mounts some fifty yards upstream and attacked the settlers on foot. They hadn't tried too hard to find the survivors, which likely meant they were mainly after horses.

Once more, he circled the place where the Shawnees had left their mounts, tying his horse to a tree and squatting down low to study their prints. The snow left clean marks, but the ground was churned up and muddy where the horses had milled about.

He let his eyes follow the low line of trees that masked the creek, but saw only untouched snow melting slowly into the earth, a half-covered log and the tracks of a rabbit. Daniel stopped, looked again, then walked thirty yards toward the trees. Another horse had stood there, away from the others. The rider had remained on his mount. Now why did he do that? Daniel wondered. Boone returned for his horse, then led the animal by the reins while he kept his eyes on the ground and followed the rider's tracks. The man had kept to the trees, following the line of the creek. Half a mile further, Daniel saw where he had stopped, gotten off his horse and peed against a tree.

Bending low, he studied the man's moccasin prints. A chill touched the back of his neck, and he went down on all fours, hands and knees pressing the cold layer of snow. It was him. By God, it was him for certain. Daniel's heart beat faster. The stride, the weight, the slight turn of the right foot all belonged to Henry Flint. Black Knife. Daniel knew if he tracked the horses back farther, he would find Flint had left the Indians and taken his path by himself.

Daniel felt a sudden swell of anger, and at the same time, a great sense of relief. His hand moved absently to the knife at his belt. He lifted it halfway out of its sheath and touched the dark lock of the girl's hair wrapped tightly around the hilt. It was Flint's way, Daniel thought, the kind of thing he would do. Stealing horses gave him no pleasure. He had waited and taken no part. Flint had other amusements that had nothing to do with horses.

Did Flint know he was here? More than likely, Daniel decided. He was cold and deadly as a snake, and as good a woodsman as any man alive. "I'm here," he said softly, looking past the trees to the north. "And now I know you're here, Flint."

When Daniel returned to camp, he found sour, disgruntled faces. Stoner was fuming. "Goddamn, Dan'l, I told you so, ja? That bastard has a mouth that needs a good blooding!"

"I don't have to ask who you're talking about."

"No, you sure as hell do not," glared the Dutchman. "He's got half these fellows scared of their shadows. Says he will lead them safely to Harrodsburg. You like that, my friend? Harrodsburg? The colonel is going to save us from the savages!"

"He's pushin' me some, ain't he?" Daniel said calmly.

Stoner looked appalled. "Pushing, Dan'l? This is what you call it? It is treason, by God!"

"We're not exactly a troop of Regulars, Mike."

"Hah!" Stoner cast a dark stormy look toward the camp and stalked off like an angry bull. Daniel looked over the faces around the fire, searching for Callaway's. Mike was right. Boone was a great deal more concerned about the colonel than he had let on. It wouldn't take much to blow the whole expedition apart right now. Damn near anything would do it. A raid by the Shawnees, another freak snow that would make it impossible to hide their tracks, or a fat little half-ass colonel, who didn't feel complete without a regiment at his back.

Chapter 32

Daniel stalked through the crowd, pushing men roughly aside, then took a place on a large rock before them. "Looks to me like an awful lot of gabbin's goin' on 'round here," he said evenly. "You ladies havin' a quiltin' party, or what?"

Most of the cutters laughed easily, but a few kept solemn faces.

"Well?" Boone's gaze touched them all. "Let's get it out, goddamn it."

"Daniel . . ." A man stepped hesitantly out of the crowd. He was Luke Mitchell, one of Twitty's crew. "Some of us was just thinking that maybe we're in over our heads out here. Kentucky's a rough place, you know?"

"No." Boone's eyes drilled him. "I don't know, Luke. Suppose you tell me about Kentucky. I just came in from Boston."

The crowd laughed and Luke colored. "I got a right to say my piece, same as anyone else."

"Yeah, he does!" called out one man behind him, and then another.

"Keep talkin'," said Daniel.

"I ain't the only one," Luke continued hotly. "There's others." A few voices urged him on. "What it looks like," said Luke, "is the Shawnees is plumb set to drive us out. They'll see us all dead 'fore we settle up Kentucky!" Angry voices chimed in. Daniel raised a hand to still them.

"If you was a Shawnee, what would you do, Luke? Damnation, the Indians have always been set to drive us out! That sure don't mean they're goin' to." His eyes swept the crowd. "Any of you fellers want to turn back, just say so. I'll be pleased to buy your land from you."

Most of the men looked startled at that, as if they had forgotten what had brought them to Kentucky. They hadn't signed on to take Dick Henderson's pay. They had signed on for land.

In the end, Luke Mitchell, Lew Draper and four others stepped forward to say they were heading back to the gap. Daniel breathed a silent sigh of relief. For a while, he had imagined the whole damn crew might desert him. He still had plenty of men, good men, well armed and ready to stake their claims in Kentucky. If the Shawnees don't hang 'bout a thousand warriors on my ass, he thought grimly.

Dick Callaway had openly supported Daniel against the dissenters, even shaming a few into staying who might have ridden off. Daniel wasn't surprised. Callaway didn't want to go back, he wanted to run the show. The moment Luke and the others rode out, he started to harangue the man who had stayed. They were naked to attack at Taylor's Fork, he said, and they would be even worse off moving up to Otter Creek. Harrodsburg was the only answer. James Harrod had a settlement started there, likely even a fort, from which they could hold off the Indians. Only when the Indian situation eased, could the expedition move safely to Otter Creek. He knew how to organize a stand and he would lead them all safely into Harrodsburg.

But while Callaway was exhorting the cutters, Daniel was sending riders out as far as Harrodsburg, the Salt River and the Kentucky to warn travelers about the Shawnees. If folks would gather at Otter Creek, Boone promised he would protect them with more than twenty well-armed, experienced men, enough to make any Shawnee war party think twice.

When Callaway discovered what Daniel had done, he raged against Boone, telling all who would listen that Daniel was determined to lead them all into a bloody massacre.

Mike Stoner and Dave Gass politely took the colonel aside and had a talk with him. Daniel flared up at the pair when he found out. "You two got no business shuttin' the man up," he said. "Callaway's got a right to say what he likes!"

"Dan'l," Stoner said blandly, "what are you talking about? We was only passing the time with our good friend."

"That's all," Gass agreed. "Nothin' more than that."

"Uh-huh." Daniel eyed them narrowly. "Then how come he ain't opened his mouth all mornin'?"

"Maybe the cat has got his tongue," Stoner suggested.

"I expect that's it," said Gass.

Daniel could get no more out of them. Whatever they had said to him, they had certainly impressed the colonel.

On March 31, Ben Cutbirth and Squire rode into camp and took Daniel quietly aside. Their dour looks told him all he needed to know. "We found all the settlers we could," reported Squire, "an' some stray hunters wanderin' about. They'll get to Otter Creek if they can."

"That's not all, though, is it?"

"No." Squire shook his head. "There's Shawnee sign everywhere, Daniel. You can't spit without hittin' an Indian."

"I ain't surprised. How many you figure?"

"Can't say," put in Ben. "Might be the same six wanderin' about that bothered us awhile back."

Daniel looked at him. "You believe that, Ben?"

"Hell, I don't know what to believe. All I know is they're out there."

"Keep it to yourselves," Daniel told them. "No use spookin' the boys any more'n we have to."

That evening he wrote a letter to Dick Henderson. The message read:

Dick,
My compliments to you, old friend. I must write this letter to acquaint you with

our misfortune here. On the twenty-fifth day of this month, a Shawnee war party fired on my company half an hour before dawn and killed Captain Twitty and his Negro. Mr. Walker was badly wounded, but I think he'll recover.

My advice to you, sir, is to come to our aid with help as soon as possible. Your presence is greatly desired, for though the men are most uneasy, they are willing to stay and risk their lives with you. Right now is the time to flusterate the Shawnees' intentions and take the country whilst we're in it. Dick, if we falter and give in to them now, we will never see an end to our troubles. This day we start from the battle ground for the mouth of Otter Creek, where we shall immediately erect a fort.

I am, sir, Your most Obedient Humble Servant,

> Daniel Boone
> April 1, 1775

Daniel sent one of his best riders with the letter the next morning. Then he gathered his men, had Felix Walker hoisted on a litter, and set out north for Otter Creek.

Dick Henderson stomped his feet to keep out the cold and pulled his heavy fur greatcoat over his shoulders. From the west face of Wallen's Ridge, he could see the broad valley sloping up to the Cumberlands. The famous gap in the mountains was lost to his sight,

veiled behind a white curtain of snow. The damn stuff
had fallen steadily, for six days now, and showed no
promise of stopping. Scouts said the weather was clear
on the other side, nearly as fine as a spring day.

But what good did that do? he asked himself
glumly. He had to get over the damn gap first, and the
way things were going, that wasn't likely to happen
soon.

When trouble came, it damn sure came in
bunches. Nothing had gone right since he had left Sycamore Shoals. Nothing! Three long weeks from the
Watauga, and here he was, squatting like a bear on the
side of a mountain and still not over the gap.

Some of the delay was his own fault. He would
admit that. Daniel had told him from the start to leave
wagons behind, but how could you tell that to a bunch
of settlers and their women? Kentucky's a grand place,
folks, and I aim to sell you some fine land there, only
be sure and don't bring anything. Lord, no, you have
to leave all your belongings behind, ma'am!

Finally he had given in to the settlers, and the
whole venture became a disaster. Folks crawled along
the roads like snails, breaking their wagons apart and
carrying them, a wheel and a plank at a time—anything to keep Ma's rocker and the bed that came all
the way from England. And in the end, of course, none
of his troubles had mattered at all. At Martin's Station,
he learned that the whole business had gone for nothing. The trail ahead was impossible. The wagons
wouldn't move another foot closer to Kentucky.

Of course, the settlers had blamed him. Some of
them were turning back now, right at the door to Ken-

tucky. Unless he did something soon, they would likely all go.

And on top of everything else, there came this frightening letter from Daniel. He had sent it on the first, and today was the seventh. What had happened between then and now? he wondered. Was Daniel alive or dead? If two had been killed already, how many more had been massacred since?

Henderson cursed and tried to light his pipe from the fire, but his fillings blew out into the snow. If only he could have kept the damn letter to himself, he thought angrily, but bad luck was still with him. The rider who had brought the message was spreading the word everywhere. Shawnees were thick as flies in Kentucky; it was risking your life to go over there. How the hell was a man supposed to sell land with everything going against him?

At supper Dick met his partners, John Luttrell and Nat Hart. They were laying for him, too. He could tell the minute he laid eyes on them.

"We must take a firm hold on this enterprise," Hart said severely, "or it will very likely slip through our fingers."

"We have a firm hold," Dick replied shortly. "We have a few problems, Nat. We'll ovecome them."

Nat raised a brow and looked ironically at Luttrell. "A few problems, Richard? Great God, man, we are practically out of business! The buyers are deserting like sheep. Another five families left at noon. They want no part of Kentucky. John, show him your note."

"What note?" Dick asked.

"I'll read it to you," said Luttrell, pulling the paper from his jacket. "A hunter sent it over the gap. 'I have discovered the scalped and slaughtered bodies of a poor family bound for Kentucky. It is a massacre here in this country.'" Luttrell looked at him. "And that, of course, is on the heels of Boone's letter."

"Who else has read it beside yourself?"

"No one. What difference does it make? Good Lord, Dick, these aren't just rumors running around this camp. Read this letter! It's all true! We are leading these people to slaughter!"

"Oh, John, come now," Henderson's face looked pained. "Those families who take to the road on their own know what they're getting into. We offer protection—armed men and safe passage. If they ignore that . . ."

"If they ignore that," Luttrell said loftily, "they can go in and claim land on their own. They don't have to buy it from the Transylvania Company."

Henderson was wondering when his partners would hit on that sore point. "They have no rights to that land. It is not theirs to claim. In time, we'll take care of them through the proper court actions."

Hart and Luttrell looked at him as if he had lost his mind. What court? they were saying with their eyes, and they were right. There were no laws or lawyers in Kentucky. It wasn't a colony or a province. It was just several million acres he had purchased from the Cherokees, against every possible pressure the Royal Governors could muster. Hart and Luttrell knew that as well as every other holder in the company. They also knew that a paper wouldn't carry them across the Cumberlands. Nothing would do that but fortitude and guts. Dick Henderson wasn't sure he had either, but he would keep trying.

He began to show his followers a Dick Henderson they had never seen before. He stomped down the valley in the cold light of dawn and stalked through the encampment, his commanding courtroom voice ringing in the frosty air. By damn, he was leaving, he told them. Right now, come hell or high water. He was taking his own provisions and pack horses and half a hundred of the finest marksmen in the land. If folks wanted to hightail it back East, why, they were welcome to do so. If they wanted lush green meadows in a virgin land, an empire to leave their children, then they had best mount up and follow! A ragged cheer went up—not nearly as loud as he had hoped for, but Henderson didn't care. He mounted his horse, raised a hand to the sky as he imagined an explorer might do, and headed across the valley.

God help me, he thought, not daring to look back, what if there's no one back there following me?

For nearly a day, Henderson felt like he imagined Boone himself might. His courage had clearly stirred the others and only a few weak souls had stayed behind. As they crossed the high summit of the Cumberland Gap, as the snow burned his cheeks and the wind howled like a demon through the pass, hope filled his heart. Below, the weather cleared almost immediately, and his settlers moved cheerfully forward. Even Hart and Luttrell began to treat him with new deference and respect.

The next day, April 9, the skies turned slate grey and a frigid rain mixed with snow pounded and pelted them. Still in sight of the gap, half a dozen families started back. By noon, the narrow trail had turned into an icy river, and they could go no farther.

At least now they can't desert, Henderson thought dismally, shivering under his blanket. They couldn't even find the way back.

When day broke on the tenth, however, he prayed for snow again. The weather was bright and clear, but it brought new disasters. Henderson was appalled when, just before noon, his column met forty men and women riding, walking, fleeing to the safety of the mountains.

The afternoon brought dozens more men with eyes full of fear and hair-raising tales of ambush, terror, blood-hungry Shawnees on the war path. With each new encounter, one of his own families lost their nerve and joined the refugees on the trek back. He begged them to stay, pleaded with them not to desert.

"Don't you know what you're giving up?" he shouted. "It's your fortune up there, your future!"

A hollow-eyed settler stared at him, holding his crying wife and child close to his side. "Mister, there ain't no future in Kentucky."

By nightfall, his whole enterprise lay shattered in pieces. A few brave followers clung to his train, but not many. The last group of stragglers had been men from Daniel's own company! They begged Henderson to turn back. Boone and the whole party were dead by now, they were sure of it!

No, Henderson thought fearfully, it can't be! Daniel's still there. He's got to be! If Boone himself was gone, then the rest were dead for sure. He had to find out. Henderson still had some men, but how many? Enough to stand off a Shawnee attack?

Before the sun came up, he walked to the head of the column and approached Will Cocke, a rangy woodsman he had hired to lead the train. It was essential to get a message to Boone, he announced, and Cocke was just the man to do it.

The man looked at him and laughed. "No disrespect, Mr. Henderson, but if you want a man to ride up through that country, you'd best look in a mirror."

"Cocke," Henderson shook his head incredulously, "I would. I would if I were qualified. I am not, and you are, sir!"

Cocke looked grim. "Qualified for what? To get my hair lifted? Hell! Near anyone's qualified for that." He paused and raised a brow. "I'll do it, mister, for an extry ten thousand acres of land."

"Done!" cried Henderson.

"Prime land, Mr. Henderson."

"The best, Mr. Cocke. I swear it! I'll write it out if you like."

"Don't have to," Cocke said dryly. "I'll remember. Only I ain't goin' alone. Not out there."

"What?" Henderson stared. "You said . . ."

"I ain't goin' alone. Take it or leave it."

Henderson trembled, certain his legs would leave him. His eyes clouded, and tears stung his cheeks, but he felt no shame at all. "Any of you?" he shouted hoarsely. "Jesus, please, our enterprise is ruined if you don't. You understand? Ruined!" He stumbled along the column, facing one man and then another. "Ten thousand acres, you hear? Just go with him. For ten thousand acres!"

Men stared at him and turned away. Finally, Cocke gave him a ragged look and jerked his horse down the trail.

"God be with you!" Henderson shouted after him. "We'll see you soon!" But he was certain they never would. Whoever rode off toward the west, he was convinced, would disappear forever from the sight of man.

Chapter 33

"By God," Stoner said darkly, "people are the only animals I put no trust in, Daniel. This is the truth!"

Daniel grinned and shook his head. Standing on the bank of the river, he looked south to the lush green meadow easing down to the water and to the broad line of sycamores beyond. Stoner was right. The hardworking men in the clearing looked nothing like the drawn and haggard lot he had led from Taylor's Fork the week before. Now they laughed and called out to one another, striding jauntily across the meadow like English lords. Three men carrying fresh-cut timber for the fort stopped to wave, and Daniel waved back. Two of the fellows had threatened to leave with Luke Mitchell and Draper. Now, they had paced off great tracts of land for themselves and talked scornfully of men who couldn't face the wilds.

They had changed, all of them, and Otter Creek

had done it, had touched them with the same kind of magic Daniel had felt the first time he saw it. They had discovered the wonder of the place, the rich soil, the fields full of game. And they had taken Boone on their shoulders, given a weary cheer, and quickly named the spot Fort Boone.

"If it ain't the thin, it's the fat," Gass complained irritably as Boone walked up. He wiped a coat of dust from his face and set his rifle aside. "Dan'l, they're not payin' no damn attention to what I say. We got 'bout half a fort standin', and it ought to be finished. I looked for my crew this mornin', and where do you think they was? Four of 'em was walkin' off plantations for themselves down the valley, an' one was out shottin' buffalo!"

Daniel frowned. Striking a healthy balance was getting to be a real problem. He had spoken that morning to Callaway who, for once, agreed with him. The problem of security was a frustrating one. The men had somehow put the Indians completely out of their minds, as if the Shawnees had vanished from the world the moment Otter Creek came into sight.

Callaway had a solution. He quickly put into effect a rigid schedule of drills, guard rosters, scout patrols and inspections that would have wearied a British grenadier. At the same time, Dave Gass doubled his labor requirements on the fort.

Since Callaway's army and Gass' workers were one and the same, the two men were at odds in less than a day. Daniel stepped in and laid down the law. "These boys ain't soldiers nor slaves neither," he explained patiently. "We got to build the fort and guard it.

That don't seem like no big problem to me." Gass and Callaway both started shouting at once. "Goddamn it, hold it!" snapped Daniel. "We got about what? Maybe thirty men, countin' the stragglers from Harrod's. You get a third of 'em for soldierin', Dick, and two-thirds go to work on the fort. We'll rotate 'em every three days."

Callaway looked appalled. "I cannot guarantee our safety with a dozen men!"

"You can and you will," Daniel said firmly. Both Gass and Callaway started to protest, but Daniel walked off.

The plan worked well for two days, and Boone was greatly pleased. Then the men started drifting back into old habits. Daniel gathered them up and gave them another talking-to, and they fell in line again for a day. After that, it was business as usual. They simply refused to change their ways.

Slowly, the fort began to rise and Otter Creek to take on the shape of a settlement. By the twelfth of April, Daniel decided the barricades were strong enough to defend against an attack, which, Daniel was certain would soon come. It baffled him that the Shawnees hadn't come down on them already. Where were they? There was plenty of sign about, and his scouts had seen war parties in the distance. The only answer that made sense chilled him to the bone—they had found Henderson's party and cut it to ribbons. It was a logical target, and far more appealing than armed men forted up on a river. There were women in the party and pack horses full of provisions. If Flint was still riding with the Indians, he would urge his Shawnee brothers to take the settlers before they reached the protection of the fort.

And Flint was there, Daniel knew. He could sense his presence, almost feel him sometimes. Wandering through the forest, Daniel would look up suddenly and stare through green branches. Something would move on a high hill, nearly out of sight. Then he would run swiftly through dark hollows and over high ridges, rifle at the ready, till he reached the spot, and there would be nothing, no sign at all that Black Knife was near. But Daniel knew he was right. His enemy was there, a wraith that stood just out of sight in the shadows.

"You want me to go look for Henderson, I will," Stoner said firmly. "He must be close, Dan'l."

"If he ain't close, he likely ain't comin'. You know that as well as I do, Mike."

Stoner frowned. "Ja. Maybe they get him, I think. You want me to see?"

"If they're in trouble or dead, there's no use riskin' a man to find out. We can't help 'em till they get here."

And if they don't get here at all, thought Daniel, then what? We have plenty of lead and powder on hand, but it won't last forever. Our lives are in Henderson's hands, and if his company's not dead, he's counting on us to give them shelter, but right now, we can't do a damn thing for each other.

On the fifteenth of April, Daniel's scouts reported a large war party to the west above Harrodsburg. The same day, Daniel himself saw two Shawnees north of Otter Creek and fired on them. What are they waiting for? he wondered. What's holding them back?

Two days later, a gaunt, hollow-eyed man rode into Otter Creek and slid wearily off his horse. "Are you Boone?" he asked. "I'm Will Cocke from Mr. Henderson's party, an' I'm goddamn glad to be here."

Boone gripped his hand and the men around him cheered. "Dick—where is he? Is the column all right?"

Someone offered Cocke a cup of water, and he drank it down fast, staining the dust on his cheeks.

"Should be here in a few days. I come about a hundred an' fifty miles, I guess. Took me seven days to do it." Cocke spit on the ground and wiped his mouth.

"Many Indians?" asked Daniel.

"Damn right." Cocke frowned. "What do you fellers do here? Grow 'em from seed?"

Daniel and the others laughed. "Mike, you can take that ride now. Take a couple of boys with you an' some spare horses." He turned back to Cocke. "Reckon you'd like some rest and a bite to eat, mister. Come on into the fort, and we'll fix you up."

Cocke stood his ground. "I can eat later," he said solemnly. "Right now I aim to stake out some land."

Boone frowned. "Right now?"

"Hell yes, right now. Dick Henderson promised me ten thousand prime acres, and I'd be pleased if one of you gentlemen'd show me what ain't taken."

Daniel stared. Ten thousand acres? Dick Henderson had promised him only two thousand for cutting the trail to Otter Creek!

After Cocke was out of hearing, Daniel took Squire and Gass aside. "When Henderson gets here, get everyone up near the fort an' keep 'em there as best you can. I don't want no folks wanderin' about stakin' off empires. There's too many Indians."

Squire shot a questioning glance at Daniel. "And where'll you be all this time?"

"Out," said Daniel. "Lookin'. Anybody else wants to know, 'specially Henderson and Callaway, I'm huntin' buffalo."

"Dan'l—" Gass started.

Boone cut him off. "That answer is no, Dave, an' 'thanks. I got to do this myself. If they're going to hit us, I want to know when and how many, and I can't spare either of you from the fort."

Squire and Gass knew better than to argue. "I know where he's going," grinned Dave. "Out to find where Will Cocke's staked his ten thousand acres."

"I'm glad you found me out," Daniel replied. "I ain't so embarrassed, now."

He slipped out of the fort after supper, leading his horse into the trees and walking through the growing shadows. After a cold camp, he started northeast before dawn, keeping to hollows and thick forests when he could.

For three days he wandered vaguely toward the Licking River, crisscrossing the land and following sign as he came to it. There were Indians about, plenty of them, and he had guessed where they were gathering. Every trail he crossed eventually turned north. Finally, he quit tracking and headed straight for the bend of the Licking. Indians held to a habit like everyone else, and the bend was one of their favorite stomping grounds.

Four days out of the fort, he left his horse under a high limestone cliff and climbed up the steep rock wall to the ridge above. Heavy foliage covered his passage, and along the ridge at the top, pines stood straight, like sentinels. Daniel chose a tree with good branches and shinnied his way up to the crown. Down the gentle slope below was the bend of the Licking. And on the flat plain beside the river were more Shawnees than he had ever seen at once, three hundred or more, he was certain. Still, it didn't take him long to pick out Henry Flint.

Dick Henderson was beside himself with joy. The long, harrowing journey, nearly a month on the trail, had taken the spirit out of him. He ached all over, and had shed thirty pounds from his portly frame. Still, when the two dozen rifles at Fort Boone fired a volley and cheered him in, he decided it was all worthwhile.

And by God, Will Cocke was still alive! Henderson, having never expected to see him again, greeted him like an old friend. Boone's men laid out great steaming portions of buffalo steak on bark platters, and the newcomers ate until they couldn't force any more food down their throats. It was a great day, the best ever, Henderson decided. A double day to celebrate, because he had ridden into Fort Boone on April 20, his fortieth birthday.

After the first good night's sleep he had enjoyed in a long time, Dick Henderson made a more careful inspection of Fort Boone. Now fully rested, he was less than enthralled about the place. Stalking across the meadow, he collared Mike Stoner. "Where's the fort?" he asked sharply. "I can't seem to find it."

Stoner raised a brow. "It is right there, Mr. Henderson. You are looking at it."

Henderson stared. "That? That's a fort? Good God, man, you can't be serious!"

"What's the matter with it?"

"What's the—why, it's—it's—everything's the matter with it!" he stormed. What Stoner called a fort looked to Henderson like a tall pigsty. The timbers were set crookedly and had been barely pounded into the ground. Henderson stomped around it and found whole sections missing.

"What the hell good is a fort if you could drive a herd of buffalo through the gaps?" he mumbled to himself. Inside, there were new horrors to see. Three small cabins were cramped tightly against the walls, only one near completion. Where were his people supposed to stay?"

"When's Daniel coming back?" he asked shortly. "I think he ought to be here."

Stoner clamped his teeth. "I don't know, sir. Soon."

"Buffalo hunting, hmmmph!" Henderson gave the Dutchman a dark look and stomped off.

He decided a bigger, better fort was the first order of business. He found a site he liked a short walk up the river and paced it off. At a general meeting, his settlers applauded in hearty agreement with his plan, then wandered off to stake out their acres.

Henderson was furious. Damnation, they were aping Boone's men to the letter—more interested in property than saving their own scalps! And that was another thing. Boone's men had taken all the choice lots near the fort. And not one had paid heed to the amount of land he had been granted!

Even his partners seemed to have no understanding of the situation. Luttrell, at least, saw the need for greater protection, but Nat Hart was totally indifferent. He was off to the west somewhere, staking off God-knew-how-many acres of his own plantation.

As the days passed, one new family after another

drifted into Fort Boone. Some had come through the gap; others had been simply wandering about and decided they liked Fort Boone better than Harrodsburg. When Henderson told them he owned all the land here, most of them looked at him as if he had lost his senses. They had never heard of Dick Henderson or The Transylvania Company, and didn't want to. They could find their own piece of land without any help from outsiders.

Jesus God, what was happening to him! This wasn't his plan at all! A fine estate on a large tract, purebred horses in the stables and vast croplands as far as he could see. That was the idea. The people who bought his land would have smaller tracts, and he would look after their interests like a responsible landowner should. They would bring him their problems, show him respect. And when it came time to choose a governor for the fourteenth colony of Kentucky, they would elect Dick Henderson.

Christ, not only did these bumpkins not know who he was, they didn't give a damn, either!

Chapter 34

Halfway down the slope, Daniel found a perch that gave him a clear view of the encampment. He was tempted to edge in closer but thought better of it. The Indians had sentries about, no doubt their sharpest-eyed young braves. He had spotted a few already, which meant there were plenty more he couldn't see.

He sat quietly under the cropping of stone, knees hunched under his chin. The sun moved past the river, hung straight overhead awhile, then angled over the ridge. Long shadows inched down the slope.

Daniel kept his watch, even after darkness filled the valley and fires glowed on the river. The long day's vigil had told him much. There were four chiefs in camp, two more important than the others. One was Cornstalk, the Shawnee who had been so badly beaten on the Kanawha. Now that was bad news, for sure. Even in defeat, Cornstalk was a powerful man among

323

his people. If he was breaking the peace, every Shawnee north of the Ohio would ride down on Kentucky.

Many meetings had taken place during the day—long, serious talks that sometimes erupted into shouting matches. More than once, voices in the harsh Shawnee tongue reached Boone across the river.

During all these talks, Daniel carefully watched the animated figure of Henry Flint. Flint never stayed in his own camp long. He spent the day visiting one chief after the other, sometimes coming back to the same spot over and over.

He's trying to sell something, Daniel decided. The man's goin' round like a peddler with his pots.

Still, he admitted ruefully, Black Knife had a great deal of status among the Shawnees. They respected him and listened to what he said.

Near midnight, when the fires on the Licking burned low, Daniel moved quietly up the slope and down the far side of the ridge to his horse. He led the mount to a trickling stream, let him chew grass awhile, then walked him back to the limestone cliff and curled up to sleep. Before dawn, he was up again, crawling down the slope to his perch.

Just as the sun came up, a band of twenty warriors thundered into camp from the south, yelping and shouting gleefully. Trotting their ponies about the morning fires, they shook their rifles and lances in the air.

Daniel sat up straight and concern narrowed his eyes. Now what the hell was that all about? Maybe they had hit the fort and wiped it out. Or maybe they had found Henderson before he could make it to Otter

Creek. For a moment, Boone thought about going for his horse and rushing back south to see for himself. But that, he decided, wouldn't help. He couldn't change whatever had happened.

In a few moments, he learned why the warriors were so excited. Another large party rode into camp and stayed a hundred yards to the east of the first group. A chill touched Daniel's spine.

Cherokees! By God, they're Cherokees, not Shawnees! We just made a treaty with them and the savages are already back in Kentucky!

A chief, with five lesser warriors at his heels, got off his horse and walked toward the camp. Cornstalk, with five of his own braves, marched solemnly out to meet him. The sun was in Daniel's eyes, but he recognized the Cherokee immediately. It was Hanging Maw. He knew the man and disliked him. He was a renegade Cherokee, a full-blood who scorned his own people and honored no man's law but his own. In his way, he was as brutal and callous as Flint. Daniel didn't like the picture at all.

Cornstalk and Hanging Maw met until noon. The other Shawnee chiefs were on hand, and so was Flint. When the meeting ended, Flint stalked back to his camp, mounted up and rode off, trailing an extra horse behind him.

It was a risk, but Daniel knew he had to take it. Even if a sentry saw him creeping up the slope, he couldn't let Black Knife get away.

Flint made it easy for him by staying close to the river. Boone picked up his tracks less than a half hour later and took up the trail a mile behind. The renegade was riding easy, using no tricks to hide his trail. He was on his own ground, among friends, and wasn't at all worried about trackers.

In midafternoon, Flint left the river and turned abruptly southwest. Daniel tried to anticipate what his quarry would do. The land opened up here, offering little cover. Flint, of course, would grow more cautious, and it would be almost impossible to track him up close. What was he up to? Daniel wondered. What would he find in the southwest? It struck him, suddenly, that the answer was crystal clear, and he grinned. The path would lead him straight to Otter Creek and the fort. They were hunting each other, both keenly aware of the other man's shadow on his path. Daniel knew he had been watched before, and Flint likely felt the same. He was headed for the fort to sniff out his enemy. Only this time, the foe was at his heels.

For nearly an hour, Daniel kept well to Flint's rear, letting the low, rolling hills come between them, never daring to move in close. Finally, when he was convinced the man would keep to his course, Daniel turned due south and kicked his horse into a run. He crossed the northern spur of the Warrior's Path, made a wide loop west, then turned northeast again. Pulling up in a dense copse of maples, he tied his horse, sat down cross-legged and waited.

The sun warmed his shoulders and the back of his neck. He moved his head now and then, so the birds would get used to him. The next time he stood up, he didn't want a startled flock taking to the air.

He didn't have to wait long. Less than an hour after Boone had crouched in the woods, Flint's horse walked past the curve of the hill. Daniel stood. He had checked his rifle a dozen times. Now he checked it again. Flint was less than fifty yards away. Setting the rifle against his shoulder, Boone let the bead slide to the center of Flint's chest. It would be easy that way. Too easy, Daniel decided. It couldn't end this way with Flint. He didn't deserve a clean death. Letting his breath whistle through his teeth, he lowered the rifle a hair and fired.

Flint's horse stumbled once and folded, a bullet in his head. The spare horse bolted and ran. Flint thought fast. There was no cover nearby, only the grove of maples from whence the shot had come. Rolling free of his horse, he grabbed his rifle and dropped behind the animal's bulk.

"Flint? It's me, Boone," Daniel called.

For a heartbeat, Flint said nothing. Finally, a voice called from behind the dead horse. "Guess I'm not surprised."

"It's time to set things straight, Flint. Put down the rifle and come on out."

Flint laughed. "And get my head shot off?"

"I don't want you that way," said Daniel. "If I did, that would've been *your* head, not your horse's."

"Then suppose I just stay right here? You sure ain't walkin' out to get me."

"I will, 'fore the sun's down. When I do, you better take your best shot. You won't get two."

Daniel watched the horse. After a long moment, the half-breed's gaunt frame rose up straight. Glaring coldly toward the trees, he tossed his rifle away. "All right, goddamn you. Let's do it."

Daniel stepped out of the trees, his own rifle steady. "Now the little hand pistol," he said quietly.

Flint hesitated, then jerked the weapon out of his

327

belt and dropped it. Daniel kept walking until they were only a few yards apart. Flint didn't move. He stood tense and ready, his good eye narrowed to a slit. Daniel laid his rifle on the grass. Before he straightened, Flint was on him like a wolf. Just as a tomahawk whipped past his head, Daniel jerked back, rolled, and let his own blade slice the renegade's thigh.

Flint cursed, backed off. He had the tomahawk in one hand, a knife in the other. Daniel held his own blade high. "This knife knows you, Flint," he said gently. "It knows you and wants you bad. That's her hair wrapped 'round the hilt. Her daddy made this blade for you and no other."

Flint's one eye widened, then he spit out a laugh. "Hell. You sure carry a grudge, Boone. Little piece of Cherokee ass an' you make a big . . ."

Daniel came in fast. Flint's blade ripped through his shirt and raised blood on his chest. Daniel groaned, then staggered back. Flint's smile turned into a snarl as he moved in for the finish. Too late he saw Daniel wasn't hurt. He had been suckered in good. Daniel's blade sang, slashing three times over Flint's belly and down between his legs.

Flint screamed, dropped the tomahawk and grabbed his vitals. Blood coursed down his leg and his face went pale with fear. "Bastard!" he yelled hoarsely. "Goddamn bastard, you ruint me!"

"Not yet," said Daniel. Hefting the knife, he walked slowly toward Flint. Flint stumbled away, his teeth grinding from his pain and shock. Daniel stalked him patiently, waiting, watching the man's eye. Cold sweat peppered the renegade's face. He feinted, drew Daniel in and cut his face. Daniel wiped blood off his cheek and came in again. Flint back off, frantically carving the air with his knife. Boone ducked, stepped inside, wove his way under the man's weapon. When the moment came, he struck fast, going for Flint's groin once more. The blade flashed once, twice, and Flint, giving a ragged cry, dropped to his knees and clutched himself. Daniel stood back and watched. The renegade thrashed about on the ground, his mouth stretched open in agony. He glared up at Boone. "Finish me. Finish me, you bastard!"

"You can finish yourself, Flint."

Deep in the thick of the forest, Daniel kept the fire banked low. The low flames flickered off Flint's naked body, staked in the narrow clearing. Flint groaned, opened his eye and shook his head. Searching about the clearing he found Daniel. "Boone, what'd you do to me?" he said weakly. "Goddamn, I hurt somethin' awful!"

Daniel smiled down at him. "I put a hot blade to your wounds, boy. Saved your life, I guess. You'd likely have bled to death."

Flint stared at him. "What for? Why'd you bother?"

" 'Cause I want you to live," Daniel said simply. "You're no good to me dead."

Flint winced. "You're not makin' sense."

"Yeah, I am. You'll see."

Flint gasped for breath and bit his lip. "I'm ruint good, ain't I? You cut me up down there."

"Yeah, you're ruint. Reckon you can still pee some though, so I wouldn't get too discouraged."

Flint choked back a cry. "Hell, kill me, Boone, but don't leave me like this!"

Daniel got up, found a thick piece of buckskin and brought it back to the fire. Flint eyed him warily. "What's that for?"

"Don't want any of your friends to hear us. Wouldn't be too good an idea, would it?" Flint started to speak but Daniel squatted down and bound the gag tightly over his mouth. Daniel stood over the moaning, thrashing renegade. "I never done this to anyone," he said evenly. "I wouldn't do it to a dog like you 'less I had to. It ain't for me or her or even for my boy. I'd just plain kill you for all that."

Daniel sat down and straddled the man's chest. Flint groaned under his gag, and Boone hit him solidly across the jaw. Then Boone hefted Flint over his own horse, and mounted the other.

Riding north all night, he reached the bend of the Licking just before dawn. Where a grove of willows masked the water a few miles downstream from the Shawnee encampment, Daniel stopped and eased himself out of the saddle. Walking back to the other horse, he bent to test the rawhide that bound Flint to the mount. Flint was naked on his back, legs tied about the horse's neck, arms stretched under the haunches. Daniel had run another line under the horse's belly, from the cord that bound Flint's hands to those that held his legs, binding Flint solid. Flint stared at him wide-eyed, straining against the gag.

"Now you can do one of two things," Boone said quietly. "You can thrash 'round some an' slip under this feller's belly and get your brains kicked out. Or you can lay real still, an' you'll make it just fine. I don't give a damn which, long as you get there."

He patted the horse's head gently, loosened the rope that held it, and gave it an easy pat on the rump. The horse blew air, then trotted slowly up the river-bank. In a few hours, it would smell the other horses and walk into the Indian camp.

The job hadn't bothered his conscience nearly as much as he had figured it would. Flint had at least been unconscious. It wasn't the same as cutting a man when he could feel it. That was Flint's game, not his.

He had carved his initials carefully into the man's chest, going deep and broad enough to scar, staunching the blood as he went. Then he had searched the woods with a brand and found some violets that would make a good dye. Mixing the substance with clay and gun-powder, he had then worked the stuff deeply into the wounds and washed Flint's chest. The wounds would heal, but they would leave a thick ridge of scar tissue that would never go away. Even if Flint could stand to wash the mix out, some of it would stick and color the scar.

Indians were fierce about their honor and pride. When they saw Flint and what Daniel had done to him, Flint's voice wouldn't ring quite as strong in their councils. That, and the fact that Boone had ruined his manhood, wouldn't leave Black Knife with much. Daniel hadn't even bothered to scalp him. He had just cut off his scalplock at the skull. The Indians would see the shame of that, too. And when Black Knife stood to exhort them into attacking the settlers, they would remember the letters that flamed on his chest and the ruin that lay between his legs. They would remember, and they would think long about it.

He slept half the day on the trail south, far from the Licking River and when he awoke it was late afternoon. Leading his horse down the rough hollow, he bent to splash water on his face. When he looked up, Captain Will was sitting his horse on the far bank, watching him quietly.

Daniel jerked up and Will raised a hand. "I do not come to fight, Wide Mouth."

"It's been awhile, Will."

"It has, Boone." He was silent a long moment, dark, somber eyes squarely meeting Daniel's. "You have settled your grievance with Black Knife."

"I guess. It was a long time coming."

Will nodded thoughtfully. "Still, all is not finished, Boone. If it does not come now, it will come sometime. Cornstalk would have peace, but I do not think he will get it. Black Fish and the others will have their way."

Daniel raised a brow. "Was Black Fish at the council?"

Captain Will nodded. "Black Fish and the Cherokees." Will spit emphatically on the ground. "I do not like doing business with Cherokees." He smiled thinly at Boone. "What you did to the half-breed will make a fine story. Do not steal too many horses, Boone." He nodded, turned his mount away, then stopped and looked over his shoulder. "Maybe we will meet in a good fight. There will be honor in it."

"There will for sure," said Daniel.

Epilogue

The Dream: September 1775

Rebecca walked up from the river, following the well-worn path back to the fort. Stopping a moment, she set down the pails and wiped sore hands on her skirt. With so many folks moving in, it was getting harder every day to get drinkable water close to the settlement. Daniel had warned her not to wander far, but what could you do? People were settling all along the river in the choicest spots, and she wasn't about to fetch up water that had God-knew-what in it.

Hefting the pails again, she rounded the bend and came out of the trees in sight of the fort. Ducks waddled down to the water, quacking and scolding. A boy drove his milk cows under the walls, bells clanging dully. Becky waved to Stoner, who was down the river.

The fort still didn't look like much. The blockhouses were complete now, but there were still large holes in the walls that sorely needed filling. The two big gate doors were lying outside, still unfinished, and there were a hundred other smaller items that needed tending. Still, she decided, the place was turning into a town. More women and children coming in had made the difference. There was wash on the line and the sound of babies crying—things that made the place feel more like a town than a camp.

And there were other signs of progress in Boonesborough. Folks were doing more than just hunting and roaming about. Crops had been planted in the fields and a number of small gardens had been dug. Squire had set up a gunsmith shop. One newcomer, named Pogue, was making wooden tubs, churns, plates, cups and a few crude chairs and tables.

Becky hesitated before walking into the fort. This was the part she didn't care for, living elbow to elbow with so many strangers. There were fifty small cabins squeezed in under the walls, and you could hear everything that happened in your neighbors' houses. It was a far cry from having your own place on the Yadkin. She never said so to Daniel, but she missed her home terribly. Especially now, with October coming on and the crisp smell of fall in the air.

The sycamores down by the river were already turning red and gold, and there was a light burr of frost on the ground. Inside the fort, there was no real season to speak of—only hard-packed earth, narrow walls and the smell of wash.

All that would change, of course, when Daniel found time to start the construction of their own place. He was too busy for that, now. With Henderson gone, responsibility for the whole settlement fell squarely on his shoulders.

Poor Dick, thought Rebecca. She had never really cared for him, but you couldn't help feeling sorry for the man. He had struggled hard to hold on, but there was just too much against him. Folks hadn't come to Kentucky to find new landlords. There was land enough for everyone here, and few saw the sense in paying for it.

At the cabin, Jemima and two of the Callaway girls were giggling over a gawky young man in a raccoon cap and buckskins. The boy saw Becky coming, turned beet-red and scooted off round a corner. Becky hid a smile as she watched him go. Lord God, were Daniel and I ever that young and stumble-footed?

The boy was one of the newcomers, and Daniel couldn't stand him. 'Course, he couldn't stand anyone paying court to Jemima—especially boys in coonskin caps. "Coonskins look best where God put 'em," he was fond of saying. "On the backs of raccoons."

Still, even Dan Boone couldn't keep the boys from flocking about his daughter. She would be thirteen in a few days, and already looked a woman. Along with the Callaway girls, Jemima was one of the major attractions of Boonesborough. That wouldn't last with more people coming, but she was queen bee now and making the most of it.

They grow up and leave so quickly, thought Rebecca. You just had to be thankful you had them for as long as you did. James had seen sixteen years of life, and poor little William, born in June, had lived only a few short days. They had buried him there in the Clinch, a few miles from where James lay. Losing a child that young in a way seemed a greater sorrow than

James' death, for she had so little to remember of William.

While Becky was cutting meat in the pot, Mary Callaway burst in, eyes blazing with anger. "Becky, you know what that Baxter woman had the nerve to say to me?"

Becky looked up at her friend. A rebellious wisp of hair hung over the woman's brow.

"I'll tell you what she said," Mary went on without waiting. "She said if my chickens got into her corn again, she'd wring their necks and drop 'em in the pot. Can you imagine?" Mary shook her head in wonder. "What am I supposed to do? Let 'em sleep with the children?"

Mary launched into a recitation of another, even more flagrant abuse by the dowdy Mrs. Baxter. Becky listened with half an ear, dropping the last bit of potato into her stew. Boonesborough's become a regular town for certain, she thought. When ladies from Virginia and North Carolina start quarrelling over chickens, there's not an Indian anywhere who would dare come between them.

Daniel spent half the morning shouting at a group of hunters who had just come in from a trek on the other side of the river. Damnation, when would the thickheads learn? They would kill six or eight buffalo, load up the choice cuts on a pack horse, and leave the rest out to rot. The herds that had grazed right outside the fort in April had already disappeared. A man had to go twenty or thirty miles now just to catch sight of a deer! What the hell was going to happen when winter came?

"We been here six months," he complained to Squire, "and the damn place is closing in on us already. One spring and a summer gone, an' already we're fresh out of meat an' up to our asses in people."

Squire grinned and shook his head. "Daniel, it's a settlement now, not a huntin' camp."

"I know what it is," Boone said grimly. Glancing out of Squire's shop, he saw Simon Kenton walking by and hailed him. He liked the young man; he was a fine woodsman, a lad with a level head on his shoulders. "When did you get back? Thought you was still up north."

Kenton stepped inside, nodded to Squire and gripped Daniel's hand. "Late last night. I was comin' in to see you." He leaned against a bench and set down his rifle. "You was right, Cap'n Boone. The Indians are gatherin' up from here to the Ohio. Not doin' much now, just gettin' ready."

Daniel nodded and rubbed his chin. "We got us a fine winter comin' up. Goin' to be short on everything 'cept Shawnees."

"You reckon they'll bother us 'fore that?" Kenton wanted to know.

"Maybe. Maybe not. If I was Black Fish or Cornstalk, I'd wait till the cold, when no one can make it 'cross the mountains with powder and lead and food."

"Be a proper time, all right."

"Well, with any luck," sighed Squire, "we'll be ready for 'em."

Daniel frowned. "Squire, we ain't ever goin' to be ready for the Shawnees. Not the number that's coming."

Boone vividly recalled another talk he'd had

337

about Indians, earlier that year. Young George Rogers Clark had been on the Clinch when he had gone back for Becky in June, and they had shared a jug of whiskey. Clark had just come from the East with plenty of startling news. While Daniel had been on the Licking after Flint, colonial militia had clashed with British troopers up in Lexington, Massachusetts. The colonials had been driven off, and a few killed. Later, though, other patriots had ambushed the redcoats at Concord and had given them a sound beating. While Daniel was still on the Clinch, news came of another big battle. His old commander George Washington was a general in the Continental Army now and had gotten himself whipped proper at a place called Bunker Hill. Things were heating up, it seemed, and were likely to get worse.

It's a strange world, Daniel mused. The officer leading the British against Washington had been a man named Gage. He too was a general, but Boone remembered him as a young lieutenant colonel under Braddock when they had moved on Fort Duquesne. Gage and Washington had been fellow officers in that campaign, and neither had liked the other. Evidently, they weren't about to grow a hell of a lot closer now.

"A war's coming," Clark had told Daniel. "Just as sure as we're sittin' here. We've gone too far to turn back."

"I kinda figured," Daniel had replied, setting down his cup. "What's it goin' to mean to folks in Kentucky. Not much, I reckon."

"It will, Dan'l. If you take my advice, you'll be ready for it. If the British have any sense at all, they'll use the wilderness to get to the colonies, come in the back door to Virginia or the Carolinas. And when they do, you can bet they'll use the Indians."

"You mean work with the Shawnees like the French did?"

"Exactly. I reckon it's happening already. In Boston, we heard Royal agents are counciling with Shawnee chiefs. The redcoats'll be buyin' Kentucky scalps this time next year. You wait and see."

"Yeah, I reckon I will," Daniel had replied.

Now, as he thought about it, Daniel figured Flint would be aiding the British. Even if he's lost face with the Shawnees, the British could use him. Maybe, Boone thought grimly, he should have killed the bastard when he had the chance.

"You look worried," Rebecca told him. "Something wrong, Daniel?"

"Nothin' new, I guess." Daniel stretched and walked over to warm his back at the fire. "Hunters are wastin' meat. I can't get the gates up or the wall finished. Same old stuff. I ain't cut out to be no town planner, Rebecca."

"You can do it as well as any," she said firmly. "Better'n most, I imagine."

"Well, I sure don't care for the job."

"You don't have to tell me that."

Daniel looked curiously about the room. "Where'd Jemima get off to? Haven't seen her since supper."

Rebecca busied herself with the patch on Israel's shirt. "Well, I suspect she's out with the Callaway girls."

Daniel caught her tone. "Rebecca, you're not lettin' her keep company with that fool in a raccoon cap!"

"He ain't a fool, Daniel. He's just young."

"Huumph! Anyone walkin' 'round with a dead critter on his head, ringtail and all . . ."

"Growed men do it."

"There's plenty of growed-up fools walkin' 'round, Becky."

"The boy kind of reminds me of you," she said.

"What?"

"Long time ago, of course."

Daniel made a face. "I damn sure never acted like that."

"Well," sighed Becky, "there was this one young suitor I had. We was at this picnic, and he was so gawky and shy he kept playin' with his knife 'stead of lookin' at me. Cut about a hundred holes in my only white dress. Ma gave me what for, I'll tell you. Can't imagine who'd marry a fool like that."

Daniel grinned. "Wonder what become of him?"

"I expect he grew up some. Maybe learned there was ways to treat a girl's dress, other than pokin' it full of holes."

Daniel walked over, lifted her out of the chair and pulled her to him. "Becky, would you still marry that fool if you had it to do over?"

Rebecca leaned her head against his shoulder. "Lord yes, Daniel! I know for sure I would. Guess I'm likely the same kind of fool he is."

Second in the Spectacular Series
THE AMERICAN INDIANS

BLACKFOOT AMBUSH

by Catherine Weber

It's 1868 and the Blackfoot reservation is seething with danger and discontent. An Indian agent has been murdered and the Blackfoot are accused. The only man who can solve the mystery of this crime is the new agent — an outlaw and killer by the name of Cole Sykes. He doesn't stand a chance until the beautiful Patricia Ashley makes him face the shattering truth. Through a maze of deceit and intrigue, the tender woman leads the vicious gunfighter to new realizations about himself — and about the Blackfoot people he is meant to serve. And the voluptuous Patricia promises a future for the man who once faced a life in prison.

Third in the Spectacular Series
THE AMERICAN INDIANS

CROW WARRIORS

by Bill Hotchkiss

A woman pursues her own destiny and learns the lessons that only the mountains can teach her...

The third volume of the AMERICAN INDIANS series — the unforgettable story of Chastity, a beautiful, free-spirited woman who refuses to conform to the Mormon way of life. Betrothed to a man she does not love, she is saved from a life she hates by the scout Aloysius Benton and the gallant Crow warrior, Big Dog, when Indians raid her wagon. Though realizing she will be banished from her own people, Chastity cannot resist the awesome power of the warrior. Yet her love for him will force her to accept a new way of life . . . among CROW WARRIORS.